VIRAGO
MODERN CLASSICS
569

Angela Thirkell

Angela Thirkell (1890–1961) was the eldest daughter of John William Mackail, a Scottish classical scholar and civil servant, and Margaret Burne-Jones. Her relatives included the pre-Raphaelite artist Edward Burne-Jones, Rudyard Kipling and Stanley Baldwin, and her godfather was J. M. Barrie. She was educated in London and Paris, and began publishing articles and stories in the 1920s. In 1931 she brought out her first book, a memoir entitled *Three Houses*, and in 1933 her comic novel *High Rising* – set in the fictional county of Barsetshire, borrowed from Trollope – met with great success. She went on to write nearly thirty Barsetshire novels, as well as several further works of fiction and non-fiction. She was twice married, and had four children.

By Angela Thirkell

Barsetshire novels

High Rising
Wild Strawberries
The Demon in the House
August Folly
Summer Half
Pomfret Towers
The Brandons
Before Lunch
Cheerfulness Breaks In
Northbridge Rectory
Marling Hall
Growing Up
The Headmistress
Miss Bunting
Peace Breaks Out

Private Enterprise
Love Among the Ruins
The Old Bank House
County Chronicle
The Duke's Daughter
Happy Returns
Jutland Cottage
What Did it Mean?
Enter Sir Robert
Never Too Late
A Double Affair
Close Quarters
Love at All Ages
Three Score and Ten

Non-fiction

Three Houses

Collected Stories

Christmas at High Rising

HIGH RISING

Angela Thirkell

Introduced by Alexander McCall Smith

virago

VIRAGO

First published in Great Britain in 1933 by Hamish Hamilton Ltd
This paperback edition published in 2012 by Virago Press
Reprinted 2012, 2013 (three times), 2014 (twice)

A CIP catalogue record for this book
is available from the British Library.

ISBN 978-1-84408-883-6

Typeset in Goudy by M Rules
Printed and bound in Great Britain by
Clays Ltd, St Ives plc

Papers used by Virago are from well-managed forests
and other responsible sources.

MIX
Paper from
responsible sources
FSC® C104740
www.fsc.org

Virago Press
An imprint of
Little, Brown Book Group
100 Victoria Embankment
London EC4Y 0DY

An Hachette UK Company
www.hachette.co.uk

www.virago.co.uk

Introduction

Angela Thirkell is today relatively unknown, by no means as familiar to readers as Benson or Trollope, or even Nancy Mitford, writers with whom she is sometimes compared. Unlike Barbara Pym, she has not enjoyed a significant moment of rediscovery; unlike Rose Macaulay, she did not write anything of quite the same status as *The Towers of Trebizond*. Yet her work has its adherents, and the republication of these two works *High Rising* and *Wild Strawberries* will be welcomed by those who feel that these unusual, charming English comedies deserve a wider audience.

She led her life in much the same milieu as that in which she set her novels. She came from a moderately distinguished family: her father became Professor of Poetry at Oxford, and her mother was the daughter of Edward Burne-Jones, the pre-Raphaelite painter. She was related to both Rudyard Kipling and Stanley Baldwin; she was the goddaughter of J. M. Barrie. Her life, though, was not always easy: there was an unhappy spell living in Australia, and two unsuccessful marriages. Financial exigency meant that she had to make her own way, first as a journalist, and then as the author of a series of novels produced to pay the bills.

Books flowed fast from her pen, and their quality was

perhaps uneven. Many of them are now largely forgotten, but amid this enthusiastic somewhat breathless literary output there are some highly enjoyable and amusing novels. *High Rising* and *Wild Strawberries* are two such. These books are very funny indeed.

The world she depicts is that of rural England in that halcyon period after the First World War when light began to dispel the stuffiness and earnestness of the Victorian and Edwardian ages. It was a good time for the upper-middle classes: they still lived in largish houses and they still had servants, even if not as many as they used to. They drove cars – made of enamel! Angela Thirkell informs us – and they entertained one another with stylish throwaway comments in which exaggeration played a major role. They were in turn delighted or enraged – all in a rather arch way – by very small things.

The social life depicted in these books is fascinating. We are by no means in Wodehouse territory – Thirkell's characters do have jobs, and they do not spend their time in an endless whirl of silliness. Occasionally, though, they express views or use language that surprises or even offends the modern ear – there is an instance of this in the wording of one of the songs in *Wild Strawberries*. But this, of course, merely reflects the attitudes of the time: it is a society in which nobody is in any doubt about his or her place. Servants observe and may comment, for example, but they must not get above themselves. Miss Grey, who takes up the position of secretary to Mr Knox in *High Rising*, is not exactly a servant, but she is an employee and should remember not to throw her weight around with her employer's friends. Of course she does not remember this, which is a major provocation to the novel's heroine, Laura Morland. One cannot help but feel sympathy for Miss Grey, who is described as having no relations to whom she can be expected to go. That was a real difficulty for women: unless you found a husband or were able to take one of the relatively few jobs that were available to you (and somebody like Miss Grey could not go into service), you were dependent on relatives. Finding a husband was therefore a deadly earnest task – almost as important as it was in the time of Jane Austen.

The children in this world were innocent and exuberant. In *High Rising* we see a lot of Laura's son, Tony, whom she brings home from his boarding school at the beginning of the book. Like most of those whom we encounter in Thirkell's novels, Tony is overstated to the point of being something of a caricature. He is as bouncy and excitable as a puppy dog, full of enthusiasm for trains, a subject by which he is obsessed. He knows all the technical details of trains – their maximum speed, and so on – and spends the 'tips' he receives from adults on the purchase of model carriages and engines. These tips are interesting. It was customary for adult visitors to give presents to the children of the house, and a boy might reasonably expect such a gift simply because he was there at the time of the visit. As a child I remember getting these tips – not earning them in any way, just getting them as of right. Today, children would be surprised if anybody gave them money and would probably immediately reject it, it having been drilled into them that such gifts are always to be refused.

Tony also has a degree of freedom unimaginable today.

Not only is he interested in model trains; his passion for railways extends to the real thing, and he is allowed to go off to the local railway station by himself. There the stationmaster permits him to sit in the signal box and also to travel in the cab on shunting engines. Whatever else is unlikely in the novels, this sounds entirely realistic. Childhood was different then.

Engaging though these period details may be, this is in itself insufficient reason to read Thirkell. What makes her novels so delightful is their humour. The affairs that occupy the minds of her characters are classic village concerns. In that respect, we could as easily be in Benson's Tilling as we are in the Risings. There are dislikes and feuds; there are romantic ambitions; there are social encounters in which people engage in highly amusing exchanges. These come thick and fast, just as they do in Tilling, and are every bit as delicious. Affection for the social comedy is not something we should have to apologise for, even if that sort of thing is eschewed in the contemporary novel. Such matters may seem unimportant, but they say a lot about human nature. Above all, though, we do not read Angela Thirkell for profundity of emotional experience; we read her for the pleasure of escape – and there is a perfectly defensible niche for escapist fiction in a balanced literary diet.

Another attraction is the coruscating wit of the dialogue and, to an extent, of the authorial observations. Angela Thirkell is perhaps the most Pym-like of any twentieth-century author, after Barbara Pym herself, of course. The essence of this quality is wry observation of the posturing of others, coupled with something that comes close to self-mockery. The various members of the Leslie family in *Wild Strawberries* are extremely funny. Lady Leslie, like Mrs Morland in *High Rising*, is a galleon in full sail, and we can only marvel at and delight in the wit of both.

The exchanges that take place between the characters in these books would look distinctly out of place in a modern novel – but therein, I believe, lies their charm. These people talk, and behave, as if they are in a Noël Coward play. In real life, a succession of insouciant sparkling observations would become tedious, but it is impossible to read these books without stopping every page or two to smile or to laugh at the sheer audacity of the characters and their ebullient enthusiasms. We are caught up by precisely those questions that illuminate the novels of Jane Austen: who will marry whom? Who will neatly be put in her place? Which men will escape and which will be caught? These are not the great questions of literature, but they are diverting, which is one of the roles of fiction. Angela Thirkell creates and peoples a world whose note can be heard today only in the tiniest of echoes, but in her books it comes through loud and clear, reminding us that the good comic novel can easily, and with grace, transcend the years that stand between us and the time of its creation.

Alexander McCall Smith

2012

I

The Prizegiving

The headmaster's wife twisted herself round in her chair to talk to Mrs Morland, who was sitting in the row just behind her.

'I can't make out,' she said reflectively, 'why all the big boys seem to be at the bottom of preparatory schools and the small ones at the top. All those lower boys who got prizes were quite large, average children, but when we get to the upper forms they all look about seven, and undersized at that. Look at the head of the Remove for instance – he is just coming up the platform steps now.'

Mrs Morland looked. In front of her was the platform, where the headmaster stood behind a rapidly diminishing pile of prizes. On each side were the assistant masters, wearing such gowns as they could muster. A shrimp-like little boy in spectacles was coming up to get his prizes.

'That's him – Wesendonck,' said the headmaster's wife. 'And what a name to send a boy to school with. Such a

I

nice child, too. I hope he will be able to carry all his prizes. I am always telling Bill to have them done up safely. Poor Bill is nearly speechless with a bad cold and all the talking today. I hope he'll get through.'

At this moment the headmaster found Master Wesendonck's tall pile of books slipping from his grasp. He juggled frantically with them for a moment and then, to the infinite joy of some two hundred boarders and day boys, they crashed to the ground in all directions. A bevy of form masters rushed forward to the rescue. Master Wesendonck, realising with immense presence of mind that his natural enemies were for once in their proper place, grovelling on the floor, stood still and did nothing, ignoring the shrieks of joy and abuse which his young friends poured upon him from the galleries of the school hall. Seldom had the time and the place and the very unfortunate name come together at such a propitious moment. Few of the jokes were funny, and none of them original, but they gave great satisfaction, and pandemonium reigned.

'Isn't Bill going to bark at them?' asked Mrs Morland anxiously; for the headmaster stood blandly surveying the tumult, making no effort to quell it.

'In about a minute,' said the headmaster's wife. 'I can see him sucking a throat lozenge. When he has swallowed it, he'll give tongue. And I can't think,' she added, surveying with some disfavour the scrum of masters on the floor, 'why on earth headmasters' wives in novels fall in love with assistant masters, or assistant masters with them for that matter. Just look at ours.'

'"Just-look-at-the-maze-in-the-house: jever-see-such-

2

maze?"' murmured Mrs Morland. Certainly, from M. Dubois, the French master, who had been so long at the school that the boys despised him now more from tradition than conviction, to Mr Ferris, the latest addition to the staff, whom the headmaster's wife was perpetually mistaking for an upper boy who had grown a good deal in the holidays, there was no face among that collection of excellent, highly educated (or athletic), hard-working, conscientious men which could, one would think, cause a flutter in any female breast.

'And yet they are mostly married,' continued the headmaster's wife, 'and the ones that aren't married are engaged. I suppose it's a law of Nature, only I wish Nature would exercise natural selection, which is one of the things she is famous for, because the masters, left to themselves, don't. What I have to bear from having masters' wives to tea—'

But at this moment the headmaster swallowed the lozenge, and in the voice of a sergeant-major who had been educated among sea-lions, simply remarked, '*Be quiet!*'

There was instantaneous silence.

'Bill barked beautifully, didn't he?' said his proud wife to Mrs Morland. 'Listen, Laura, wait till the other horrible parents have gone, and have some tea with me. Bring Tony, too, if you like.'

'All right, Amy, but I can't stay long. I'm driving down to the cottage.'

The rest of the prizes were distributed without mishap, and boys and parents began to surge out of the hall. Laura waited by the entrance to claim her own child, whom she could barely recognise in his revolting Eton collar. When Tony was

3

first sent to school, Laura had rung up the headmaster's wife, an old friend, to ask if the regulation Eton suit, which nothing, she said, would ever induce her to let Tony appear in at home, was really necessary for Sundays. Amy had asked what kind of shape Tony was, and hearing that he was a strongly built, thick-set little boy, said, 'Of course not. He'd look ghastly in Etons. Get him a blue serge suit for best.' So the Eton collar was the only concession to school respectability. Which all goes to show what a very sterling woman Amy Birkett was. But as little boys all look exactly alike, with hair twirling round and round from a starting point on the backs of their heads, round bulging cheeks, and napes that still have some of the charm of the nursery about them, it was not easy to spot Tony, especially as the whole school was reduced to a common denominator by the unnatural cleanliness enforced upon it for the prizegiving ceremony. At last something tugging at her arm made itself visible as Tony.

'Mother, did you hear the noise the chaps made when Donkey's books went down? Did you hear me, Mother? I was yelling

"Donk's an ass,

Bottom of the class."

Mother, did you hear it?'

Laura wondered, as she had often wondered with the three older boys, why one's offspring are under some kind of compulsion to alienate one's affections at first sight by their conceit, egoism, and appalling self-satisfaction. But, recognising the inevitable, she said yes, she had heard, and told him to get his things ready and then come to Mr Birkett's study for tea.

'Oh, Mother, must I?'

'Why not?'

'Go to tea with Mrs Birky? Oh, Mother, I couldn't. She'd think my hair wasn't properly brushed or something. She goes off pop if you aren't tidy.'

Laura, wondering, as before, why one's gently bred and nurtured children have such a degradingly common streak in them, merely repeated her order to Tony. His soft face assumed a sulky expression, which, however, cleared up immediately as he caught sight of Master Wesendonck, surrounded by his admiring mother and sisters. He walked past the group, repeating in a loud, abstracted voice his famous distich,

> 'Donk's an ass,
> Bottom of the class,'

and was rewarded by a friendly attack from the victim of the libel. The two little boys disappeared in a scuffle of arms and legs into the boarders' quarters. Laura, feeling rather guilty towards the Wesendonck family, slipped into the large classroom where the common herd of parents were being fed. The school sergeant, a huge, powerful, gentle creature, was stationed at the door to prevent boys getting in and eating the parents' tea.

'Good afternoon, sergeant,' said Laura. 'How is Tony getting on?'

'Nicely, Mrs Morland. I wouldn't say but what he mightn't be as good as young Dick was. Talks too much, though. Funny, if you come to think of it, his elder brothers weren't at all talkative young gentlemen, but young Tony, well, he wasn't behind the door when tongues were given out. Still, he's shaping well. I hope we shall see you at our Boxing Competition next term, Mrs Morland.'

Without waiting for her answer, he made a plunge into the tea-room, and brought out two small boys by the scruff of the neck.

'Mother or no mother,' he said severely, 'orders are given, and none of you boys goes into the tea-room. Get along with you.'

Letting Laura through, he stood like Apollyon, blocking the doorway to the boys outside.

Laura wandered through the tea-room, but could not see Amy anywhere. Presently her great friend, Edward, came up to her. Edward, who had enlisted at sixteen 'for company', had found his ideal job after the war as factotum and friend of all mankind at the school, with the company which he so much loved perpetually renewed. He could clean boots like an officer's servant and patch them like a real cobbler; clean knives and sharpen them; mend the boys' bats, skates, racquets, cameras; cut hair; sing any popular song ever written; repair the headmaster's wireless and drive his car. When the whole kitchen staff went down with influenza, was it not Edward who held the breach for two days, cooking boiled beef and dumplings in the copper? When the sanatorium overflowed during the same epidemic, was it not Edward who took his turn as night nurse in the temporary hospital, and sang the convalescents to sleep with highly unsuitable songs from Flanders? On that blissful occasion when the local power station failed and all the school lights went out, and the Birketts were away, and Johnson and Butters collided in a dark passage where they had no business

6

to be, and Johnson had a bleeding lip and Butters an eye-brow laid open, was it not Edward who had the wits to run them both over in one of the masters' cars to the doctor's house and get them sewn up at once, returning so swiftly that no one had time to think of any serious mischief to do? There was even a tradition that, in a crisis, Edward had taken the place of nursery-maid in Mrs Birkett's nursery and wheeled her two little girls in a perambulator. But this was looked upon as going a little too far, and was slurred over by the school. One didn't like to associate Edward in any way with those two great gawky girls, Rose and Geraldine. At least that was what the young chivalry of England felt.

'If you were looking for Mrs Birkett, madam,' said the omniscient Edward, 'she is gone over to the house and hopes you'll follow. She said she couldn't stand no more parents at any price, madam, if you understand me.'

Laura thanked him, and wound her way through the crowd of parents and across to the headmaster's house, where she found Amy in the study.

'Bill was so exhausted and voiceless that I've sent him to lie down for a bit,' said Amy. 'I expect he had a touch of flu. Come and sit down and tell me about the family. Is Gerald enjoying China?'

'It's Dick who is in China, at least somewhere about on the China station, whatever that is. He quite likes it, and he loves the ship.'

'Oh, it's Gerald who's in Burma, then. How's he getting on?'

'No, that's John. He's getting on nicely. He hopes to get back next Christmas. Gerald is the one who explores. He has got a good paying job with some Americans in Mexico. He says it's great fun. It sounds horrid.'

'I'm sorry, Laura dear, that I mix your family up so. It's so confusing of you to have four boys. And whenever I got used to a Morland Minor, his elder brother would leave us and his younger brother come on, and then he was Major and there was a new Minor. Most confusing. But I'm glad they're all well. Things are easier now, aren't they?'

'If you mean money, yes. Gerald and John are self-supporting, bless them, and Dick almost. So really they cost me nothing except presents, and holidays when they come back. There's only Tony now.'

'But he'll get scholarships, like Gerald.'

'Tony has a splendid natural resistance to learning in any form,' said Laura, in a resigned voice. 'I expect he'll be a pig-farmer.'

'Then you can live on bacon, and not work so hard. Are you always writing?'

'Mostly. But it's much easier now than when I had three at school and Tony at home. I am actually saving up for my old age.'

'Come in,' called Amy, to a knock at the door. Tony came in. He had evidently got at somebody's brilliantine. His hair was irregularly parted down the middle and slabbed shiningly down on each side, and he brought with him a powerful odour of synthetic honey and flowers.

'Foul child!' cried Amy, 'what have you been doing? Have some tea.'

Tony appeared to be accustomed to his headmaster's wife, for he evinced no discomposure, and seating himself, replied, 'It's only a little Johnson's hair fixative, Mrs Birkett. Two of the chaps poured it on for me, and I brushed it down. Did you hear the noise, Mrs Birkett, when Wesendonck's books fell down? I was shouting like anything.'

'Hear it?' said Amy. 'Why, you broke both Mr Birkett's ear-drums and he has gone to bed.'

Tony looked alarmed.

'If this weren't a tea party and the end of the term and Christmas next week,' said Laura, 'I would kill you, Tony. Look at your suit.'

Indeed, signs of the whole-hearted way in which the two unspecified chaps had entered into the spirit of the fixative job were visible on Tony's collar and all down his jacket and waistcoat.

'Oh, that's all right,' said Tony, 'we wiped the rest off the floor with Swift-Hetherington's gym shorts and then matron came in and went off pop.'

'Well, thank heaven you're going,' said the headmaster's wife.

'You'll come to me for a few days in the holidays, won't you, Amy?' said Laura, as they kissed goodbye.

'Love to. Bill is taking the girls to Switzerland for a fortnight. I'll let you know the dates and invite myself for a night or two.'

'My love to Bill. I hope he'll be all right again.'

'Oh, he'll be all right. It's just end-of-term fatigue, and a lot of worry with a stupid secretary. We had what we thought a very good woman in the summer, but she went mad or something at the beginning of this term, and we had to change, which meant a lot of extra work.'

'Bad luck,' said Laura.

'Goodbye, Tony, and happy holidays.'

'Goodbye, Mrs Birkett, and thank you very much for having me to tea,' said Tony, looking so seraphic that his mother had to concentrate her mind on his disgusting hair and suit to keep herself from hugging him on the spot.

Laura and Tony got into the car and set off on the twenty-mile drive home.

'Well, darling, I'm very pleased to meet you again,' said Laura as they sped along.

'I know,' said Tony briefly. 'I say, Mother, how old, really, are you?'

'Forty-five, really, but I don't always look my age.'

'That's all right,' said Tony, with such relief in his voice that Laura had to ask why.

'Swift-Hetherington said he knew how old his mother was and he betted I didn't know how old mine was. So I betted him mine was older than his was, anyway, and I'm right.'

'So what do you win?' asked Laura, amused.

'I don't *win* anything, Mother. I just betted him.'

'I see.'

Evidently the vice of gambling was not wrecking Tony's life, in spite of his misleading phraseology.

'Oh, Mother,' began Tony again, 'are we going to the flat for Christmas, or the cottage?'

'Oh, didn't I tell you? The cottage.'

'I see. Of course I left my railway at the flat, and I had specially made plans to play with it these holidays. That would happen.'

He sank into the depths of gloom.

'I did happen to think of that, too, Tony, and I brought the railway. It is on the back of the car.'

'Thanks, Mother, but I'm afraid it's no use. You see, I can't play with it unless I have some new points for shunting, right-hand curve, and if I haven't got my savings bank book and the railway catalogue I can't get them. That's all. It's just all no good.'

'As a matter of fact, you'll find the catalogue in the railway box, and I have very kindly brought your bank book with me.'

'Thank you,' said Tony, and fell into a mystic dream of fresh railway systems on a more ambitious scale than before.

Laura was looking forward to a holiday at the cottage after a hard-working autumn in town. When her husband had died, Tony was only a few months old, and there was very little money. Laura had written for magazines for some years past, in a desultory way, but now the problem of earning money was serious. She had considered the question carefully, and decided that, next to racing, murder, and sport, the great reading public of England (female section) likes to read about clothes. With real industry she got introductions, went over big department stores, visited smart dressmaking friends, talked to girls she knew who had become buyers or highbrow window-dressers, and settled down to write best-sellers. Her prevision was justified, and she now had a large, steady reading public, who apparently could not hear too much about the mysteries of the wholesale and retail clothes business. One of her novels had even been dramatised with considerable success, its central scene being the workroom of the famous Madame Koska, where a minion of a rival firm got taken on as a bodice hand, and made notes of advance season models. But a judgment fell on her when, in the handsome traveller for a French silk manufacturer, she recognised the lover she had robbed and left some years ago. How he also recognised her, the struggle in his breast between love and duty, how the honour of the dressmaking world got the upper hand, how he denounced her to Madame Koska, how Madame forgave her, how the mannequins struck half an hour before Madame's spring opening, how the minion went on and wore forty-eight frocks with such ravishing grace that Madame Koska took five thousand pounds' worth of orders in that afternoon alone: all this is too long and improbable to relate. But, most luckily, it suited the public taste, and so did the others, and Laura had educated Gerald and John, and got Dick into the Navy, and now there was really no anxiety and only the inscrutable Tony to be dealt with. She was quite contented, and never took herself seriously, though she took a lot of trouble over her books. If she had been more introspective, she might have wondered at herself for doing so much in ten years, and being able to afford a small flat in London, and a reasonable little house in the country, and a middle-class car. The only thing that did occasionally make her admire herself a little was that she actually had a secretary. Not a real full-time secretary, for Miss Todd lived in the village with her mother, and only came up for the mornings, but still, a secretary.

This had been forced upon her when, a couple of years earlier, she had been asked, to her great alarm, to do some articles on women's fashions for an American paper. The money was too good to refuse, so Laura, whose own idea of dress was hurried bargains in the sales, collected a mass of information in exclusive shops and took it down to the cottage, to work it up. Here she was found one morning, in tears, by her friend Miss Todd. Miss Todd sat down, took her hat off, and asked what had happened. Laura, amid sobs and snuffles, said she couldn't, couldn't do it. There was a serial to get on with, about a mannequin who wouldn't pose in any silk but pure British artificial, and so somehow married a Cabinet minister; there was a second series of 'Tales from Madame Koska's Showroom' to be finished; money was wanted to help Gerald through an extra year at Oxford, which was to lead to a fellowship and ultimately to exploration; but how, oh, how would she ever do it all? And she cried bitterly, and her hair began to come down, while Miss Todd lent an intelligent ear.

Presently Miss Todd said:

'Stop crying, Mrs Morland, and I'll tell you something. What do you think I love most in the world?'

Surprised by this curious attempt at consolation, Laura did stop. Pushing her dishevelled hair off her tear-sodden face, she thought for a moment, and then said:

'Your mother.'

'No,' said Miss Todd. 'Clothes.'

Laura sat up, and forgot her own pressing troubles entirely. This was very interesting. Heaven knew that for a woman who made a good income out of writing about them, she, Laura, knew as little personally about clothes as need be. But Miss Todd. She stared. Miss Todd, who was certainly forty, who was celebrated for filial piety to an ailing and impoverished mother, who had apparently had one tweed suit and one black evening dress for ever and ever, who never left High Rising (for so the village was agreeably called) except to take her mother to Bournemouth for a fortnight, who— But, as Laura went on staring, some of Miss Todd's better qualities, ignored until this outburst drew attention to them, began to impress themselves on her eye, which was trained to look at the appearance of others, though it always disregarded that of its owner. Miss Todd hadn't a bad figure, she hadn't bad hands, her feet were undeniably good in her shabby old brogues, if her hair hadn't obviously been cut at home it would look very pretty, her teeth all looked good, thought Laura enviously. In fact, not at all an unattractive creature, Miss Todd, if once it occurred to you to look at her at all.

Under this prolonged scrutiny Miss Todd appeared to think some explanation necessary.

'Not that I don't love Mother,' she stated calmly, 'because I do. One gets fond of them, you know. But she's a bit dotty, and she's got a bit of a heart, so it doesn't do to concentrate on her.'

Again Laura had to readjust ideas. Everyone knew that old Mrs Todd was slightly mad. While she was still able to get about alone, she had formed a habit of ordering groceries, meat, and boots, on a gigantic scale, from the village store. Miss Todd had been obliged to explain this to Mr Reid at the shop, who obligingly humoured the old lady and took her orders with great respect. Now, Laura knew vaguely, she had been kept to the house for some months, but she hadn't realised that Miss Todd had, for all this time, been uncomplainingly nursing a rather mad mother, with a heart into the bargain. Her opinion of Miss Todd rose even higher.

'Well, Anne,' she said, distractedly running a knitting-needle through her hair, 'I dare say you are right. You've been a brick. But where do clothes come in?'

Miss Todd's eyes glowed with a holy flame. 'Mrs Morland,' she said impressively, 'they save my life. That's why I read all your books. I don't care for good literature, but when I read about clothes, it's like taking opium. I forget all about Mother, and death, and dividends, and I *revel*. I know I couldn't wear them. I'm not the type, even if I could afford them. But they mean a lot to me, and your books have been an awful help to me, so . . .'

Here she broke off in embarrassment. Laura was immensely interested. Here was her real public, made flesh in Anne Todd. Laura herself had no illusions as to her books being, in any high sense of the word, literature, but she knew they had an appeal, and here was the person to whom they appealed. She gazed again upon Miss Todd, who sat with her knees wide apart and her toes turned in, her eyes shining, her cheeks red as flame. What was the matter with Miss Todd?

'So,' continued Miss Todd, seeing that no help was forth-coming from Laura, 'I thought when I found you crying, perhaps I could help you. There. I've said it. Mother doesn't need me all day. She stays in bed in the morning with the wireless, and Louisa can keep an eye on her. But if I could come up here between breakfast and lunch, and type things, or help you a bit … I did do a secretary course, you know, before Mother got so difficult … Oh, Mrs Morland, do say yes.'

Laura's hair came right down with emotion. 'Pick up some hairpins for me, Anne, and you can come every day, and you can do this awful American stuff for me.'

Miss Todd, on her hands and knees, handed hairpins to Laura. 'Mrs Morland, you are an angel,' she said.

'But,' said Laura, her articulation rather impeded by a mouthful of large tortoiseshell pins, and suddenly wondering if she had been rash, 'do you think you can really do it?'

'Of course,' said Miss Todd, standing up and jamming her hat on. 'Give me all that stuff, Mrs Morland, and tell me how many thousand words, and I'll get it all into shape for you by the day after tomorrow.'

Quite hypnotised, Laura handed a bundle of papers and sketches to Miss Todd, who left the house at once, without saying goodbye. With rising but bewildered spirits, Laura stuck the last hairpin into her head, and sat down to cope with Madame Koska, whose best tailor was turning out, very improbably, to be an Austrian grand duke, fallen on bad times. What with Madame Koska's difficulties in refusing the grand duke's suit and yet retaining his services, and her own lucky gift of being able to shelve her less pressing troubles till they had to be faced, Laura never gave the American articles another thought till, two days later, Miss Todd turned up with a parcel of typescript.

'Here you are,' said Miss Todd. 'You'll find it's not bad.'

Laura read it, found it not bad, and invited Miss Todd to stay to lunch.

'Can't,' said Miss Todd. 'You know we haven't got the telephone, and Mother expects me. But if you like it, that's all right. I loved doing it.'

'But I must pay you, Anne. You see I am to get—'

'Never mind about that, Mrs Morland,' said Miss Todd firmly. 'That's not my business, and anyway you collected all the material – I only put it together.'

'But, my dear child, we can't leave it like that. Sit down and have some sense.'

After a good deal of protesting on Miss Todd's part she agreed, under pressure, to come every morning while Laura was at the cottage, to accept a weekly salary at such times, to type at the usual rates any manuscripts sent her while Laura was away, and to take ten per cent on anything she actually wrote from Laura's notes. More than this Laura could not induce her to accept.

Several other people, finding this unexpected treasure among them, had tried to seduce Miss Todd from her allegiance, but she was singularly unmoved. Even when George Knox, the very successful writer of biographies, who lived a mile away at Low Rising, asked her to come as permanent secretary, and offered her a cottage in his grounds for herself and her mother, she declined.

'You see, Mrs Morland,' she said to Laura, who was scolding her for refusing such a good offer, 'I don't care so much for literature – it's the subject of clothes that appeals to me. With Mr Knox it would be dates, and philosophy, and highbrow stuff. I like Mr Knox, and I like the girl – Sibyl's a good child – but my place is with you. And I couldn't move Mother if I wanted to. With a heart you never know, and here we are with Dr Ford almost next door, and she can look at the street and see what's happening. At Low Rising she wouldn't see anyone. If she died, I wouldn't say— But you come first, Mrs Morland.'

So Miss Todd remained as Laura's secretary and what Laura called the prop of her declining years. And old Mrs Todd got gently madder, and her heart gave a little more anxiety, but Miss Todd, sustained by clothes, remained perfectly serene, and if she occasionally shed a tear about her aged mamma's uncertain health, only Laura knew.

2

High Rising

Now, as they drove along towards High Rising, Laura became vaguely conscious that Tony was asking a question. He suffered from what his mother called a determination of words to the mouth, and nothing except sleep appeared to check his flow of valueless conversation.

'Mother, which *do* you think?'

'Think about what, darling?'

'Oh, Mother, I've been *telling* you.'

'I'm sorry, Tony. I had to pay attention to the driving, and I didn't quite hear. Tell me again.'

'Well, I could get a Great Western model engine for seventeen shillings, but there is a much better L.M.S. one for twenty-five shillings. Which do you think?'

'I should think the Great Western, if it only costs seventeen shillings and the other is twenty-five.'

'Yes, but, Mother, you don't see. The Great Western would only pull a coal truck and one coach, but the L.M.S. would pull three coaches quite easily.'

'Well, what about the L.M.S. then?'

'Yes, but, Mother, then I'd have an L.M.S. engine and Great Western coaches. Didn't you know my coaches were all Great Western?'

'I'm sorry, Tony, I'd forgotten that.'

'Well, Mother, considering I was telling you all about them I thought you would know. Mother, which *would* you say?'

'Look, Tony,' said his mother, stifling a desire to kill him, 'there's Mr Reid's shop. We shall be home in a minute.'

'But which do you think, Mother? A Great Western to go with the coaches, or do you think an L.M.S.?'

'Let's have a look at the whole railway tomorrow, Tony,' said Laura, temporising, 'and then I'll tell you. Here we are.'

They turned up the short drive, and found the front door open, with light shining from it. A very fat woman in a grey flannel dress, girt with a tremendous checked apron, came out to meet them.

'Well, Stoker, here we are,' said Laura. 'How's everything?'

'Quite all right.'

'You and Tony get the things out, and I'll run the car into the garage. Are the doors open?'

'Yes, and supper's all ready. I thought you and Master Tony would have it together as you're alone. Here, Master Tony, come and help with your trunk.'

But Tony had already secured his railway box from the back of the car and disappeared.

'Don't do it alone, Stoker,' said Laura, as her maid

prepared to lift Tony's trunk into the house. 'You'll hurt yourself.'

'Hurt myself?' said Stoker scornfully. 'Not unless I was to burst, and that *would* be a bursting.'

Seeing her so determined, Laura put the car away. When she got back to the house she found that Tony had already unpacked most of his railway all over the drawing-room floor, flung his coat and cap on the sofa, and settled down to the construction of a permanent way.

'No, Tony,' said his mother firmly. 'Put all those things back in the box and take them upstairs. You know you have your own play-room. I will *not* have your rubbish all over the drawing-room floor. And take your clothes off the sofa and go and wash for supper at once.'

'But, Mother, you wanted to see the railway, because of settling about the engines.'

'I don't want to see the railway now, or ever,' cried Laura, goaded to exasperation, 'at least not this evening, and not in the drawing-room. Pack it up at once.'

Unwillingly, with a delicious, pink, sulky face, Tony put his engine and lines away, piled his coat and cap on the box, and staggered from the room, with faint groans at the tyranny under which he lived.

'No, not in the hall. Right upstairs,' shouted his mother.

Tony reappeared at the door.

'I only thought you wanted me to hang my coat and cap up,' he explained in an exhausted voice.

Laura flung her own coat and hat on a chair and sat down. Darling Tony. How awful it was to be a person of one idea. The elder boys said she spoiled him. It was not so much that she deliberately gave way to Tony, she pointed out to them, as that, after bringing three of them up, she was too exhausted to do anything about the fourth. When, for about a quarter of a century, you have been fighting strong young creatures with a natural bias towards dirt, untidiness and carelessness, quite unmoved by noise, looking upon loud, unmeaning quarrels and abuse as the essence of polite conversation, oblivious of all convenience and comfort but their own, your resistance weakens. Tony was no more trying than Gerald had been – oh, those firstborn, how they take it out on one's ignorance of their ways – or John, or Dick, but she was older, and less able to deal with his self-sufficient complacency. She had sent him to school at an earlier age than his brothers, partly so that he should not be an only child under petticoat government; partly, as she remarked, to break his spirit. She fondly hoped that after a term or two at school he would find his own level, and be clouted over the head by his unappreciative contemporaries. But not at all. He returned from school rather more self-centred than before, talking even more, and, if possible, less interestingly. Why the other boys hadn't killed him, his doting mother couldn't conceive. There seemed to be some peculiar power in youngest sons which made them resistant to all outside disapproval. When he was checked in his flow of speech, he merely took breath, waited for an opening, and began again. Laura could only hope that this tenacity of purpose would serve him in after life. It would either do that, or alienate all his friends completely.

A noise like the sweep in the next-door chimney when

you aren't expecting him was heard coming down the stairs, and her hateful, adorable son burst into the room.

'Supper's ready, Mother, and old Stokes is just going to ring the bell.'

'Have you washed, Tony, and why haven't you changed your boots?'

'I couldn't, Mother. My other shoes aren't unpacked.'

'Well, there are some bedroom slippers upstairs. Put them on. And show me your hands.'

Tony reluctantly exhibited two grey hands, fringed with black, diversified by a few streaks of lighter colour.

'Where did you wash, Tony?'

'In the bathroom.'

'Yes. One second under the tap and then wipe the dirt off on a clean towel. Off you go, and put some water in the basin.' As her son left the room in offended silence, she continued her recommendations in a louder voice. 'And turn your sleeves up, and use the nailbrush, and when you've washed your hands, rinse them properly, and then clean your nails in my room if you haven't enough sense to unpack your own bag. And don't forget to change your boots,' she wound up at the top of her voice. Then, with great and well-founded want of faith, she followed him upstairs, stood over him while he moodily continued his toilet, and showed a marked want of sympathy while he groaned over the knots in his bootlaces, knots which, as she unkindly pointed out, could only have been put there by himself. The result was so clean, so pink, and so inviting, that she had to hug it, to which it submitted with an excellent grace, putting its arms tight round her neck, and lifting its feet off the floor.

'Mercy, mercy! you're strangling me!' she cried.

Tony pushed his hard, pink cheek firmly against hers, and let himself down.

'Come on, Mrs M,' he said, leading the way downstairs, 'old Stokes wants us for supper.'

When they got to the dining-room, Stoker was standing before the fire with her arms folded. Laura often wished that Stoker didn't feel it due to herself to wait at table with her massive arms bare to the elbow, but in matters affecting dress, Stoker was neither to hold nor to bind. She had entered Laura's service soon after Gerald, the eldest, was born, with a very lukewarm reference from her former place, and nothing but her air of good-nature to recommend her. On this Laura engaged her, and never regretted it. She was an excellent cook, a devoted slave to the boys, and absolutely trustworthy. Manners she had none. Of her mistress's housekeeping powers she had no opinion at all, and Laura had long ago given up any attempt to control her, or to interfere in the battles which raged between her and each successive house-parlourmaid in the early days. After every particularly fierce battle she was accustomed to give Laura notice, which Laura always accepted, saying, 'All right, Stoker, but you are a fool, you know!' After two days of awful sulks the notice was always withdrawn with voluble explanations, and things would go on as before. By the time the two elder boys were at school, Stoker decided that a house-parlourmaid was an unnecessary expense, and from that moment she reigned supreme from top to bottom of the house. For Laura's husband, that ineffectual and unla-mented gentleman, she had a kind contempt, which took the outward form of always alluding to him in his lifetime as 'the boys' father', which didn't prevent her going to his funeral in widow's weeds which left Laura in the shade, and having hysterics on the way home. Whether she was Miss or Mrs, Laura had never dared to ask her. The London tradesmen, with whom she liked to exchange loud and pointless badinage at the kitchen window, called her Miss, until a fateful day when the Milk, so she told Laura, had called her Miss once too often. What she meant Laura never dared to enquire, but after her next Sunday out, Stoker appeared with a broad band of silver-gilt on the third finger of her left hand, bearing in embossed lettering the mystic inscription *Bethel I'll raise*. Gradually she let it be known that the ring had belonged to her mother, an old lady of well-known piety, support of a peculiar sect, but when Laura enquired whether the ring embodied an allusion to the chapel she favoured, Stoker darkly replied that her mother was long since dead and no one knew what the Lord had seen fit to do with her, but that's what the Milk would get if he tried it on again. She then took to herself the prefix Mrs, under the shelter of which title she felt at liberty to go to more outrageous verbal lengths than ever, especially with the Milk. By good fortune she took a liking to Miss Todd, with whom she commiserated loudly on her unmarried state, bringing to her notice the various bachelors of the neighbourhood, none of whom Miss Todd had the slightest wish to marry.

'Now, how about Dr Ford, miss?' she would say, as if she were recommending a cut from a good joint. 'You won't do much better, and neither of you are getting any younger, as they say. Or Mr Knox over at Low Rising? He's been a widower these four years now, and there's Miss Sibyl needs someone to look after her, for we all know her poor mother wasn't much to boast of, lying ill on her back till death her did part. Think of it, miss.'

Miss Todd thanked Stoker warmly, but didn't feel called upon to think of it.

'Soup's hot now,' said Stoker, getting her massive form sideways through the door to the kitchen. 'Eat it while I see to the fish.'

'Oh, Stokes, no meat tonight?' asked Tony.

'No, Master Tony. Young blood like yours doesn't need no heating at night. There's fried fish, and I've done some chips, too.'

'Chips! Good for you, Stokes,' cried Tony, letting the soup slide backwards out of his spoon in his rapture.

'Mrs Birkett was quite right when she called you a foul child,' said Laura dispassionately. 'Wipe that soup off your waistcoat, Tony. No, not with the tablecloth. What's a table napkin for?'

Tony, like most small boys, had a curious antipathy to unfolding his table napkin, which remained in its pristine folds all through the week, merely getting greyer and more smeared on the outside.

When Stoker had removed the soup plates and brought in the fish and fried potatoes, she settled herself in an easy attitude against the kitchen door, nursing her elbows, and began to impart information.

'Just as well I come down a week before you,' she began. 'There's always more than enough to do. I tell you, when I saw the way things were, I felt my back open and shut with the nerves.'

'I'm very sorry, Stoker,' said Laura. 'That must have been awful. But hadn't you Mr Knox's Annie's sister to help you? I told you to get her if you needed help.'

'Annie's sister!' exclaimed Stoker, with withering contempt. After a dramatic pause she added, 'What that one is you wouldn't know if I was to tell you.'

'Well, what's wrong? I thought you liked her.'

'There's many a slip between does and did,' was Stoker's enigmatic reply. 'When a girl spends half the morning talking to the young fellow that brings the wood, and sweeps the dirt under the drawing-room carpet, where it may be, for all she cares, to the present day, for I said to her, "There it stays, to show the mistress the way you work" – there's no talk of liking.'

'That's very sad, Stoker. Suppose you sweep it up, and we needn't have the girl again.'

'I did sweep it up. I wasn't going to have the house left like a dust-bin for you to see. But I told Mr Knox's Annie what I thought of the girl, and she'll sort her. And what do you think of the news at Low Rising?'

'What news, Stoker?' asked Laura, who sometimes vainly hoped that by using Stoker's name rather often she might gently hint to her that some form of address would occasionally be acceptable – even Mrs Morland, if Stoker's soul were above ma'am or mum. But Stoker had her own code of etiquette, and though she freely gave Laura's friends their titles, and never omitted the word 'master' when speaking to, or of, one of the boys, she chose to express her deep devotion and pitying condescension to her mistress by never addressing her otherwise than as 'you'.

'They've got a new girl.'

'Is Annie leaving, then?'

'Annie? No.' On this word, long drawn out, she disappeared into the kitchen, returning with a fresh supply of potatoes which she placed before Tony, and continued:

'Annie, she wouldn't go. No; sectary.'

'Oh, a new secretary?'

'That's right. Miss James, it seems, was took suddenly.'

'Do you mean she died?'

'Died? No. There was trouble in her family, and she had to leave, beginning of October that was, and Mr Knox got a new girl, Miss Una Grey she calls herself,' said Stoker, as if the secretary were indulging in a sinful alias.

'Well, I hope she has settled down. It must have been very annoying for Mr Knox. Tony, if you must eat potatoes in your fingers, which I don't really mind, at least don't wipe your hands down that unlucky suit. Go into the kitchen and rinse them. You can take away, Stoker.'

When Stoker came back, followed by Tony, who was gloatingly bearing a chocolate pudding, she took up her former position and went on with her news.

'You may well ask me,' she announced, though Laura had shown no intention of asking anything of the sort, 'about Miss Grey. Mr Knox's Annie says there'll be more than one change in the family before long.'

'What do you mean, Stoker?'

'Sectaries have been known to marry their Masters before now, and Annie says she pities poor Miss Sibyl if such were to be, and she will hand in her notice the very day the banns are put up.'

'Rubbish, Stoker. You and Annie have been gossiping as usual. You have tried to marry poor Mr Knox to every secretary he has had, and to Miss Sibyl's governesses, and to Mrs Knox's nurse. You are just as bad as Annie's sister. Bring me my coffee in the drawing-room now. I'm tired to death.'

Taking no notice of Stoker's sibylline mutterings, she escaped, leaving Tony to give Stoker a highly coloured account of his doings at school, and how the masters went in terror of his mordant tongue.

In the drawing-room she found a pile of letters waiting. Most of them were business, or proofs, which could wait till tomorrow, but presently she came upon one in her publisher's well-known handwriting. If he had taken the trouble to write himself, it meant he had something personal to say. It turned out to be a suggestion that he should come down on Saturday for the day, to talk over a possible cheap reissue of some of her books.

Laura looked up at the shelf of her novels, with Adrian Coates's name on their backs. She had been very lucky, she thought, to fall into the hands of so agreeable and helpful a publisher. Soon after she first decided that she must try to earn money by writing, she had met him at dinner, and inquired earnestly how many thousand words one needed to make a novel. Adrian was charmed, and rather touched, by this delightfully vague widow with four sons. He had not been long in business and was anxiously looking out for good writers whom he might add to his list, so he asked her if she would have lunch with him.

'If you are really writing a book I would very much like to see it when it is ready,' he said.

'You mightn't like it,' said Laura, in her deep voice. 'It's not highbrow. I've just got to work, that's all. You see my husband was nothing but an expense to me while he was alive, and naturally he is no help to me now he's dead, though, of course, less expensive, so I thought if I could write some rather good bad books, it would help with the boys' education.'

'Good bad books?'

'Yes. Not very good books, you know, but good of a second-rate kind. That's all I could do,' she said gravely.

So in time her first story went to Adrian, who recognising in it a touch of good badness almost amounting to genius, gave her a contract for two more. Her novels had been steadily successful, and she and Adrian had had a very agreeable partnership over them. She looked upon him as a contemporary of her eldest son – after all, he was only ten years older – while he found it difficult to remember that she was almost old enough to be his mother. Owing to honest dealings on one side and conscientious hard work on the other, their relations had always been very friendly. Adrian's only complaint about Laura was that she was too unconscious of her own worth, and would belittle herself as a hack writer of rubbish when she was turning out good, workmanlike stuff. Laura's only complaint against Adrian was that he didn't read her letters carefully enough, which may have been true, though to a busy man they were at times infuriating, as the business parts were sandwiched in among accounts of the boys' progress, and general reflections on the conduct of life.

Of course Adrian should come down for Saturday, and

she wrote a postcard to that effect. Stoker came in with the coffee.

'I want this to go tonight, Stoker. Tony can run to the pillar-box with it. What's he doing?'

'Helping wash up.'

'Oh, all right. But send him up to bed soon, Stoker, it's getting late. What's the news of Mrs Todd?'

'Miss Todd took her away to Bournemouth. She rang up today to say her poor mother was feeling the benefit and she'd be back on Saturday and you wasn't to bother about any business letters till she came. And there's a telephone message from Mr Knox. Miss Sibyl and him is coming over this evening to see you.'

'Oh, Stoker, why didn't you tell me before? Here I am all dirty and untidy.'

'You'll do all right,' said Stoker robustly. 'If Mr Knox wants to see you he can take it or leave it. That's them now. I hear the car.'

Taking the card for the post, Stoker went out and opened the front door. A pretty, dark girl of about twenty, with an ill-assured manner, got out of the car.

'Good evening, miss,' said Stoker. 'Where's Mr Knox? He said on the telephone you was both coming.'

'I know, Stoker, but he found he couldn't. Is Mrs Morland there?'

'Well, that is a pity,' said the hospitable Stoker. 'It's always nice to have a gentleman. Mrs Morland will be disappointed.' Flinging open the drawing-room door, she announced, 'Here's Miss Sibyl, but you needn't worry about not being dressed. Mr Knox isn't coming.'

31

'Dear Sibyl, how nice of you to come,' said Laura reaching out a hand. 'Come near the fire. What's the matter with your father?'

'Oh, nothing. At least I didn't think it was much, but he had a little cold, and Miss Grey thought he had better stay in. He's near the end of a book, you know, and Miss Grey's awfully keen on it, and she's afraid he'll get worse and not be able to get on with it. He sent his love and hoped you wouldn't mind.'

'Dear me, of course not. I'm really rather glad, because I'm all dirty and untidy. What have you been doing?'

'Oh, nothing much.'

'Not typing?'

'No, not much. You see Miss Grey's frightfully good at it, and she thinks it's better if only one of us does it. And her typing is really much better than mine.'

'And what about your own work? Have you been writing anything?'

Sibyl blushed painfully. 'I wish you wouldn't, Mrs Morland. You're so clever, and I know I can't ever do anything half as good as yours, and it makes me feel so mortified.'

Laura laughed. 'Good heavens, child. I'm a pot-boiler, that's all. I look to you to do the Risings real credit, to rescue them from the disgrace of lowbrow novels that I've brought upon them. High Rising's pretty low at present. You must follow your father's footsteps and make Low Rising a star.'

'Coffee for you, miss,' said Stoker, bursting in with a tray. 'Better than what your Annie makes.'

'Thank you, Stoker. But we're having much better coffee

now. Miss Grey makes it herself in a kind of machine, and Daddy likes it very much. But I'm afraid Annie isn't pleased.'

'Listen to me, miss,' said Stoker impressively, wrapping her arms up in her apron as she spoke, 'a young lady like you doesn't know what coffee made in the dining-room means. Extra trays to carry and twice the washing up. You shouldn't let her do it.'

'But I can't help it, Stoker. I did tell Miss Grey that I thought Annie would be hurt, but she laughed. I don't think she quite understands Annie.'

'Send Tony to bed now,' interrupted Laura, who began to fear that Stoker would favour them with her company indefinitely, 'and tell him I'll come up to see him in half an hour, and he must have a bath, whether he wants it or not. And now, Sibyl,' she continued, as Stoker left the room with a burst of song, 'what is all this about Miss Grey? Stoker is full of some gossip or other. She and your Annie are the death of all our reputations.'

'Well, there's nothing much really. Miss James's sister got ill about the beginning of October and she had to go, so Daddy advertised and of course he got shoals of answers. He didn't know which to take, so he made me choose one, and I thought Una Grey sounded a nice name, and she wasn't too old, so we asked her to come on approval for a week, and Daddy and I liked her very much, or we shouldn't have kept her.'

'You don't like her so much now, then?'

'No, not really.'

'What's the matter? Isn't she competent?'

33

'Oh, yes, she's terribly competent and Daddy likes her awfully. I'm the one that doesn't care for her so much. You see, she's very clever, and I feel so small and unhelpful beside her – I expect it's really a horrid kind of jealousy.'

'But what is there to be jealous of?'

'Nothing really, I suppose. Only I feel less and less use to Daddy. I'm not very good at housekeeping, or typing, and Miss Grey is so good at both, so there doesn't seem to be anything for me to do. But Daddy is terribly pleased with her, so I suppose it's all right. Only Annie and cook and I have conversations sometimes when she is shut up with Daddy, and we wish we had Miss James again.'

'But she isn't unkind to you, is she?' asked Laura, sticking a few hairpins more firmly into her head, as if in preparation for an onslaught on Miss Grey.

'Oh, no, she's very kind and asked me to call her Una, but I couldn't quite do it, which is awkward, especially as she has called me Miss Knox ever since. She means to be very nice, I know, and encourage me; but she frightens me, Mrs Morland. She is always talking about how I must go and live in London, and meet lots of people, to help my writing, and she will make Daddy and me go out to dinner when we would much rather not, because she says she can't bear us to stay in on her account. And then Daddy writes to whoever it is and says may he bring his secretary, and people don't want an extra woman, but they don't like to say no. And if she isn't asked out with us, Mrs Morland, an awful thing happens. Her face goes scarlet, and she gets quite ill and goes to bed for a day or two. Of course, it is lovely to have her upstairs and have Daddy to myself again, but Annie does so hate taking her meals up, and then I have to do it, and she won't speak to me. Then, when she comes down, Daddy is so sorry for her that he gives in more than ever. And the awful thing is that he won't think of dismissing her, ever, because she has no home to go to and only distant relations, who despise her for being a secretary.'

Laura listened to this outburst with some perplexity. She had looked upon Sibyl as a kind of daughter since Mrs Knox died, and was prepared to fight for Sibyl's rights. But girls did exaggerate, and a girl like Sibyl, who had always lived at home with an adoring father, might easily make too much of Miss Grey's attitude. Possibly it might be quite a good thing for Sibyl to be in town for a bit and learn to stand on her own feet and make her own friends. However, she put aside Sibyl's speech for further consideration, resolved to judge for herself, and to get the opinion of Anne Todd, whose views were always worth considering. So she led the talk into safer channels, and delighted Sibyl by telling her some of the plot of the book she was working on. Sibyl, before she went, invited Tony to come and help with a little rough shooting on the following day and come back to Low Rising for tea, where Laura might meet him. Laura jumped inwardly at the prospect of seeing Miss Grey, and begged Sibyl not to let Tony kill himself, or, as a second thought, anyone else. Sibyl promised to put him in charge of the gardener, who would keep him out of mischief. Then she got into her car, and drove away.

Laura was genuinely puzzled and a little upset by this new and disturbing element in the quiet life of the two Risings, but a yell from Tony sent Miss Grey out of her head.

'What's the matter?' she shouted up the stairs.

There was dead silence, so she went up. Tony was sitting in a bath full of boiling water, with all the soaps, sponges, nailbrushes, loofahs and toothbrushes floating on the surface.

'Did you hear me, Mother?' he inquired as she came in. 'I was being the South Wales Express going into the Severn Tunnel. This is the Severn, with all the boats on it. Now, watch.'

Uttering another piercing shriek, he plunged under the water, there making a loud gurgling which Laura took to be the noise of an engine going through a tunnel.

'Come out at once, Tony, and don't splash the water about. You've been far too long already. Stoker has enough to do without your flooding the bathroom.'

Tony emerged, his hair dripping down his face, and plunged into the bath-towel which Laura was holding for him.

'Thank heaven you have washed that horrible stuff off your hair,' she remarked.

'Mother, did you see me go under the water? Did you hear the whistle? Mother, do you think old Stokes heard me?'

'Get all those things out of the bath, and clean your teeth, and come along to bed,' said Laura. 'Sibyl has asked you to go over for some shooting tomorrow and have tea there, and you can't go if you dawdle.'

Tony, by now in what he called his pyjama-legs, executed a dance of joy, while his mother picked up his clothes and examined them. The result was not satisfactory.

'Right through the seats again,' she said hopelessly. 'And

a hole in the middle of your jersey, as usual. Why on earth do little boys keep spikes in the middle of their stomachs? I can't account for it any other way. And why matron can't darn your stockings with a wool that matches, I can't think. I suppose I'll have to get Miss Todd to re-foot them all before you go back.'

'Mother,' began Tony, who had abstracted his mind during this jeremiad, 'it's a good thing we don't live on a planet where there isn't any air, or we couldn't breathe at all. We couldn't move either. Even a rocket car couldn't move. I wonder how we would manage. I suppose we'd have to wear gas masks and breathe oxygen. Mother, do you know what oxygen is?'

'No, I don't, and I don't care,' cried Laura, pushing Tony into his bedroom.

'Oh, Mother, don't you know that? We did an experiment about it in the lab last week. Mother, how do you think people could get on without oxygen?'

'Get into bed, Tony, and stop gabbling.'

'I thought you liked me to fold up my clothes,' said Tony sanctimoniously. 'Matron goes off pop if we don't fold them at school.'

'Leave them alone and get into bed!' shouted Laura.

Tony turned head over heels down the bed and dashed under cover, immediately poking up an anxious face to inquire, 'Where's Neddy?'

'I'll get him,' said Laura, who was sorting out Tony's ragamuffin attire. Opening a drawer, she extracted a stuffed donkey with a red flannel saddle, and threw him across to Tony. After rummaging a little more, she pulled out a foxcub's tail, mounted on a handle, with the inscription *Risings Hunt November, 1828*, which was a mistake of a century on the part of the local naturalist, but Laura had never liked to have it altered. On this cub Tony had been blooded, at the instigation of Gerald and John. He hadn't enjoyed the ceremony at all, but another and smaller boy had been frightened and cried, which had made Tony boast quite unbearably of his superior pluck and true-blue-ness.

'And here's Foxy,' said Laura, throwing it.

Tony caught them both with a scream of joy and arranged them carefully, one on each side.

'You great baby,' said his doting mother.

'But Neddy and Foxy like it, Mother. And really Neddy is quite a trouble, because he takes up so much room he nearly knocks me out of bed.'

'Put him on the table, then.'

'Oh, Mother, he'd be cold. Mother, how would you like it if you were put on a table all night?'

'The contingency would never occur,' said Laura, and hugged her son tightly. Just as she was going out of the room, Tony's voice was raised. 'Mother?'

'Well, what is it?'

'Oh, Mother, do you know, the Cheltenham Flier does over seventy, part of the way. I should think it could do over eighty easily. Mother, did you ever go in the Cheltenham Flier? Mother—'

Laura shut the door and reeled downstairs. Four weeks of this to come. Nearer five than four. Thank heaven it was the country, where he would be out all day, and would certainly amuse himself. Oh, the exhaustingness of the healthy young! Laura had once offered to edit a book called *Why I Hate my Children*, but though Adrian Coates had offered her every encouragement, and every mother of her acquaintance had offered to contribute, it had never taken shape. Perhaps, she thought, as she stood by Tony's bed an hour later, they wouldn't be so nice if they weren't so hateful.

There lay her demon son, in abandoned repose. His cheeks, so cool and firm in the day, had turned to softest rose-petal jelly, and looked as if they might melt upon the pillow. His mouth was fit for poets to sing. His hands – spotlessly clean for a brief space – still had dimples where later bony knuckles would be. Foxy was pressed to his heart, while Neddy, taking, as Tony had predicted, the middle of the bed, had pushed his master half over the edge.

Laura picked up the heavy, deeply unconscious body, and laid it back in the middle of the bed. Neddy she put revengefully on the table. Then she tucked the bed-clothes in, kissed her adorable hateful child, who never stirred and, turning out the light, left the room.

3

Low Rising

Holiday breakfasts were a ritual in which Tony and Stoker shared in equal ecstasy. As one who has been long in prison pent, Tony welcomed the extra hour which nine o'clock breakfast gave him, and the delicate inventions which Stoker, with the true cook's worship of a hearty male appetite, laid upon his plate. When he came down on the following morning a sausage, a fried egg and a piece of fried toast, together with the remains of last night's chips, were keeping hot for him under a cover. Of all these he rapturously partook, while expatiating to his mother on the meagre diet supplied by the housemaster's wife. According to Tony the diet consisted of starvation alternating with poisoned food, but so long as his face was so round, and his body so obviously well-nourished, Laura paid scant attention to his complaints. Directly after breakfast, she sent him off with sandwiches to join the shooters at Low Rising, and after half an hour's monologue from Stoker on life in its various aspects, she escaped to her room. Here, except for the occasional annoyance of having to get up and put coal on the fire, she hoped to do a long, conscientious morning's work on the typewriter, though typing one's own manuscript was poor fun, and she rarely did it now, except when Miss Todd was away.

But it was one of the days when the typewriter exhibits original sin in some of its more striking forms. That her own manuscript, written in pencil in threepenny exercise books, was mostly illegible, was not, as Laura in fairness admitted, the machine's fault; but there was no other fault which it left untried. To begin with, the evil day when the ribbon must be changed had been too long deferred. To do this job, Laura put on a large overall, turned her sleeves up, and after hunting for some time in a pile of papers, produced the Instruction Book of the Harrington Portable Typewriter. Any real author, she felt, without rancour, would, after having used the same kind of typewriter for about twenty years, remember offhand how to change a ribbon, but no vestige of remembrance ever clung to Laura's mind. The diagrams in the book were undoubtedly meant to be helpful, but they were always drawn from an angle at which you had never seen your machine, nor ever probably could, and assumed that you would remember which was Catch Point Release Lever and which Left Hand Spacer Stop – or words very much to that effect. Before you could change the ribbon you had to press Release Knob A either to the right or the left. Then you lifted the old spool from one side, manoeuvred the ribbon from a small gridiron in the middle, and took off the spool on the left. By the time you had done this, and removed a little spring clip from the empty spool, not only did all your fingers and thumbs look as though you were a Bertillon fan, but the clip, with the liveliness of necessary inanimate objects, had sprung high into the air and vanished. Laura could not see it anywhere on the carpet, so with a sinking heart she gently shook the machine. A rattle inside it told her that the worst had happened, and the spring clip had gone to earth. With a hearty curse she got a screwdriver from a drawer, wearily took the machine off its stand, rescued the clip, and screwed the typewriter firmly down again. She then refreshed her memory with a glance at the instructions, pushed Release Knob A in whichever direction she had not pushed it before, without being quite sure which that was, and reversed the unthreading process with a fresh black ribbon which, being new to the work, entered wholeheartedly into the spirit of the thing, and inked her so thoroughly that her fingerprints would have been entirely choked and valueless from Scotland Yard's point of view. For an instant she contemplated living a wider and fuller life by cleaning the type as well, but reflecting that even a small bottle of petrol in a room with a fire had been known to cause severe injuries to be sustained by people in the papers, she contented herself with picking the dirt out of the 'e' and the 'a' with a hairpin. By the time this was accomplished, and the hairpin replaced, her face was so streaked with ink that there was nothing for it but to go to the bathroom and have a thorough wash, which meant that she had to shout to Stoker for the special soap from the garage, which again let loose the floods of

Stoker's eloquence upon her. But at last, with fingers only faintly blue-black, she sat down to work.

After typing three lines, she looked at her page, and observed that the writing had become fainter and fainter, and was now only an adumbration of itself. She groaned.

'Of course I would,' she said aloud. 'I pushed the Release Knob the wrong way to start with.'

With a set face she altered the knob, wound the ribbon, which appeared to be at least a hundred yards long, from one spool to the other, pushed the knob back in the right direction and started again. Fate then relented, and after the trifling set-back of typing a whole page with the carbon the wrong way round, so that she had to re-type the sheet for her second copy, and the maddening way in which portable typewriters, however you may try to stabilise them with mats of felt or rubber, walk about all over your table like a planchette, knocking paper and inkstands on to the floor, she was able to work steadily till a late lunch.

The light was already fading as she set out to walk to Low Rising. High Rising was a pretty, unpretentious village consisting of one street, whose more imposing houses were vaguely Georgian. Laura's house stood at the end, so that she had no more than a mile to walk to Low Rising, which was only a church, a vicarage, a farm, and a handful of cottages. The Knoxes' house stood apart, down a turning of its own which led to nowhere in particular, and behind it fields stretched away to the slopes of the hills. As Laura walked along the field-path, which followed the little river Rising, she tried to imagine the kind of person this unknown Miss Grey would be. Probably one of those over-educated young

43

women who knew everything, and would help George Knox with dates and references. Naturally Sibyl, who had never had any education to speak of, would feel small. There was something about educated women that had that effect.

As she turned out of the fields by the church, Dr Ford came driving past, and pulled up when he saw her. They exchanged a few words and Laura asked about Mrs Todd.

'She has no right to go on living with that heart,' said the doctor. 'But Miss Todd keeps her going, and she may live till ninety, or she may drop down dead in a moment. Your Miss Todd will be glad to have you back. She's a good girl and doesn't have much fun.'

'I'm afraid she doesn't get much with me,' said Laura seriously.

'That's as you look at it. Can I give you a lift?'

'No, thanks. I'm going to the Knoxes'. I expect you have come from there.'

'Yes, getting my half-guinea under false pretences. Mr Knox is perfectly well, but his daughter got scared and sent for me.'

'Oh, did she? I thought it was the secretary.'

'Quite up in our local gossip as usual. That's my friend Stoker, I suppose.'

'Oh, no. Sibyl came over last night, and she said the secretary was worried. But she thought it was nothing.'

'It was certainly the secretary who rang me up, but she said Miss Knox wanted me to come. Have a look at the secretary, Mrs Morland, she is interesting. Tony's all right. I saw him with Sibyl, and he hadn't blown his own head off, or anybody else's.'

Dr Ford drove away. It was nearly dark as Laura crossed the green and walked down the willow avenue beside the brook. It was a lonely walk, and had a slightly haunted reputation, which occasionally caused one of Mr Knox's maids to have hysterics and give notice. But, being local girls, their mothers usually made them take it back. At the far end stood the Knoxes' house, lonely among the water-meadows, often surrounded by thick white mists, a little sinister, but Laura was not imaginative except in the matter of plot and incident.

The front door, ordinarily left open, was shut this evening, and Laura had to ring. It was opened by Mr Knox's Annie, who beamed a welcome.

'Mr Knox in, Annie?'

'I think so, mum. The master's up with Miss Grey in the study. Miss Sibyl and Master Tony are with the dogs in the yard; they'll be here in a minute.'

Laura stepped gratefully from the chill December dusk into the sitting-room. Low Rising Manor House still looked like the farmer's home which it had been for several hundred years, and George Knox, most annoyingly, would stick to oil lamps, which threw dark shadows among the beams of the ceiling and into the corners of the room. If George wanted to be really period, Laura had said to him, after a distracting evening with an ill-trimmed lamp, he had better have rushlights, which had the additional advantage of being less likely to set the house on fire. The living-room was long and low with windows to the ground. Above it was a similar room, where George Knox worked, looking down the willow avenue towards Low Rising. A fire was blazing in the large open fireplace, where a kettle, another of George's trying Wardour Street ways, was swinging over the flames on a hook. She sat down by the hearth, secretly quite relieved to know that Tony was alive. Pride would never allow her to inquire, but she was always glad when the shooting expeditions were over. Presently she heard a step coming down the stairs, and a young woman opened the door.

'You must excuse me,' said the newcomer. 'I believe you are Mrs Morland. Miss Knox told me you were coming today. Mr Knox is very busy, but he is coming down, just for tea.'

'Certainly I'll excuse you,' said Laura, 'though I haven't the faintest idea what for. You are Miss Grey, of course.'

'Has Miss Knox been telling you about me?' asked Miss Grey.

'Oh, yes, and Dr Ford, and my devoted maid, Stoker. We gossip very quickly here, Miss Grey, and I've been looking forward to meeting you.'

She held out her hand, without getting up. Miss Grey hesitated, then touched it without enthusiasm and moved away to the tea-table.

I'm ashamed of myself, thought Laura, for nearly being rude at sight. But I *won't* be patronised by a chit in George's house. And why should she ask if Sibyl has been talking about her? Why should she think that anyone wants to talk about her? Impertinence.

Then Sibyl and Tony burst into the room, followed by George Knox, large, loosely framed, violent in gesture and speech, kind and timorous at heart.

'My dear, dear Laura,' he cried, sweeping her into a vast embrace, 'this is divine. I must kiss you, on both sides of your face owing to my French blood. I was half asleep upstairs, desiccated in mind, ageing in body, and now here you are and everything lives again. You have met Miss Grey, who helps Sibyl to delude an old man into thinking he can still do a little work.'

'Don't be an ass, George,' said Laura, upon whom George's flights of fancy had long ceased to have any effect. 'You're not much older than I am, and I hope neither of us is desiccated yet. How's the book?'

'Getting on; getting on. And yours, my dear Laura?'

'Mine doesn't matter, as you very well know. It is a literary hack's day-labour. You offend me by asking, but as you *will* inquire, the Mysterious Mannequin is turning out to be in de Valera's pay, and is trying to smuggle model gowns into the Free State, to help Dublin to lead the world of fashion.'

George Knox roared with laughter. Laura glanced at Miss Grey, who was scowling into the teapot. 'I thought so,' said Laura to herself. 'Irish of course. First the voice, and a very pretty one, and this finishes it. Why did nobody mention it?'

Miss Grey was certainly interesting to look at, as Dr Ford had hinted, and attractive too. She was of middle height, with a charming figure; fair, straight, silky hair cut short like a page's; large grey-black eyes and a delicate complexion. At the moment her rather heavy chin was sulkily sticking out and her face distorted with anger, as she made the tea in a shadowy corner, but Laura could see that she would look very pretty and very appealing, so long as she controlled herself. And the devil's own temper, too, she thought, though she won't let George see it, and Sibyl only suspects it. I wish Anne Todd were here.

Sibyl and Tony were too busy eating to talk much, so George had the field to himself. Miss Grey sulked privately, and Laura listened.

'It is delightful, dear, dear Laura, to hear all about your book. We must have many talks about it, now that you are again among us. I long to hear more. We shall have a long talk and you shall tell me everything. I am having infinite trouble myself with my life of Edward the Sixth which is nearly finished. A much neglected figure, poor kinglet; personally, I mean. Think what it must have been to have such elder sisters as Mary and Elizabeth – practically aunts – and what aunts! And so many uncles! Some day I shall write a book about the Great Uncles of history. Great Uncles, I mean, of course, not great-uncles. They appear to me to have been the curse of England. From the days of Arthur – whose nephew Mordred, by the way, had no high opinion of his uncle, *et pour cause*, my dear Laura, if you read your Malory carefully – to the days of Victoria, uncles have always been in the ascendant. I go no further on account of my intense loyalty. I challenge you to name more than two English kings who did not suffer the intolerable tyranny of uncles.'

'Canute,' said Laura promptly, 'and Alfred, and Richard the Third.'

'You laugh at me, Laura. Richard was, of course, so essentially an uncle himself that we cannot think of him in the capacity of nephew, but I fear you cannot claim him. As for Canute and Alfred, I used the expression English kings, of

48

course, in its usual connotation; that is, meaning all kings who were not English, or all kings since the Conquest, at which date, as you are aware, the kings and queens of England begin. And mark me, Laura, none of the royal uncles, so far as we know, ever tipped a nephew. In fact, they would sooner put out their eyes, or smother them in the Tower, than part with the half-sovereign, rose noble, angel, call it what you will, which is the rightful perquisite of a nephew. The more I see of uncles, the better I like aunts. And you, my dear Laura, are the aunt incarnate, perfection.'

'Well, George, I'm not, if that helps you at all. I am a mother and I hope to be a grandmother, but an aunt I cannot be. Sisters and brothers have I none, nor had my husband either, but this child's mother,' said she, point-ing accusingly at Tony across the table, 'is my mother's daughter.'

Tony looked startled.

'Can I give you some more tea, Mrs Morland?' said Miss Grey, who was now looking normal again.

And stop me talking, thought Laura. 'No, thank you; it was delicious,' she said aloud. 'And it's all right, Tony, Mr Knox and I were only speaking in parables.'

'But you've got it all wrong, Mother. It is a man looking at his own portrait, and he says—'

'All right, Tony,' said Sibyl, quickly pushing a doughnut at him. 'They were only talking nonsense. Hurry up and finish your tea.'

Laura felt she must do something civil to Miss Grey, so she inquired whether she was very busy.

'Yes, we are – very busy. While Miss Knox was out with

the shooters today, we put in a hard day's work. There is very little time left before Mr Knox's book has to go to the printer, and every moment is precious.'

'Couldn't I help?' asked Sibyl, rather timidly, but encouraged by Laura's presence. 'I know your typing is better than mine, but if you are very busy, I would like so much to give you and Daddy a hand.'

'What do you think, Mr Knox?' asked Miss Grey, not looking at Sibyl. 'Doesn't it seem rather a shame that Miss Knox, who loves being out of doors, should sit at the typewriter while you have a secretary?' The words 'and a good one' were almost audible in her tone.

'But it would be so good for Sibyl to practise her typing, Miss Grey,' Laura put in kindly. 'She will get out of practice if she never works.'

'I feel sure Mr Knox won't want Miss Knox to be kept indoors working for him all day,' was the answer.

'You ought to get out too, Miss Grey,' said Laura with some malice. 'Oughtn't she, George?'

But a scuffle between two dogs who had crept in under the table and were being fed by Tony, prevented any pronouncement from George.

'Take those dogs out, Tony,' said Miss Grey sharply.

Laura at once resented this order to her son. The woman had been absurdly cold and rude all teatime, and it couldn't be tolerated. Rising majestically, she said, ignoring Miss Grey, 'Well, George, we must go. It's been a pleasure to see you, and tell you all about my book. Next time you must tell me about yours. How are your quarrels with Johns and Fairfield?'

'Raging, as ever. All publishers are a race inhuman, set apart, flourishing in wickedness, but probably doomed to eternal fires.'

'Don't exaggerate, George. You are celebrated in the whole book world for your grasping ways. Publishers fly at the sight of you. You should be kind, and never grasping, and ask no questions, and they will eat out of your hand, like my charming Adrian Coates!'

'Ah, woman, woman! Always at the mercy of a smooth face and a flattering tongue. If Coates eats out of your hand, it is because he finds it pays him. If he ate less, you would have more.'

'Be quiet, George, you are disgusting. I get just as good terms from Adrian as you do from your men, without accusing him of being a Jew all the time. And as for a smooth face, I know nothing about its smoothness, and I'll thank you to keep your tongue off a widow woman.'

Here Laura and George both broke down and laughed uproariously. Mixed emotions were struggling in Miss Grey's face. Obviously she was puzzled by their peculiar, if not very brilliant brand of humour, and not a little shocked to see her employer making himself a motley to the view. But there was something else; perhaps curiosity. Her face softened to a charming smile. 'Is Mr Adrian Coates your publisher, then, Mrs Morland?' she asked, in a soft, eager voice, quite unlike her previous tones.

'He is that,' responded Laura with equal suavity.

Miss Grey actually blushed, though whether at Laura's slight assumption of a brogue, or for some other reason, Laura couldn't be sure.

51

'I have read his poems,' was Miss Grey's surprising statement.

'Those must be his early ones. He hasn't written anything since.'

'I thought them lovely. And I have seen his photograph in a newspaper article. I think he is wonderful.'

This was most unusual. How annoyed Adrian would be, thought Laura, to have these early poems admired. He had rashly flown into print with them when he was still at Oxford, and was now not only thoroughly ashamed of them, but had ever since forsworn the Muse.

'Well, you must meet him some time and talk about them,' said Laura brightly. Then turning to George she said goodbye, adding, 'I suppose you and Sibyl are going to Italy quite soon now.'

'As a matter of fact, Italy is off,' said George.

'But why?'

'It – seemed advisable,' was all George would say. Laura, baffled, shook hands, refusing the farewell accolade, and smiled to Miss Grey, who came forward to shake hands very prettily. Sibyl came to the door with Laura and Tony.

'I'm sorry Italy is off,' said Laura. 'The exchange, I suppose?'

Sibyl looked nervously around. 'Miss Grey persuaded Daddy not to go,' she said softly. 'She said he must get his new book planned out, and Italy would be better in May. Oh, Mrs Morland, I don't want to be horrid, but I think she really wanted to be sure of staying here. It's beastly of me to mind, but I was so looking forward to Italy with Daddy. I think she was afraid that when Edward the Sixth was finished he mightn't want her any more, so she wanted him to get well into another book so that he would need her.'

'I'm sorry about Italy, too, my dear, but keep a sense of proportion. Come and talk to me and Anne Todd if you're worried. And I want you to come over to tea on Saturday. Adrian is coming, and I'd like you to meet him. It may be useful for you, as you are writing.'

Sibyl shuffled nervously from one foot to another, and as Laura kissed her, she felt that the child's cheeks were burning hot. Why this embarrassment over Adrian?

'It's awfully good of you, Mrs Morland, but really I'd rather not. You and Mr Coates are sure to have heaps to talk about, and I'd be in the way.'

'Nonsense, child. I wouldn't ask you if I didn't want you. And I don't want your father. He breathes up too much air. Come alone. Goodbye, dear.'

As Laura and Tony disappeared into the darkness, Sibyl lingered at the door, pink-faced and terrified. She watched the light of Tony's torch flickering down the avenue till they turned the corner. 'Oh, I wish people wouldn't. Oh, if only they wouldn't,' she sighed, and then turned and went indoors.

4

Christmas Eve

On Saturday morning, which was also Christmas Eve, Dr Ford had a letter from Miss Todd at Bournemouth. She said her mother had not been quite so well for the last two days, but they were coming back according to plan, and would Dr Ford be kind enough to look in directly after lunch if he was free. This letter sent Dr Ford hurrying to his desk to consult the railway guide. Not seeing it, he rang the bell, which was answered by Mr Knox's Annie's aunt, a placid widow, who managed Dr Ford and his house with a firm hand. She had been cook to his predecessor and had married the gardener, but continued to live in the house. Her husband's death some years later was borne with philosophy, and any devotion she may have felt for him was transferred not to her employer in particular, but to the house and, as it were, to the status of doctorhood which surrounded it. After the old doctor's death she was left as caretaker, and when Dr Ford bought the house and practice from his widow, no one questioned her right to stay on as housekeeper. She cooked, washed, and cleaned, with occasional help from Mr Knox's Annie's sister, of whose work she held much the same opinion as Stoker, though slightly more bitter on account of the relationship, and never minded how late or irregular meal times were.

Dr Ford was a very energetic middle-aged man, with private means, good friends with all his patients. Some of them complained that in the winter he gave more time to hunting than to their complaints, but when there was anything real to do, his devotion was untiring, and his noisy two-seater was heard from one end of the district to the other. Naturally the village had married him to the old doctor's widow, to Mrs Morland, to Miss Todd, to Miss Knox, and to several other unconscious females whose names do not concern us. But years passed by, and Dr Ford still showed no symptoms of matrimony. Mr Knox's Annie's aunt, to whom it will perhaps be more convenient to allude by her name of Mrs Mallow, would listen with remote toleration to the village talk of marriage, but without encouragement. She would have been quite pleased to see a nice mistress established in the house, whom she could manage and spoil, but Something told her, so Mrs Mallow said, that it was not to be. There were certain signs, only known to those who had long lived in doctors' houses and so become affiliated to the profession and its mysteries, which told Mrs Mallow that a bachelor's house it would ever be. Whether one of the signs was a packet of old letters tied up with ribbon, discovered by Mrs Mallow during a spring cleaning, it would be indiscreet to inquire, and as the letters were from his grandfather to his father, and were kept by the doctor for the sake of the very forcible language in which the old gentleman expressed his opinion of his son's adherence to the Oxford Movement, it is improbable that they exercised any influence upon the doctor's matrimonial intentions. He hadn't the faintest idea of marrying anyone, or hadn't till this winter, when old Mrs Todd had needed more frequent attention, and propinquity had been at its fatal work. Dr Ford was apt to judge women by their sick-room manner, and rarely had he seen such a kind, firm, and perfect manner as Miss Todd's.

After one unusually trying day when the old lady had insisted on sending for him three times, ostensibly because she had palpitations, but really to tell him to order an ambulance from the county hospital to take her revolting little dog for a drive, he had expressed his opinion to Miss Todd.

'I wish your mother were certifiable,' said he frankly, kicking the revolting little dog quite kindly off the hearth-rug. 'A week of it would kill me, and you have to stick it day in, day out.'

'Oh, it might be worse,' said Miss Todd. 'It's quite harmless, and Louisa is rather proud of her. It's quite a distinction to be in service where there's a dotty old lady. What sometimes gets me down is answering the same question ten times in an hour. So long as I don't go dotty myself, and the money lasts out, it'll be all right.'

'Well, you're a good woman. And as for the money – don't look at me with an independent expression, for that's only stupid pride – I may as well say that there's nothing I can do for your mother, unless her heart or her mental

56

condition suddenly get worse, so it's no use coming as a doctor. But if you'll let me drop in occasionally and give a friendly look round, that won't hurt anyone.'

Miss Todd gulped. 'I'll take your charity,' she said. 'There isn't anyone else's in the world I'd take,' and went out of the room in tears.

The subject of money was not mentioned again at the time, but when Miss Todd began going to Mrs Morland as secretary, she insisted on having an account from Dr Ford, much to his annoyance. He persuaded, he blustered, he was almost pathetic, but Miss Todd stood firm. All he could do was to talk to her in her front garden instead of in her drawing-room, and put her fees, which she luckily paid in cash, into his safe, in an envelope marked *Property of Miss Anne Todd left with me for safe keeping*.

Mrs Mallow answered the bell, carrying a large live duck by the legs.

'Annie's mother's brought a duck this morning, sir. If I can get it reasonable, would you like it for your dinner? It's a nice fat bird,' she added, poking the unhappy duck which emitted a loud quack.

'Put the animal the right way up!' shouted the doctor. 'Do you think I can eat anything I've seen carried about upside-down? Good God, woman, the poor creature's blood will go to its head.'

Mrs Mallow mildly put the duck on the floor, where it felt far from at its ease, and rushed backwards and forwards, squawking and flapping its wings.

'You was wanting something, sir?' she asked.

'The railway guide,' snapped the doctor.

57

'What you haven't used for shaving papers, sir, is in the dressing-room. I'll get it.'

She came back with the remains of a railway guide in her hand.

'Confound it. I've used up to Exeter,' said Dr Ford angrily, 'and I wanted Bournemouth.'

'Shall I telephone to the station, sir?' asked Mrs Mallow.

'No, I will. And take that bird away, and don't let me see it again.'

Mrs Mallow, without appearing to exert herself at all, caught the duck, and departed as serenely as she had come, holding it by the legs, head downwards. A minute afterwards it breathed its last under Annie's mother's experienced hands, and was much appreciated by the doctor the following evening.

Having got the time of Miss Todd's arrival from the station-master at Stoke Dry, Dr Ford went out on his rounds, timing them so that he would meet the Bournemouth train. Miss Todd was already helping her mother out of the carriage when he arrived, so he helped to get the old lady down and carried the suitcases.

'I'll drive you home myself,' he said, 'and have a look at your mother as soon as she's rested.'

They all packed into the two-seater, where Mrs Todd, whose intellect, if not her heart, appeared to have derived benefit from the sea air, conversed in a sprightly way about their hotel at Bournemouth and the shops.

'Shops were the trouble,' said Miss Todd, who had acquired the habit of speaking of her maternal parent as if she were stone deaf. 'Mother wanted to give orders on her usual scale. But when I told them she was dotty, they were quite decent. The hotel people thought she was very rich and a bit eccentric. How do you think she looks?'

'Wait till I've seen her properly. What about you? Not much of a rest, was it?'

'Mrs Morland back?' asked Miss Todd, ignoring his question.

'Yes. She and Tony came down on Tuesday. And I have a message for you. She says, will you come up to tea this afternoon. Her publisher is coming, and she may want you about some business. But not if it is inconvenient, she said.'

'I'll come. I've missed the work terribly. Will you be an angel and ring her up for me and let her know? Mother will be all right. You can have a chat with her when you come, and then our Louisa will love to hear all about Bournemouth, and give Mother her tea.'

'I might drop in and give you a lift back.'

'Hardly worth while, unless you are coming back that way.'

'I am.'

Mrs Todd was safely decanted into her own house and received by Louisa and the revolting little dog, while Dr Ford went home to lunch.

Adrian Coates, driving himself down from London in a rather glorious car, got to High Rising in time for lunch. If Adrian had a touch of Jewish blood, it was all to the good in his business capacity and in his dark handsomeness. One could hardly question Adrian himself about it, but the suspicion was an immense comfort to such of his brother publishers as were being less successful on a purely Christian basis. They had nearly all, at various times, attempted to wrest Laura from his clutches, but she preferred to remain there. Johns and Fairfield, of whom we have already heard Mr Knox's extremely untrustworthy opinion, had laid determined siege to her.

'You should consider your own interests a little, Mrs Morland,' said Johns (or Fairfield), persuasively, at a lunch party given by George Knox at his instigation. 'Our friend Coates is a remarkable man in his way, a real flair for discovering talent, as we know; excellent at preparing the ground; but he has not, cannot in the nature of things, have the standing we have. With our immense resources we can give you double the advertisement you are at present having. If you have something new and delightful in preparation, and are not yet committed to Coates, may we have the pleasure of having a first sight of your manuscript?'

'Well, you see,' said Laura, 'what I say about advertising is, if you spend all that money on advertisements, it's got to come off my royalties, hasn't it?'

At this striking view of the uses of advertisement, Mr Johns (whom we may as well call by that name, for Laura never discovered, or remembered to ask, which of the firm he was) was so staggered that he had nothing to say. So Laura calmly continued, 'And I like dealing with my publisher direct. If I came to you I'd have to see underlings half the time, but I can always see Adrian whenever I like. And then he hasn't got a wife, so there's no bother about being asked to dinners and that sort of thing.'

Again Mr Johns was stupefied, though Laura had not the slightest idea that he was celebrated for the appallingly dull banquets which his lion-hunting American wife forced him to give four or five times a year.

'So thank you ever so much,' said Laura, turning her charming tired eyes on Mr Johns, and pushing some loose ends of hair under her hat, 'but really I think I'm very well as I am, and anyway I've got a new contract for three more books on very good terms.'

This was pure showing off, as Laura had very little notion of what terms, good or bad, should be. But as she got a good deal more money on each book she wrote, she was quite contented – and if she had known it, she was getting very good treatment as well.

Luckily George Knox had been deserted by the lady on his other side for a few moments, which he had employed in listening to this peculiar conversation. He could hardly wait for lunch to be over, so eager was he to get Laura alone.

'Oh, you pearl, you pearl,' he exclaimed, taking both her hands and waving them up and down. 'By Jove, I like the way you tackled that devil. Dull dinner parties! When I think of his wife and the agonies – eternal agonies, dear Laura – that I have to sit through, it does me good to think of the way you set him down.'

Poor Laura, much distressed, offered to go and apologise to Mr Johns, but was dissuaded by George Knox, who said it would only make matters worse. With his usual indiscretion he then told everyone he met what had happened, including Adrian, who was immensely pleased and touched by Laura's confidence, and delighted by the snub to Johns.

'That woman is a heavenly fool,' he confided to George

Knox. 'She appears to take anything I do for her in the business line as a personal favour, and thanks me for what she is paying for. If I were a swindler— But look here, Knox, to take a leaf out of Johns's book, what about letting me see a manuscript of yours?'

This was not very seriously meant, but George Knox used such overwhelming wealth of verbiage and circumlocution in refusing the suggestion, that Adrian heartily regretted his mild joke.

As Adrian drew up at Laura's door, Tony came round the corner of the house, with an abstracted air.

'Hullo, Tony,' said Adrian, getting out.

'Hullo, sir. Oh, Mr Coates, what would you say was the best name for an engine? Princess Elizabeth or Titley Court?'

'Princess Elizabeth, undoubtedly.'

Tony's face fell.

'But Princess Elizabeth is only a two-four-nought, and the Titley Court is four-six-nought.'

'What on earth does that mean?'

'Oh, sir, didn't you know that? The Princess Elizabeth has two bogey wheels and four driving wheels, and the Titley Court has four bogies and six driving wheels. Titley Court is a lovely engine. It costs thirteen guineas, and I am going to save up. I got about two pounds ten last Christmas, so if I saved up every year, I could get the Titley Court in nearly six years.'

Unable to stem this flood of information, Adrian went into the house, followed by the railway expert.

'You see, sir, I could get the Titley Court in clockwork, or steam driven with methylated spirit, or coal. And if I had coal, I could get a real tank to fill the boiler from. Wouldn't it look splendid if I had an accident, and the Titley Court was really derailed, and lay puffing out steam?'

'Go and wash, Tony,' said his mother, appearing from upstairs. 'Come in, Adrian, and take your coat off. Your hands are as cold as ice. It's beginning to freeze, I think. Had you better put a rug over the radiator?'

'It's got a little quilt-affair of its own, thank you. But I'm terribly hungry.'

'That's good news,' said Stoker from the dining-room door. 'Here's lunch, and I do like to see a gentleman hungry. It's a steak-and-kidney pudding, Mr Coates. Do you good – you're not so stout as you was.'

'Bless you for the kind word, Stoker.'

'Dr Ford rang up,' said Stoker to her mistress, as she handed the vegetables, 'to say Miss Todd will be up to tea, and he will look in and fetch her.'

'Thanks, Stoker, you needn't wait. Not,' she added as Stoker left the room, 'that it's any good saying that, because she'll be back with the next course soon, and start talking again, and I can't send her away twice. I sometimes wish I could lock her and Tony and George Knox up in a cell, and see which would talk the other to death.'

'I'd back Tony,' said Adrian, with conviction. 'He has youth on his side as well as unholy fluency.'

'Mother,' began the subject of this unsympathetic comment, 'Mr Coates thinks Princess Elizabeth, but he didn't know the Titley Court was really a better engine. You see, the Princess Elizabeth is only two-four-nought, and the Titley Court—'

63

'Be quiet, Tony. I apologise for this nursery meal, Adrian. Tell me what you have come about, if it isn't a bore.'

Adrian plunged into an explanation of cheap editions, their advantages and disadvantages, which lasted through apple fritters and cheese. He was so carried away by his own enthusiasm that Laura remarked, without heat:

'I think I'll put you in the cell too, Adrian. Poor Stoker hasn't been able to get a word in since we started lunch. Yes, Tony, you can be excused. Coffee in the drawing-room, please, Stoker.'

The business in hand took some time to discuss, and it is doubtful whether Laura was much wiser at the end than at the beginning, for all her air of intelligence. But Adrian had clarified his own plans to himself, and laid the foundation of an edition which was to help a good deal towards supporting Laura's old age. Also Laura was not paying much attention, being wrapt in pleasant day-dreams about Adrian and Sibyl. What could be more delightful than to interest Adrian in Sibyl through her writing, and so begin a romance? Laura had never succeeded in persuading Sibyl to show her anything, and the child showed a commendable disinclination to rush into print in early youth. George Knox had spoken with enthusiasm of what Sibyl was going to do, though with a spaciousness which left Laura rather vague as to whether Sibyl was writing a novel, a short story, poetry, a play, biography, or literary essays. Something she must have in her, with that father, brought up among books as she was. Perhaps Miss Grey's plan for getting her to London would really be a good thing, and give her self-confidence. At any rate, she and

Adrian should meet that very day; that could do no harm. And perhaps George Knox would let Adrian publish all his books if he married his daughter, thought the ignorant Laura.

She was roused from these pleasant speculations by a touch on her arm, and returning to daily life with a jerk, saw that Adrian was solemnly handing her two large hairpins.

'Have you heard a single word I've been saying, Laura?' he asked in affectionate exasperation. 'You have been lying back in your chair with pins dropping from your head like the last rose of summer, and quite obviously not paying the slightest attention. I know my conversation is dull, but when I'm trying to make your fortune, Laura dear, don't you think you might try to understand?'

'I'm very sorry,' said Laura, replacing the pins, 'but it's no good my saying anything, because you always know better than I do, and anyway it will be your fortune as well as mine. And I expect you are still quite honest. What do you want me to do? Go to one of those literary agents and pay him to make bad blood between us?'

To this novel view of a literary agent's functions, Adrian could say nothing. So Laura went on, 'Nonsense, Adrian. You send me a contract, and I'll get George Knox to read it, and he will say everything is a hundred per cent too little, and that will give me a pretty good idea that your terms are all right.'

'Laura, you will drive me mad. Is this the way to do business? George Knox is a grasping, over-reaching old owl. For heaven's sake don't take his advice. Get your lawyer on to it, but not Knox.'

'I never meant to. When I see reason to mistrust you, Adrian, I'll make a frightful row. Till then, what you say goes.'

'Which makes you more of a weight on my conscience than ten grasping authors,' said Adrian resignedly.

'Then that's all right. Now don't be too hard on George, because his daughter is coming to tea and she is writing something – I don't know what – and if it is at all in your line you might get in ahead of Johns and Fairfield. I know George thinks well of it, but no one has seen it. So be nice to the child, because she is young and shy. By the way, you have a new admirer in this neighbourhood.'

'Who?'

'George's secretary. She has a secret passion for you, on account of your poems, and she has your photograph out of some paper.'

'Good God,' said Adrian, 'I must be getting back to town at once.'

'All right. She isn't coming to tea. It's only Sibyl Knox and Anne Todd, whom you do know. I thought we might need her. And I said tea at four, so you can get back in plenty of time. I suppose you wouldn't care to go and see Tony's railway before tea? He would so love it.'

Adrian, who liked to please the goose that laid his golden eggs, and also was genuinely fond of the goose's child, in spite of its tongue, pulled himself out of his chair and went upstairs. He had not been long gone when a car drove up. Laura heard Stoker answer the bell. Then that faithful creature appeared mysteriously at the drawing-room door and made incomprehensible signs to Laura, who

66

told her to come and say what it was. Stoker, shutting the door cautiously behind her, advanced with a conspirator's tread.

'What is the matter, Stoker?'

'Do you know who is at the door?'

'How can I know unless you tell me?'

'She's come,' said Stoker, with an air of gloomy triumph.

'Who has come? Really, Stoker, one can't get any sense out of you these holidays. Is it Miss Knox?'

'Yes, and no, as you might say.'

'For heaven's sake, who or what is it?'

'Miss Sibyl's come, but she's brought That One with her.'

'Miss Grey, I suppose?'

Stoker nodded portentously.

'Well, that's most annoying, especially as I didn't ask her and don't want her, but it can't be helped, and you needn't behave like a banshee about it. Where are they?'

'I told them to go in the dining-room while I found you. You don't want to see Her, do you?' asked Stoker, pointing her thumb over her shoulder.

'Oh, Stoker, you are an ass. Show them in at once, and tell Mr Coates – he's upstairs with Tony.'

Stoker's face fell, but she left the room and returned with the guests. To Laura's horror she announced Sibyl with a flourish, and then said to Miss Grey, 'Who shall I say, miss? Mrs Morland didn't tell me there'd be two.'

'Come in, Miss Grey,' cried Laura, rushing to the rescue. 'How nice that you could come. You must be frightfully cold, aren't you?'

To her further embarrassment Stoker said, 'Pleased to see

you, miss,' in a stage aside to Sibyl, and left the room, banging the door. Laura ploughed feverishly on, 'I'm so glad you managed to get out. I hope that means Mr Knox's book is getting on well. It's a delicious drive from Low Rising, isn't it?'

'It's just lovely,' said Miss Grey, without a trace of her former sulky manner. 'I couldn't resist the afternoon, so I started with Miss Knox, meaning to go back to tea, but we found the afternoon was getting on, and she persuaded me to come in with her. I do hope, Mrs Morland, I'm not being pushing, but I've heard so much of you from Mr Knox that I felt I really knew you quite well.'

Laura answered civilly, but was inwardly consumed with fury at the woman's impertinence. How dare she talk as if she and George Knox had been discussing their neighbour? Sibyl knew quite well that she was at liberty to bring anyone she liked to Laura's house, but Laura was pretty sure that Sibyl had not suggested this afternoon's outing. It was a black lookout if one could never see George and Sibyl again without this incubus squatting down beside them. She did not dare to exchange glances with Sibyl, and was thankful when tea arrived, with Adrian and Tony on its heels.

'Adrian,' she said, 'I want you to know a very dear friend of mine, Sibyl Knox, a kind of adopted daughter.' Not till they had shaken hands did she introduce Miss Grey, adding with a meaning look at Adrian, 'Miss Grey is doing some secretarial work for George Knox at present.'

She saw Adrian blench at the news and cast an appealing glance at her.

'There's a chair by Miss Knox, Adrian,' she said, 'and I

want you by me, Miss Grey. I do hope you are enjoying our part of the country.'

'I just love it. And I enjoy working for Mr Knox enormously – it's a privilege.'

'You've been with him all the autumn, haven't you? You weren't here in the summer holidays, when I was last down.'

'No, I had another position then, where I wasn't very happy.'

'Bad luck,' said Laura, who didn't at all want to hear about Miss Grey's unhappiness.

'It was a little difficult, Mrs Morland. I was very much misunderstood.'

'Oh, well, that happens to all of us,' said Laura cheerfully.

Miss Grey turned her large, expressive eyes on Laura and murmured, with a slight added touch of her pretty brogue, 'Yes, I know, but most people have someone to go to with their troubles. I am such a homeless person,' which forced Laura, against her will, to say something conventional about hoping Miss Grey would feel quite at home at Low Rising.

'Indeed I do. Mr Knox is kindness itself and so is Miss Knox. It is lovely to be in a house where there are no petty feelings. When I had to give up my last position, largely through my employer's wife, I had nowhere to go, and no one to turn to. So you can imagine how lucky I think myself to have got this job, where everyone is so kind, and all Mr Knox's friends are so interesting. I have always loved your wonderful books, Mrs Morland, if you don't mind my saying so, and I have been so looking forward to meeting you. And it's a great privilege to meet Mr Coates today. I hardly hoped for such luck.'

Laura's distaste for this well-spoken young woman deepened. What interest was it to her to know that Miss Grey was disliked by her late employer's wife? I'd have loathed her myself, she thought, if she was rude one minute and all over me the next. Luckily Miss Grey, having apparently given Laura her share of flattery for the time, turned to Tony and began to talk about dogs, a subject upon which they both became quite human, so Laura was able to cast an eye on what she already called her young couple, who were getting on very well. Although Miss Grey's presence put a slight constraint on her, Sibyl was much more herself. But some anxiety, which she could not altogether shake off, was evidently still weighing on her mind. Under cover of Miss Grey's animated description of an Airedale she had had as a girl, Sibyl said to Adrian, 'Do you think it is a good thing to talk to authors about their works?'

As Adrian's professional experience of them was that they rarely wanted to talk about anything else, he said, 'Yes,' heartily. Sibyl looked confused.

'Even poetry?' she asked nervously.

'I should think so.'

'Oh,' and she looked ready to cry.

Adrian was rather perplexed. Had this girl been writing poetry by any chance and wanted him to look at it? Otherwise, why introduce the subject like that? 'Am I speaking to a poet?' he asked.

'Oh, no. But I am; that's the trouble.'

She looked so confiding and worried that Adrian had to ask her if he could help.

'Well, you see, an awful thing has happened. Daddy's secretary – you know, over there – loves your poems, and she made me read them, because we were to meet you here today. At least, Mrs Morland asked me to come, and she wanted to come too, so I couldn't very well say no, but I knew it would be awful.'

'I'm getting a bit confused. What is it exactly that is awful? Is it me? Or going to tea with Mrs Morland?' Sybil shook her head violently, but still cast appealing glances at him, as if praying to be helped out of some difficulty. 'Or is it my poems you don't like?'

Sibyl blushed painfully. 'I'm terribly sorry, Mr Coates. I did try to, because she wanted me to be able to tell you how much I liked them and ask you to come and see us some time. And I know I'm a fool, and anyway I can't ever understand poetry except the bits in anthologies, but I couldn't understand yours at all. I'm so very, very sorry.'

'Dear Miss Knox, I don't know when I've had a more comforting thing said to me.'

'Do you mean one needn't like them?'

'One not only needn't, but one would be an abject ass if one did – with all respect to your father's secretary. Early poems are a thing it takes years to live down. If only you knew how many people have told me they liked those shameful, half-baked verses of mine, in the hopes that I would want to publish their even worse prose, you would be surprised. I was just a conceited undergraduate with doting parents, and that's the truth of it. The poems, if you can call them that, were a disgrace to civilisation, and I've never written another line and never shall.'

71

Sibyl's face showed what seemed to Adrian quite dispro-
portionate relief as she said, 'I'm so glad. I feel much safer.
Then you aren't an author at all now?'

'Not a bit, and never shall be. But I am speaking to one,
I believe. Mrs Morland tells me you are writing. May one ask
what?'

'But you said one's first things were awful.'

'Not always by any means,' said Adrian laughing. 'I feel
sure there must be something very interesting and delicious
to come from you, Miss Knox.'

Sibyl sank into the depths of embarrassment again and sat
miserably twisting her hands together, but Miss Grey saved
her from any further questioning by getting up and saying
they must go, as Mr Knox would be waiting for her. Before
Laura could burst with indignation over Miss Grey's assumption of leadership, Stoker threw open the door, stating,
'Someone you *will* be glad to see. Miss Todd.'

Miss Todd's arrival kept the Low Rising party for a few
minutes. Miss Todd engaged Miss Grey in conversation
about Bournemouth, and varieties of typewriter, while Sibyl,
quite happy again, sparkled at Adrian. Then, at a look from
Miss Grey, she got up and began saying goodbye.

'Don't you think, Miss Knox,' said Miss Grey, 'that we
might take it upon ourselves to ask Mrs Morland to bring
Mr Coates over to us when he is next here? I am sure your
father would like it.'

'Oh, yes,' said Sibyl, resuming her harried air.

'Mr Coates is coming to me for the New Year weekend,'
said Laura, interested to see how far Miss Grey would go.
Miss Grey then suggested that they should dine at Low

Rising on New Year's Eve. Laura, knowing that Adrian could easily have enough of George Knox, was beginning to hedge, when Adrian expressed his approval of the plan. So, like a kind match-maker, she accepted, subject to ratification from Mr Knox, and the ladies took their leave.

Laura, Miss Todd, and Adrian then had a short professional talk, after which Adrian went back to town, Tony clinging to his running board as far as the end of the drive.

'Mother, Mother,' cried Tony, bursting, round-eyed, a minute later, into the drawing-room, where Laura and Miss Todd were sitting comfortably by the fire. 'What do you think has happened?'

Laura had a moment's sick fear. 'Not an accident? Nothing's happened to Adrian?'

'Mother, how could you! Of course not. Look, Mother; look, Miss Todd!'

Speechless with emotion, he exhibited a pound note, Adrian's Christmas tip. Laura pushed him out of the room, recommending him to tell Stoker, and sat down exhausted. After a moment's peaceful silence, Miss Todd remarked, 'So that's the woman.'

Laura, still smarting under her wrongs, told Miss Todd all that had happened that afternoon, and her indignation at Miss Grey's behaviour. Miss Todd listened calmly.

'I'm glad all the same. I wanted to get a look at her. You see, with you being away all autumn, I didn't see much of the Knoxes, and if Sibyl ran in for a moment, it was while her father and Miss Grey were working and she was alone. I can tell you all about her now, Mrs Morland.'

'Do you know her, then?'

'No. But we serfs,' (which was Miss Todd's invariable way of mentioning her status as secretary to a well-known authoress) 'have a secret understanding of each other. She's a queer fish, Mrs Morland. I wouldn't say a bad egg, but a neurotic, and possibly a dangerous egg. Of course she's after Mr Knox, and she'll very likely get him. She is the sort that always gets her employer. Sibyl will be her difficulty. That woman is a fool to take airs like that, inviting guests to the house in front of Sibyl. The child is too ignorant and too shy to stand up for herself. I wonder where she was before, and how much damage she's done already.'

'Oh, Anne, how sinister.'

'Fairly sinister, but might be worse. It's a good thing you are down for the holidays.'

'But I can't do anything – I can't interfere.'

'No, but you are a counter-attraction.'

'Rubbish, Anne.'

'Rubbish, perhaps, but I'm right about Miss Grey. Trust one serf to see through another. Ask Dr Ford,' said she, as the doctor came into the room, ' whether Miss Grey isn't a queer fish.'

'Well, that sounds less disagreeable than being a neurotic egg, Anne. How do you do, Dr Ford. As Miss Grey isn't your patient, could we gossip about her?'

Dr Ford proved to be refreshingly free from gossip inhibitions, and gave it as his opinion that the new secretary was certainly a neurotic egg, and would be a nuisance if she went on unchecked.

'I don't mind about Knox,' he declared. 'If he can't keep a woman off at his age, he's a fool; but I don't like it for

Sibyl. The girl is very young for her age, and easily bullied. She might have fallen for Miss Grey, for the woman has a way with her. But as she hasn't, she may be persecuted a good deal. Ever seen Miss Grey in one of her tempers?' Neither of them had. 'All right, wait till you do. All I hope is that she will lose her temper with Sibyl while Knox is there. He adores the child, and that would settle Miss Grey's hash.'

'But how did you see her in a temper?' asked Miss Todd.

'Professional secrets.'

'Not now,' said Miss Todd. 'It's too serious. Out with it.'

Dr Ford, who only wanted to be pressed, continued his story.

'It was in November some time, and the Knoxes were asked to dinner at Castle Rising. Miss Grey seems to have said she was Cinderella so loud and so often, and sat so firmly in the ashes, that Knox got uncomfortable and asked if she could come too. It wasn't at all convenient, because Lady Stoke was away and the earl only wanted the Knoxes in a friendly sort of way – this he told me himself. But Miss Grey got her invitation, and then Sibyl went down with flu and she was pretty bad. So Knox said they wouldn't go – quite right too – the child was running a raging temperature and those maids are fools. He didn't like to tell Miss Grey, so I had to. It was an interesting experience, and she went off the handle completely. Then she pulled herself together and said it was her nerves that were worn out with nursing Sibyl. She's a good nurse all right, I grant her that, but a woman who can lose her temper like that before a stranger, has something wrong with her. I'd like to get her analysed.'

'I hope it's all right for Sibyl,' said Laura, made quite uncomfortable by Dr Ford's indiscretions.

'Quite all right,' he reassured her. 'Miss Grey has the wits to know that Sibyl is everything to her father. If he were in love, that might be another matter. She might do a good deal to hurt anyone George Knox happened to care for, if it got in her way.'

Everyone felt depressed by this conversation, and it was for once a relief when Tony came in. They then played Consequences, a stipulation being previously made by Laura that Tony was not to use any upsetting expressions from school. When the results were read, Tony tried to keep up his detached attitude, but his mouth dimpled and twitched till he had a fit of delicious giggles.

'Mother, listen to this,' he said, reading the paper in front of him in a voice weak with laughter: ' "Squinting Dr Ford met golden-haired Stoker at the station; he said to her, Where is Tony? and she said to him, Miss Grey is a wonky fool, and the consequences were the engine ran off the lines, and the world said A Happy Christmas." Mother, she is a fool, isn't she?'

'Yes, I thought that was your contribution, Tony, and very near the border-line,' said his mother.

'But she is, isn't she, Dr Ford? We always said her brain was wonky?'

'Who said? You and Stoker?' Laura began, but as Dr Ford got up, she lost the thread of her sentence. The doctor collected Miss Todd and took her off in the two-seater. As they stopped at her door, she said, 'I want to hear about Mamma. Come in for a moment. I promise not to ask for a bill.'

On those conditions Dr Ford accompanied her into the little drawing-room, and there told her that Mrs Todd was as uncertifiable as ever and a little weaker about the heart. 'Nothing to be frightened of, but something might happen at any minute – though I don't think it will – or she may go on for years, wearing you to death.'

'Rather fierce, aren't you?' asked Miss Todd. 'I could kill the poor old thing sometimes, but heaven knows I don't want to lose her, and I do my best to be decent. She's all I've got.'

'I think decent quite an understatement, Miss Todd. But remember, if she did suddenly die, it won't be your fault. You're doing all you humanly can. The rest is out of your hands.'

'I know, I know. Well, thanks for telling me. I'm going to have a cry now, so goodbye.'

Before Dr Ford could offer any consolation, he was hustled kindly out of the house and the door was shut behind him. He went home and ate his solitary dinner, with a vision of Miss Todd, pride and valour laid aside, having her cry all alone, before she went up to her mother for the evening. He nearly got up and went back to her, but reflecting that she would again be armoured against herself he thought better of it, and went on eating with undiminished appetite.

5

Embarrassing Evening

Saturday having been Christmas Eve, Christmas Day, not unnaturally, followed on Sunday. Tony collected thirty-five shillings in tips, apart from Adrian's gift, and became so insupportable on the subject of trains that Laura had to ban them altogether during meals. Luckily the hounds met twice during the week, which faintly distracted Tony's attention from railway systems, and he was able to give her a mass of authoritative and mostly erroneous information about hunting. Both these pleasures were happily combined on the day when the fox crossed the line just above Stoke Dry station, and Tony, following on foot, was fortunate enough to arrive by short cuts just as the London Express, which ignored Stoke Dry, thundered past, killing one hound outright and knocking another, yelping loudly, head over heels down the embankment, with a broken leg, and causing a young horse to have hysterics. Tony, who had shed bitter and unmanly tears over the corpse, was transported to the seventh heaven by being allowed to drive home with the local vet and see the survivor's leg set, and spent most of his spare time for the next few days talking to the invalid.

Stoker drowned her animosity against Mr Knox's Annie's sister in the excitement of Christmas time, when extra help was always wanted. The kitchen, and indeed the whole house, so rang to their shrieks and songs that Laura gave up trying to write, and spent three days in bed, reading detective stories.

Dr Ford had Christmas lunch with the Todds, and insisted on spending the afternoon with old Mrs Todd, while Louisa went off for the rest of the day, and Miss Todd helped with the vicarage Christmas tree. Luckily old Mrs Todd was perfectly sane about cards, so they passed an ungodly afternoon, playing double dummy bridge. Dr Ford found the old lady a serious opponent, losing one-and-threepence-halfpenny to her at a halfpenny a hundred. Then he made tea for her, and she went to sleep till Miss Todd came back and released him.

What happened at Low Rising, no one knew, but later in the week Mr Knox's Annie bicycled over to see Stoker and to ask her to waive the lien which she had on her sister's services, as they would be required for the weekend.

'She's having dinner at half-past eight on Saturday,' said Annie, when seated with her sister and Stoker in the warm kitchen.

'Bolshie,' said Stoker, 'that's what she is. What for do you let her do it?'

'Oh, I don't mind,' said Annie easily, 'I can always give in my notice.'

'Oh, Annie, you know Mother wouldn't let you,' spoke up Annie's sister.

'Who asked you, young Flo. Anyway, you've got to come over to us on Sunday, if Mrs Stoker doesn't need you.'

Stoker was only too delighted to get a spy into the enemy's camp, and the kitchen had a long, delightful conversation about 'Madam', as Annie called Miss Grey, with a very poor imitation of her accent. Annie expressed her opinion that Madam was soft on Mr Coates, as she had seen his photo in Madam's drawer when she was dusting. Stoker replied that heaven knew young Flo was bad enough at her dusting, but she didn't have no call to go dusting inside drawers as well as out in this house and Annie hadn't no call to put ideas into young Flo's head. This being taken personally, conversation became acrimonious, till Annie mentioned the preparations that were being made at Low Rising for the New Year's Eve dinner.

'Dinner at half-past eight, Mrs Stoker, as I said. There's your lady coming, and Dr Ford, and Mr Coates, and our lot makes six. Turkey and all, just like Christmas over again. We shan't get washed up till lord knows when. And then master's to make punch in the sitting-room, and they all drink the New Year in.'

Even Stoker was temporarily overpowered by this news, and Annie felt a delightful glow of superiority, till young Flo let the lid of the teapot fall off into a cup and break it. Annie and Stoker then united against Flo, charging her with greed for wanting more tea at all, uppishness for helping herself without being asked, and general clumsiness and depravity. Annie pitied Stoker for having young Flo in the kitchen, and Stoker commiserated with Annie over the probable destruction among Mr Knox's glass and china when young Flo helped to wash up. Young Flo, an adenoidal, half-witted young woman, took it all in good part, and did penance by taking two empty bottles into the yard and breaking them, being incited thereto by Stoker, who said that if you broke once you always broke three times, and she believed in getting it over.

So time passed till New Year's Eve, when Adrian came down to Laura till Monday. Tony had been sent to bed early after a blissful day spent at Stoke Dry with the station-master, who had allowed him to act as aide in the signal-box and the goods yard, and even ride in the cab of the engine while it shunted some trucks.

Laura and Adrian were dressed and having a cocktail before starting for the Knoxes', when Laura suddenly told Adrian to be quiet, and rushed to the door, which she opened, listening intently. Adrian heard nothing, but her over-sensitive mother's ear had evidently heard some sound.

'It's Tony – something's wrong,' she gasped, running upstairs, followed, more slowly, by Adrian.

She was quite right. From Tony's room came a sound of gentle, heartbroken sobs. With a mother's familiar feeling of sick agony she opened the door. Tony was sitting up in bed with the reading lamp alight, a piece of paper in one hand, and a pencil in the other, crying uncontrollably.

'My darling, what is it, what is it?' cried Laura, kneeling down by the bed, in total abandonment.

Tony's sobs checked his speech, but at last he managed to get out the words: 'I've written a poem – and it's so beautiful, Mother.' Then turning to Laura he buried his head on her shoulder. Gradually his sobs subsided and Laura, pulling a chair up to his bed, sat down and asked about the poem.

'It's about a moorhen. We shot some the other day and I wrote a poem about it, and it is so marvellous, Mother,' and his lips began to tremble again.

'My darling, can I read it?'

'I'll read it to you, Mother, but it's very, very sad, and will make you cry.'

'Never mind, darling. I'd love to hear it, and so would Mr Coates. Come in, Adrian, and shut the door.'

Much comforted, and not displeased with the unexpected addition to his audience, Tony sniffed loudly, rubbed his eyes with the back of his hands, and prepared to read.

'The name of it is "By Marsh and Mallow, Fern and Glen",' he announced.

'Jolly good title,' said Adrian kindly.

'It's a very sad name,' said Tony reproachfully.

'Never mind, darling,' said Laura. 'Let's have the poem.'

Tony cleared his throat and read:

> 'By marsh and mallow,
> Fern and glen,
> By marsh and mallow,
> Went they then.
>
> 'By marsh and mallow,
> The moorhen,
> By marsh and mallow,
> Went she then.

'By marsh and mallow,
When, ah, then,
A hunter sallow
Shot that poor moorhen.

'By marsh and mallow,
Fern and glen,
By marsh and mallow,
Ne'er again.'

It is idle to state that his foolish mother's eyes were full of tears by the end of the reading. 'Darling,' she gasped, 'it is frightfully sad.'

'I knew you'd cry,' said Tony complacently. 'I cried like anything. Isn't it marvellous, Mother?'

'Laura,' said Adrian, 'I loved Tony's poem, especially that bit where the metre goes a bit queer, and he's a much better poet than ever I was, and we'll publish it with his collected works; but do you realise that it is nearly half-past eight, and even my car can't do it in under ten minutes, on a dark night and a road I don't know.'

'I'm coming,' said Laura, wiping her eyes. 'Thank you, Tony. It's a sad poem. Now go to sleep, and don't, please, be unhappy, and forget about moorhens.'

Tony hugged his mother violently and lay down. Just as she and Adrian were leaving the room, he called, 'Mother.'

'What?'

'Mother, Sibyl's asked me to go shooting again on Monday. Isn't it lovely? Can I go?'

'Yes, darling. Goodnight.'

Laura quickly shut the door. She and Adrian looked at each other and began to laugh. In fact, they laughed so much that Laura nearly fell down the last two steps, and Adrian had to support her.

'I do have peculiar children,' she said, as she got into Adrian's big car.

'He's all right though,' said Adrian. 'He keeps his poetry in a watertight compartment. Do you know, Laura dear, I always think of you when I go to funerals.'

'How sweet of you. Why?'

'When the clergyman reads the bit about "Let us now praise famous men", I think you have a version for yourself which says "Let us now praise famous children".'

Laura laughed. Adrian laughed too, but very affectionately. He had liked the picture of Laura hugging her poetic son. He had been vaguely conscious for the last week of a surge of domestic feeling in him, and Laura fitted perfectly into the picture. Laura, with her tempestuous brown hair, her shabby black velvet, to which she somehow gave an air of sceptred pall, her red silk shawl falling off her shoulders, tears in her eyes, clasping the elegist to her heart. Dear Laura.

Long, long were Adrian and Laura to remember that New Year's Eve as perhaps the most uncomfortable dinner party either of them had ever been at. When they arrived, a little late, the Knoxes, Miss Grey and Dr Ford were already assembled. Laura had privately resolved to be as nice as possible to Miss Grey, but to see that Adrian got as good an innings as possible with Sibyl. Tony's description of Miss Grey as 'wonky in the brain' seemed very suitable. What was it he had said? 'We always said her brain was wonky.' It was a curious way to put it – 'we always said'. Probably with his child's intuition he had sized her up at once and thought her wonky from the beginning – vulgar child. But she dismissed this from her thoughts as George Knox handed her to the seat next to him. She found Dr Ford on her other side, then Sibyl, then Adrian, and then Miss Grey, who was thus sitting next to George as well.

'Well,' said Laura, as they sat down, 'I must say, George, your women do you credit tonight.'

And so they did. Laura's rather noble, battered beauty stood apart, without competing. Miss Grey's sleek golden hair shone in the lamplight, and in her pale green gown she looked like a water-maiden. The dark-haired, dark-eyed Sibyl, in red, was sparkling unconsciously for Adrian. Both looked extremely attractive.

'It is you who honour us, dear Laura,' said her host. 'You are indeed a goddess tonight. You make me think of Mrs Siddons, in your sables.'

'More likely Mrs Crummles, George. How's Edward the Sixth?'

'Ah, there, my dear Laura, you touch upon a sore point. He has stuck. The kind Miss Grey and I struggled in vain today. The poor boy is slowly dying, while the whole of England waits, breathless. But I'm damned if I can get him polished off,' said George, violently.

'Why don't you drop him for a month, and go abroad?'

'I shall, Laura. I knew you would be my succour, my shield. Edward's obsequies shall be deferred. Sibyl,' he shouted across the table to his daughter, 'Laura is right, she is always right. We must go abroad. I am stale, and probably flat and unprofitable too.'

'How lovely, Daddy.'

Miss Grey had been talking with much animation to Adrian, but at George Knox's outburst she turned round.

'Oh, Mr Knox, you can't. There would be nothing better for you and Miss Knox than to get abroad to sunshine, and I wouldn't a bit mind staying at home in the cold, but you know your publisher must have the book by the end of February. How I wish I could finish it for you.'

'Yes, why don't you?' said Dr Ford. 'It would do Knox and Sibyl all the good in the world to get right away from here.'

Miss Grey seemed to detect some *arrière-pensée* in his words, for the scowl which Laura had seen on their first meeting passed across her face.

George Knox was petulant at this interruption of his plans. Laura and Dr Ford, talking village gossip, were each conscious that the other was watching Miss Grey as she soothed her employer, making every use of her large, fine eyes.

'What's your special job here tonight, Mrs Morland?' asked Dr Ford, seeing that both the other couples were well occupied.

'To look after Sibyl and Adrian,' said Laura, in a low voice. 'What's yours?'

'A watching brief for Miss Todd. That's the type that gets insane with jealousy.'

'Who, Anne?' asked Laura, alarmed.

'No – someone else. They're quite capable of poisoning

86

people, or of putting their own heads in gas ovens. Both are unpleasant situations.'

'But why should she?'

'You are one reason. Sibyl's another. She's like a donkey between two bundles of hay tonight.' Upon which, Dr Ford, who rarely laughed, permitted himself a short bark.

Adrian and Sibyl were exchanging repartees which both evidently found amusing, but Miss Grey, having placated George Knox, turned quickly to Adrian and cut in.

'I must tell you, Mr Coates, how I admire those wonderful poems.'

'Poems, Miss Grey? Forgive me if I don't quite understand.'

'Ah, yes, you do. That little book called *The Golden Dustbin*.'

Adrian looked appealingly at Laura, but her attention was entirely absorbed by George Knox, who was laying down a theory that the Reformation had caused a set-back of some hundred years in domestic sanitation. Adrian was furious at being dragged away so rudely from Sibyl, and even more furious at the mention of his early indiscretion.

'Oh, *The Golden Dust-bin*.'

'Yes, by A. C. But of course we know who that was. They are marvellous.'

'We don't speak of them,' said Adrian, assuming a tragic expression.

'Why?'

'My poor brother is a sore subject, Miss Grey.'

'Your brother?'

'Why, yes, I assumed that you knew of his tragic end.'

'Indeed and I didn't. But what has that to do with the poems?'

'Everything,' said Adrian, who felt that having committed himself so far, he might as well go on and get what fun he could out of the position. 'We were twins. He was Alfred. He was all that I am not,' said Adrian modestly, 'with the face of a young god. But he had the seeds of disease in his mind, and was incapable of receiving any education. Those little poems, Miss Grey, were inspired by Nature alone. Exhausted by the effort, the frail body could not sustain the ardent spirit. He died. Better so. Forgive me if I do not pursue what is a painful subject.'

Miss Grey's large eyes opened wide. 'Ah, the poor fellow,' she exclaimed. 'Then, you are not a poet?'

'Not a bit,' said Adrian cheerfully, feeling his feet at last upon firm ground.

At this moment, George Knox, finding his audience of one insufficient, prepared to gather the whole table.

'The Reformation, my dear Laura,' he announced, crushing all other conversation with the booming of his voice, 'was one of the greatest misfortunes England ever knew. Not from a religious point of view, for of that I do not judge, being a Catholic by birth, a Presbyterian by marriage, and nothing by conviction, but from a purely social standpoint.'

He glared round him, inviting opposition. Miss Grey was heard to say she thanked God she was a Protestant. Adrian stared at this irrelevant statement. Laura and Dr Ford exchanged amused, but anxious glances, knowing this particular hobbyhorse of George Knox's of old. Sybil was quite obviously only thinking of Adrian.

'No, no,' continued George Knox ferociously, 'not religion – drains, drains, my dear Laura. If there was one thing the world before the Reformation thoroughly understood, it was Drains. Look at Norman castles. Show me the Norman castle you can explore without falling down a thirty-foot shaft at every corner.'

His audience, fascinated but nervous, waited with some trepidation for his further views. Hitting the table violently, he proceeded, 'Look at Tintern,' as if it had just come into the room. 'Look at Tintern. A perfect example of drainage from the kitchen to the river. All laid bare for us today. Then look at the Elizabethan Manor House; look at Hampton Court. Where, I ask you, are your drains? In their place—'

But here the whole company rallied and flung itself into the breach. Laura loudly volunteered a great deal of inside information about the wholesale silk trade in France to Dr Ford, while Adrian, forgetting his recent brush with Miss Grey, gave her a feverish account of his last visit to America and accepted her comments with equanimity. George Knox gradually simmered down and was presently able to join in the general conversation. It was not till dinner was nearly over that Laura realised what Dr Ford had meant by the donkey between two bundles of hay. Miss Grey was obviously distracted between George Knox and Adrian. She wanted attention from them both, but as fast as she turned to one, the other would slip through her fingers. If she interrupted Adrian's talk with Sibyl, then Knox would monopolise Laura. If she broke into the talk between Knox and Laura, Adrian was only too ready to turn to Sibyl's dark eyes. Laura felt half amused at the young woman, half sorry for her.

Dinner was long and very good, so that when Sibyl, prompted by Miss Grey, got up and collected her ladies, it was already after ten. As they pushed their chairs back, Laura murmured to Dr Ford, 'This is quite impossible. If I get hold of George after dinner, will you tackle the Incubus?'

'It wouldn't often be a pleasure, but this time it will be,' said the doctor, who was pleased to see Sibyl looking so happy.

When they got into the sitting-room, Laura tried hard to make the conversation general, but Miss Grey was obviously thinking of something else. She was not rude, as on the first evening, but very absent-minded, so that at last Laura and Sibyl gave up trying to interest her. Presently she roused herself and said, 'That was a terrible misfortune, Mrs Morland, about poor Mr Coates's brother.'

'But he hasn't got a brother. How do you mean?'

'I mean the one that died, the brother who wrote *The Golden Dust-bin*, poor fellow.'

'But Adrian wrote *The Golden Dust-bin*. He is ashamed of it now, because the poems were so very bad,' said Laura, quite forgetting Miss Grey's enthusiasm.

'But he said it was a twin brother called Alfred, who was clever and rather peculiar and died young. You must be mistaken, Mrs Morland.'

'Not a bit. He is all the brothers of his father's house – though not all the sisters too,' said Laura, much to Miss Grey's bewilderment.

'I don't understand then at all. Didn't Mr Coates write those poems?'

'Yes, he wrote them all right, but I'm afraid, Miss Grey, he has been pulling your leg a bit. It's very rude of him,' said kind Laura, who hated to see even an Incubus uncomfortable, 'but he is very shy, and that's his form of humour.'

'It's laughing at me he was, then!' cried Miss Grey, her face once more assuming its ugly look.

'Oh, no, Miss Grey,' put in Sibyl, 'he was only joking. You mustn't take him so seriously.'

Miss Grey's face turned scarlet. 'Faith—' she began, then checked herself, glared balefully at them both, and whisked out of the room, slamming the door violently. Poor Sibyl looked frightened and tearful, and said she had better go and see if Miss Grey was ill, but was dissuaded by Laura, who felt that any further scene would mean hysterics.

'I wish we could go home now,' she said to Sibyl. 'I don't mean to sound ungrateful, and it's been a lovely party, but Miss Grey hasn't somehow been a help, and it is strongly borne in upon me, Sibyl, that Adrian and your father will not be exactly the better for staying too long in the diningroom. Adrian has to drive me home, and if your father gets going they'll sit there till midnight, and your father's wine is too good to waste on a motorist.'

'I did think of that,' said Sibyl in a practical way, 'and I asked Dr Ford to bring them along soon. I know what it is when Daddy and the port get together, and he doesn't notice the time at all. But you'll have to stay till the New Year, Mrs Morland, or it won't be like other New Years.' So Laura promised.

Dr Ford was as good as his word and in a short time the gentlemen appeared. George Knox did ask where Miss Grey was, but when Laura said she had had to go and see about something in the house, he seemed satisfied. Adrian lost no time in getting Sibyl to himself, and Dr Ford joined Laura in baiting George Knox.

'Now the servants aren't here,' said Dr Ford, 'Knox ought to get rid of some of those inhibitions about drains. Out with them, Knox.'

George Knox required no encouragement to enlarge upon this entrancing topic, and Laura laughed so much that her hair, as usual, began to fall down.

'Dear Laura, it is worth laying all my life's work at your feet,' said George, 'for you to laugh at, to spurn, to deride, if it makes you loose your witch-locks so beautifully. I could make a garland of your hair, and crown myself tonight, while I drink punch in your divine company.'

It was unfortunate that Miss Grey should have chosen this moment to make her re-entry and hear George's speech. She cast a furious look in Laura's direction and seated herself at a distance from both parties. She was pale, but quite self-possessed again, and made no effort to monopolise either Adrian or George Knox. In fact, when Dr Ford got up and joined her, she appeared quite resigned to his company.

Shortly before twelve Annie, supported by a giggling Flo in the background, brought in an immense array of bottles and put them on the table. George Knox then prepared a powerful brew of punch, supposed to be a recipe hereditary in his family, but really varying according to the state of his cellar. This year the materials were copious and extremely varied and Laura, who had seen what went into it, wondered if she could warn Adrian without hurting George's feelings. But before she could find an opportunity, twelve o'clock had struck, and the New Year had begun. George Knox industriously ladled out glasses of punch from his witch's cauldron.

'Happy New Year to everyone,' said Laura. 'You and Sibyl, George, and you, Miss Grey, and Dr Ford and you, Adrian, coupled with the name of Anne Todd.'

The toast was enthusiastically drunk.

'Now I'll give one,' said Miss Grey. 'To Mr Knox's next book, and may it be the greatest success of all, except the one that comes after it – the one we are just beginning.'

If wishes could kill, four people in the room would have been murderers at that moment.

'And I'll drink to Miss Grey,' said George Knox, 'and long may she help me.'

Laura, Dr Ford, and Sibyl could not but drink, but their eyes met, prophesying disaster.

'And I'll say one more,' said Adrian. 'Your boys, Laura, dear.'

Upon this, what with the emotions of the evening and George's punch, Laura nearly cried, but just managed to pull herself together and say 'Thank you.' She was also a little worried about Adrian. Where Laura, Miss Grey and Sibyl had sipped from choice, and Dr Ford from professional principles, Adrian had drunk more deeply, and George had filled his glass for him several times. He looked extremely handsome and a little blurred. Laura was anxious to bring this nightmare evening to an end as soon as possible, and hoped that the cold night air would steady her cavalier. Goodnights were said. As Dr Ford got into the two-seater, he pressed Laura's hand. 'Thank you,' he said, 'for remembering Anne Todd,' and he drove off.

Adrian tucked his big fur rug round Laura, and started the car. His driving was certainly not so steady as she might have wished. Luckily the road wasn't frozen, otherwise a skid might have landed them in the brook, which would have been very uncomfortable, if not exactly dangerous.

'Don't go too fast here, Adrian,' said Laura, as they turned into the high road. 'It's rather narrow before we get to High Rising, and there may be belated revellers.'

Adrian obediently slackened speed, but the wheel was wobbling perilously. As they reached the narrowest part of the road, they saw a car just in front. The Demon of Mixed Drinks, seeing his chance, caused Adrian to accelerate furiously, without sounding his horn. The car in front did not pull over to the left. Adrian tried to go round it. Laura, feeling a smash inevitable, pulled the rug right over her head and thought agonisingly of Tony. The car ran along the grass edge, which slightly checked its speed. Adrian, recovering his senses rather too late, jammed on the brakes and the car fell over on its side, against a low bank. Laura, still muffled in the rug, was thrown violently against Adrian, and waited for death, but death was otherwise engaged. 'Damn!' said Adrian very loudly, and turned the engine off. They lay in complete silence and darkness, for the headlights had evidently been broken, heaped up together on the steering-wheel.

'Laura,' said Adrian, in a shaken voice. 'Are you all right?'

Laura, who was finding considerable difficulty in unwinding herself, said crossly that she was. And what, she added

94

with some asperity, did he think they were to do now? As Adrian was jammed under the low steering-wheel, with Laura and the fur rug on top of him, he could obviously do nothing. With a good deal of difficulty Laura got herself out of the rug, and, kneeling heavily on Adrian's body, tried to open the door which was uppermost.

'It's stuck, of course,' she said coldly. 'Do we spend the night here? It may be respectable, in view of the limited opportunities, but it's not my idea of comfort.'

Adrian, with heaves and jerks, managed to get himself out from under Laura and the wheel, and wriggled over on to the back seat. The other door was also jammed, and so was the window.

'Is your window working, Laura?' he asked. By great good luck it was, so Adrian climbed back into the front seat, trampling on Laura as little as possible, and with considerable difficulty got out of the window on to the grass.

'Come on, Laura,' he said. 'I'll give you a hand.'

'How can I get out of a small window above my head, you soft gobbin,' said Laura angrily. 'I'll never take you to a party again.'

But as it would have been cold and uncomfortable to spend the night alone in an overturned car, she consented to try, first pushing the rug through the window, with instructions to Adrian to put it where she was most likely to fall.

'You'd better come head foremost,' Adrian advised. 'Put your arms round my neck, and I'll help to haul you out.' It is no joke to haul a fine figure of a woman out of a small window, but Adrian, though annoyingly conscious that he was kicking the lovely enamel of his car unmercifully, hauled and pulled, till at last Laura was extricated.

'Well, thank heaven I made you put the rug there,' said Laura, getting up and twisting her hair into a bundle. 'Nobody'll steal your car. Come straight home and I'll tell you what I think of you there.' Accepting Adrian's arm, she picked up her skirts and they walked the remaining few hundred yards in silence. In silence Laura unlocked the front door and led the way into the drawing-room, where there was still a good fire, and a tray of drinks, two thermos flasks, and sandwiches, left by the thoughtful Stoker.

'I can't tell you how sorry I am, Laura. I've never done such a silly thing before. Are you sure you aren't hurt? You'd better have a stiff drink and go straight to bed,' said Adrian abjectly, hoping to flee from the wrath to come.

'What you need, Adrian – take your coat off and sit down there – is to join the Blue Ribbon Army for a year. I've never been so ashamed of you in my life. I've no objection to your partaking freely of George Knox's excellent vintages all through dinner, but when it comes to overdoing it with punch, just before you drive a lady home, words almost fail me – but thank goodness, not quite. I should have thought a man of your age who had been at Bump Suppers and Authors' Benevolent Society Dinners and what not,' said Laura, unjustly confounding two quite separate festivities, 'would have the wits to know how strong George's punch was. George is a fool, anyway, but that is no reason why you should be one. Here am I, trying to give you a Happy New Year, and all you do for me is to run a car – your own car, thank God, and I hope it isn't insured – into a ditch and frighten me out of my wits, and drag me out of a window like a dead sheep, all because you and George Knox are a couple of idiots. I hate you both.'

Upon which Laura's hair began to come down again, her much tried nerves gave way, and she cried bitterly.

Adrian got up and stood aghast. Laura was perfectly right. There had been some intoxication in the evening which had made him quite oblivious of what he drank. He supposed the punch had been strong, and of course he ought to have noticed it. Never before had he done such a silly thing with a car, and never would he again. It was unforgivable in him to have frightened her like that. And now she was in tears and all his fault. What a beginning to the New Year. He had come down looking forward so much to this weekend, to talks with Laura, to seeing that delicious Sibyl Knox again. Now Laura would tell Sibyl he was a confirmed drunkard. No, she wouldn't, she was too kind, too noble. Dear Laura. What a brute (said he to himself for the second or third time, being still a little confused) he had been. She was all alone, with four children to support, and he had made her cry. How could he make amends, how show a devotion which would atone for his horrible folly?

Laura, rather enjoying the very rare self-indulgence of tears, found her handkerchief inadequate.

'Handkerchief, please, Adrian,' she said in a snuffling voice, stretching out her hand behind her. A handkerchief was pressed into her hand, and at the same time, to her great surprise, a manly arm came round her waist, and a kiss of respectful devotion was placed on the top of her head.

97

'Laura, dear,' said the voice of her publisher, thick with emotion and the remains of George Knox's punch, 'can you ever forgive me? When I think of you so brave, all alone, and what I have been, I could kill myself. Laura, couldn't you marry me, and let me bear your burdens, and be a father to your boys?'

Laura, who belonged to the school of Miss Skiffins, unwound Adrian's arm and blew her nose violently. Then, without a word, she opened one of the thermos flasks, poured out a large cup of black coffee, and handed it to Adrian.

'Sit down and drink this at once,' said she, not unkindly, 'while I tell you all about yourself.'

Adrian, already horror-struck at his own precipitancy, sat down obediently, with the cup in his hand.

'You may be a good publisher,' Laura began, keeping the advantage which a standing position gave her, 'but you are the world's most blethering ass, Adrian Coates. If I really wanted to punish you, I'd accept you on the spot. Do you think I want a husband, and if I did do you think I'd want you? I'm old enough to be your mother, or at least I would be in India. And as for being a father to my boys, do you think three independent young men who are earning their own livings need a father? Bah! As for Tony he doesn't require one. We get on very well, thank you. Bear my burdens, indeed. You great mass of incompetence and conceit, you revolt me. You really do. Here, drink that coffee.'

Adrian finished his coffee, and began to feel really and soberly ashamed.

'I can only say, Laura, that I was a bit shaken by the car upsetting. Yes, I know it was my fault, but you were so plucky about it, and I admire you so tremendously, and I do want to help you.'

'Listen to me, Adrian. I knew a young man once, at least he wasn't so young as all that, but he thought he was. Well, he went to some races somewhere with a girl, and coming back late they had a motor smash, and just because he was over-excited he proposed to her at once and she accepted him. And the next thing was, it was broken off in *The Times*. You don't want to be broken off in *The Times*. And I'll tell you something else. You're in love with Sibyl Knox.'

'You are perfectly right, as usual,' said Adrian, and dropping his head into his hands he groaned loudly.

'Don't make that noise,' snapped Laura. 'You might at least be grateful to me. I've done everything I can to help you, and Sibyl is a darling girl, and all I get for it is you behaving like a Tom Fool.'

'Sorry, Laura. A thousand times sorry,' said Adrian, at last completely sobered. 'May I ask forgiveness?'

Laura began to laugh. 'You may, my poor nincompoop, and I'll give it gladly. Only you are to promise me you'll get engaged to Sibyl as soon as she'll have you. Shake hands. And now,' she continued, 'eat some sandwiches, and you can pour out coffee for us both, with milk this time, and we'll talk about Sibyl. It's going to be an awkward job, Adrian, because of the Incubus, but I can help you quite a lot while I'm down here. One thing is that you've offended her so much, I believe, by your quite unnecessary lies about brother Alfred' – Adrian looked a little ashamed – 'that her girlish passion for you is entirely shattered. But she's a jealous cat, and if she thinks Sibyl has hopes of you, she'll probably make a nuisance of herself on general principles. However, I'm very likely exaggerating. It's poor George Knox that she seems to be really after and we'll have to rescue him somehow.'

'You can if anyone can. Oh, Laura, do you think I have any chance with Sibyl?'

'Of course you have. She never sees a man from year's end to year's end, except the locals,' said Laura unkindly. 'Oh, Adrian, don't forget about her writing – you must do what you can for her.'

'Of course I will. I'm sure it is something exquisite. But I hope she won't want to patronise literature when we are married,' he said anxiously. 'There's quite enough of that in the trade already. Think of Mrs Johns, and a dozen more.'

'That's all right. Living with George Knox must give one a sickener of literature. Besides, if I know anything of her she'll want to breed dogs and have a large family.'

'You're rather premature, Laura. But of course, a family would be desirable. When I saw you and Tony tonight, Laura, something came over me – I'd never felt it before—'

'Sentiment,' said Laura judicially. 'You get attacks of it. I've seen you as sentimental as a love-bird because of twins in a double perambulator. You want a family of your own. That will clear your mind of cant. Now go to bed at once. Stoker shall bring you up some breakfast, and I don't want to see you or hear of you till lunch tomorrow. I'll see about the car. If my friend at the garage is shut, being Sunday, I'll see the farmer about it – he's a friend of mine, too, and he'll oblige with some horses. Off you go.'

She hustled Adrian upstairs, and sat down at her desk, where she rapidly sketched a draft for a story, based on the events of the night, her role being played by a rich countess, Adrian's by a young dress designer of genius, while Sibyl was represented by the mannequin of poor estate but noble birth, so much beloved by her readers. As for Miss Grey, she could not decide whether she should be a Russian anarchist, or a White Slave agent who specialised in poor but highly connected mannequins, so she queried this and went to bed, where she read part of an enchanting story called *Death in the Potting Shed,* till she went to sleep. Peace and darkness reigned.

6

New Year's Day

'Happy New Year, darling,' said Laura, going into Tony's room next morning. 'And church this morning, so try to look clean.'

'Oh, Mother, need I? I had something very important to do with my train today.'

'Yes, you must. I'm sorry about the train, but we must go to church once in the holidays, or the vicar would be disappointed,' said Laura, feeling that to go to church on social grounds was perhaps a little better than not going at all. Besides, one ought to have the Church Service as part of one's background on account of the beauty of the language. 'And what about saying Happy New Year?' she added.

'Happy New Year,' said Tony grudgingly. 'I hope they'll have some decent hymns.' However, by breakfast time he was quite in spirits again. Laura told him that they had had an accident last night, but before she could give any details, Tony had embarked on a long, dull and circumstantial account of an accident which had occurred to a Scotch express in 1907. But on hearing that Mr Brown of the garage was going to jack the car up that afternoon, he temporarily forgot about trains, and rushed off to make arrangements with the vet to take the foxhound, whose leg was nearly well, to see the fun.

Church with Tony was apt to be an anxious business. School chapel was his standard of public worship, and any departure from its procedure was looked upon with suspicion. A further complication was that he could not easily find his way about the Prayer Book, but deeply resented any offers of assistance, preferring to turn over the pages himself with disturbing loudness. As the first hymn was given out, his face cleared. 'We often have that in chapel,' he whispered to Laura. But when the harmonium played the opening bars, he remarked audibly, 'Wrong tune,' shut his hymn-book and looked about him in bored despair. It was only in keeping with things that he should lose the sixpence that Laura had given him for the plate, and disturb the other occupants of the pew by hunting among their legs, but the sixpence was not discovered till, during the blessing, Tony, to his mother's horror, pulled out a filthy grey handkerchief, from which the sixpence bounded into the aisle and disappeared down the hot-air grating. Tony looked at his mother with a persecuted face, shrugged his shoulders, and gave it up.

The Knox family were all there, as neither George's Catholicism nor his Presbyterianism prevented him from supporting the vicar, who was a great friend. Laura had a few words with them after church, but could not ask Sibyl in public what had happened last night after the guests had gone. But she managed to say, 'Adrian sends his love. We had a little accident last night, but no bones broken, and luckily no glass either, so I've kept him in bed.'

'Oh, that was the car we passed in the road?'

'Yes, they are going to get it out after lunch. Tony is going to help, and it might amuse you to watch. I must catch Anne Todd. Anne! Anne!' she called, 'come back to lunch. You can tell your Louisa and then come on to me. It's her day in, isn't it?'

'Love to,' said Miss Todd. 'I'll be with you at half-past.'

When Laura got back, she found a chastened Adrian reading his own advertisements in the Sunday papers. 'Now,' she said, 'not a word about last night. That's forgotten. Brown is going to get your car out this afternoon. He's had a look, and he thinks there's very little damage except the lamps, which he can fix, and the enamel, which I must say you deserve. I told Sibyl they were going to move the car, but I didn't particularly mention that you would be there.'

'Angel Laura. Did you have a good church?'

'Tony was an exhaustion to the spirit,' said Laura, 'and they had one of those psalms about Thy molars gnash upon me exceeding hard and my loins are spilled abroad on the ground, and I nearly got the giggles.'

Adrian couldn't help laughing at Laura's version, which pleased Laura so much that she laughed too.

'Darling, you are such an entertainer,' said he.

'Glad of that,' answered his hostess, 'but keep your darlings for Sibyl.'

'Very well, Mrs Morland.'

'Mr Coates,' said Tony, 'did you know one of the hounds got run over? I'm going to bring him to see your car got out of the ditch this afternoon. It would be such a treat for him. It was a marvellous engine that ran over him, the very latest type.'

'That must have been a comfort for the dog.'

'He rolled all down the embankment, poor thing, and yelped like anything, and his leg was broken. I wish you had seen the train, Mr Coates. It had eight coaches and a post-office sorting van, and the engine was a four-six-nought like the Titley Court. Mother, could I have my railway in the garden next summer? I could make a splendid embankment. The trains would look marvellous dashing round the garden, wouldn't they? I'm going to get a small goods-engine with that pound you gave me, sir, a small tank-engine to haul trucks. It really costs twenty-one shillings, but it will be your present all the same.'

'Would another shilling be any help?' asked Adrian, feeling in his pocket.

'Oh, sir, thank you.' Tony went bright pink. 'I shall call the new engine the Adrian Coates, after you, sir. Oh, Miss Todd,' he addressed that entering lady, 'look what Mr Coates has given me. Now I can get a guinea tank-engine for the goods trucks. Would you like to look at the railway, Miss Todd?'

'After lunch, Tony.'

Lunch being a close time for trains, the grown-ups were able to indulge in fairly reasonable conversation. Laura dismissed Tony as soon as he had finished pudding, after which they were able to let go over last night's dinner party, taking the subject with them into the drawing-room. Adrian soon became restless, so Laura sent him off to superintend the righting of his car, while she continued the conversation with Miss Todd. Anne was delighted to hear of Sibyl's conquest, and relieved to know that Adrian had quenched Miss Grey's passion. She quite agreed with Laura that the Incubus was likely to be a nuisance to the young lovers on general principles.

'But I can do my bit while you are away,' she said. 'The Incubus is coming once a week to the Women's Institute – where I may say she is cordially disliked by most of our members – preparing to be the great lady of the Risings, I suppose, and I'm going to make great friends with her. Such great friends that if Mr Coates happens to come down and wants to see Sibyl I shall have an engagement with my dear Miss Grey, and take such offence if she suggests breaking it that she won't dare. Also I shall get the low-down on her views on Mr Knox. I'm not a bad sleuth, Mrs Morland.'

If anyone else had said that, Laura would have laughed, but her confidence in Anne Todd was unshakable, and she felt a good deal reassured. If she and Miss Todd were working for Sibyl, things wouldn't be so bad.

'Has he spoken yet?' inquired Miss Todd.

'No. As a matter of fact, he was offering honourable matrimony to me last night, or more properly this morning. You see, the accident and George's punch had upset him a bit, and he had a vague idea he wanted to propose to somebody, so he proposed to me at one o'clock this morning. So he can't very well propose to Sibyl the same day.'

Miss Todd was filled with admiration for her employer's calmness, and promised eternal secrecy on the subject, a promise which she faithfully kept.

'I admit,' said Laura wistfully, 'it was nice to have an arm round one. I don't in the least want to marry again, Anne, but I do badly want a Platonic arm sometimes. I expect you do too,' she added, with her disconcerting directness.

'No,' said Miss Todd, 'I don't think I really do. But it isn't likely to occur. I don't attract arms.'

They both sighed, and then laughed.

'Did I tell you, Anne, that Amy Birkett is coming for a few days before school begins?'

'Good. I like Mrs Birkett. And I have an idea she may be a help.' But what the idea was, Miss Todd wouldn't say.

Adrian found a happy crowd assisting, in the Gallic sense, at the exhumation of his car. In the front row of spectators was Tony, perched up on a bank, nursing the convalescent foxhound. Dr Ford had stopped in his two-seater to watch, Mrs Mallow and Mrs Knox's Annie were present in their Sunday clothes, even young Flo had managed to escape from her mother for an hour. Adrian felt extremely uncomfortable. He had made a fool of himself last night. Probably it was all over the village that he had been blind drunk and driven his car into the ditch. Dr Ford hailed him.

'Bad luck, Coates. Those speeding cars are the devil.'

'I wasn't speeding, really.'

'No, no, I mean the other car. I saw your car in the ditch this morning and then I met Brown from the garage, and he told me you'd been forced off the road by some idiot going at seventy or eighty.'

'I suppose Mrs Morland told him.'

'Yes. She rang him up after breakfast, while you were still idling in bed, I suppose. She wasn't hurt, I hope?'

'No. She was splendidly plucky.'

'So were you, and a jolly good driver too. It takes some nerve to upset one's car deliberately. You didn't get the fellow's number?'

'Unfortunately not.'

'Well, see you again before long.' Dr Ford rattled off. Blessed, blessed Laura.

After a word with Mr Brown, who was disinclined, through long experience, to encourage amateur help, Adrian climbed the bank and sat with Tony, who was kindly directing the hound's attention to the more interesting parts of the salvage operations. Presently Sibyl Knox came past, taking her dogs for a walk.

'Hullo, Tony,' she said. 'How's poor old Ruby?' Then, seeing Adrian, she climbed the bank and sat down beside him.

'What bad luck, Mr Coates, about your car,' said she, handing the dogs' leads across to Tony. 'We heard all about it from Annie, our parlourmaid. She's a great friend of Brown at the garage. I hope Mrs Morland wasn't hurt.'

'No, thank heaven. She was perfectly splendid.'

'I'm sure she was. And I do think it was perfectly splendid of you,' she said, turning dark, adoring eyes on him, 'to be so quick. Brown told Annie it was the neatest job he's ever seen, to get your car out of the way and not smash it up. I am so thankful you weren't hurt – either of you.'

Adrian realised that the price he would have to pay for Laura's kindness was to feel like a liar and a hypocrite. But nothing could induce him to betray Laura, so he would have to bear it.

'I don't think they'll have finished for some time,' he said. 'It's rather cold for you here. Don't your dogs want to go on with their walk? Here, Tony, hand over the leads.'

As Sibyl made no objection, they set off along the road. The dogs, who had to be kept on their leads because of cars, were a thorough nuisance, sometimes plaiting themselves together and having to be disentangled, sometimes winding themselves round the nearest human legs, sometimes rushing forward with an eagerness that nearly wrenched Adrian's wrists out of their sockets, and at other times requiring to be dragged, sitting, along the ground. But Adrian loved every minute of it, and so did Sibyl, and if what they said was folly, it was the folly which is new to every new lover. Before they parted Adrian begged Sibyl to let him see what she was writing, but she wouldn't make any promise, except that he should be the first to see it, whenever it was finished. He held her hand a little longer than was necessary, laying his other hand over hers, and then walked back to High Rising, full of happiness. The crowd had dispersed, the car was in Mr Brown's garage and would be fit by tomorrow morning to take up to town, where more extensive repairs could be done.

'Better luck next time, sir,' said Mr Brown, when Adrian had paid his bill. 'You're some driver to do what you done.

Just laid her neatly on her side as if she was a baby. Thank you, sir. Good day.'

Laura was sitting by the fire when he got in. 'Did you have a nice walk?' she asked.

'Perfect. You were so right, Laura, so right. But I feel further away from her than ever after the impossible position you've put me in.'

'How, Adrian?'

'Oh, Laura, heaping coals of fire on me. Apparently the whole village – and what is far worse, Sibyl – think I am your noble protector and the world's most brilliant driver. I can't live up to it.'

'You've got to,' said Laura, with her amused expression. 'I'm not going to have Sibyl worried, or my publisher gossiped about. You must bear your cross, Adrian.'

'Dearest of women – quite truthfully that, because Sibyl is only a child, bless her – you are all that is kind and generous, and I am your most undeserving, grateful worshipper.'

'Bless you, Adrian, dear, that's all right. I am just the solitary-hearted, and I like to see the children enjoying themselves …'

After that people dropped in for tea, and as Laura went to bed before dinner, tired by her weekend experiences, and Adrian left very early next morning, he did not see her again for some time.

7

An Author at Home

Before the end of the holidays Amy Birkett paid her promised visit to Laura. Her train was due at Stoke Dry soon after lunch, so Laura, with Tony, drove down to meet her. At Tony's earnest request they went half an hour too early, so that he might see the down express go through the station, and watch Sid Brown, whose brother was Mr Brown of the garage, change the points in the signal-box and shut the level-crossing gates. Laura, unworthy of such joys, sat in the car with a book, looking out at intervals to see if her son was in any particular mischief, but as he remained invisible, she concluded that he was with the station-master, who was Mrs Mallow's nephew by marriage. After twenty minutes or so had passed she looked out for the fourth or fifth time, and her eye was caught by Tony descending the ramp at the end of the platform and establishing himself in a crouching position in the middle of the line. She opened the window and shouted to her son, who looked up with a bored expression and resumed his mysterious work. Half in rage, half in panic, she got out of the car and dashed through the little booking office on to the platform.

'Tony,' she yelled, 'come off the line at once.'

Tony adopted the attitude of one who has a faint idea that he may have heard something, but thinks on the whole that he hasn't.

'Tony,' she yelled again, 'come here at once.'

Tony slowly raised himself, and came up the platform towards her with an injured expression.

'Why didn't you come when I called you?' asked the justly indignant Laura.

'I didn't hear you till the third time.'

'What were you doing on the line, you idiot?'

'Mother, the level-crossing gates were shut, and the down express went through five minutes ago, and there's no train till Mrs Birkett's one.'

'That doesn't matter in the least. You know perfectly well you have no business on the line. I shall tell Mr Mallow not to allow you in the station again if you do such idiotic things.'

'But, Mother, I was only laying a threepenny bit on the line to see if it would be squashed into a sixpence. Mother, can I go and see where it is when Mrs Birkett's train has gone?'

'No, you can't.'

'Oh, Mother!'

'Well, you can't, that's all. Do you think I want my youngest son squashed into a corpse six feet long?'

At this Tony was pleased to be amused, and there was no further difficulty.

As Mrs Birkett's train drew up, Tony caught sight of the foolish, amiable face of a golden cocker spaniel at a carriage window. 'Oh, Mother,' he shrieked, 'Mrs Birky has brought Sylvia; look, look!' He dashed off down the platform in pursuit of Sylvia's face. Mrs Birkett, opening the carriage door, was nearly pulled out head foremost by Sylvia's anxiety to talk to Tony.

'Oh, my dear Sylvia, do you remember me, then?' cried Tony, on his knees, hugging the affectionate Sylvia, and submitting with every appearance of enjoyment to having his face licked all over.

'Oh, Mrs Birkett, Sylvia is so pleased to see me. Mother, can I take Sylvia to look for the threepenny bit when the train has gone? It would be such a treat for her.'

But Laura unsympathetically hustled Tony and Sylvia into the car, and they drove off.

Amy was enthusiastically received by Stoker, who had a great affection for 'that Mrs Bucket', as she preferred to call her.

'We *are* pleased to see you here,' she announced, as she brought tea in. 'High time you came to us again, Mrs Bucket.'

'Thank you, Stoker. And how have you been keeping?'

'I'm splendid,' said Stoker, folding her large arms over her capacious bosom defiantly. 'Dr Ford says I ought to reduce a bit, but that's his fun. Mrs Morland and me, we don't hold with reducing.'

'Not exactly a compliment to your figure, Laura,' said Amy, as Stoker left the room.

'But, my dear, I don't pretend to figure. I prefer to be matronly.'

'Well, it suits you. How are things going?'

'If by things you mean writing, Amy, not too well. First there was Christmas, and then there was the New Year, and there's always Tony. I don't count on doing much in the holidays. And how are your affairs?'

'Bill and the girls are safely in Switzerland, breaking their legs on skis. We have finished spring-cleaning the school, and matron is having a lovely holiday with her married sister at Weston-super-Mare, and sends me picture postcards. Our invaluable Edward has been to a scouts' training school, and come back even more covered with badges than he was before. On the whole, things look well for next term, barring the chance of infantile diseases, of course. The only bad news is that Mr Ferris is engaged. I knew he would. And he brought her to see me.'

'The usual sort?' asked Laura sympathetically.

'Yes, indeed. Typical assistant-master's wife. Another to ask to tea. And you can't think, Laura, how *awful* it is to have them to tea, because they all hate each other, and I don't like to inflict them on my real friends. I can't think why it is that headmasters and men who are destined to be house-masters marry the right kind of wife and the others don't. I mean, without undue modesty, I make a fairly good headmaster's wife, and if Bill were in any other profession he needn't be ashamed of me. But obviously none of those assistant-masters' wives could rise above a suburban tennis club. It's very depressing and mysterious.'

'I've often noticed the same thing about the clergy,' said Laura. 'Archdeacons and bishops and such-like have really good wives; often they are Honourables, or even Lady

Agneses. But just look at the wives of the inferior clergy. There must be an unseen providence to see that men destined for eminence in the Church, or the scholastic world, should have what one can only call, looking at you, Amy, suitable helpmeets. Or is it helpmates? People write to the newspapers every now and then about it, but I can never remember what they say.'

'Say partners. And have you noticed another thing about the higher clergy, Laura? They always have suitable Christian names. The guardian angel of the Church of England makes men who are going to be bishops be christened Talbot Devereux, or Cyril Cyprian, and then, of course, they are bound to rise.'

'And it's just as peculiar in the Roman Catholic Church,' said Laura, pushing her hair off her forehead in a very unbecoming way. 'If you see announcements of preachers for Lent outside the Oratory, they are all called Monsignor Cuthbert Bede Wilkinson, or Dom Boniface Chrysostom Butts. Not that I know what Dom is exactly. It is some sort of liqueur as well. Of course the Roman Catholic clergy don't have the worry of having to find suitable wives to rise with, so perhaps it's easier for them. An unsuitable wife must be such an incubus. And talking of incubuses, you know George Knox?'

'I've never met him. I've heard you talk about him. Is he an incubus? I thought you rather liked him.'

'Oh, I'm very fond of George. No, he's not an incubus, it's his secretary. Amy, she is the most peculiar woman. She seems to be a kind of blight. I believe she's awfully good at her work, and certainly she has made George stick to this book and get it done in time, which is unheard of for George, but she is bullying him horribly, though he doesn't know it. And I believe, and so does Anne Todd, that she means to marry him.'

'Would that matter? Authors often marry secretaries, don't they? And so do lots of people.'

'No, it wouldn't always matter; but in this case it would. She's quite unsuitable, and she is taking airs as if she were mistress of the house already, and not being very kind to George's daughter, who is a darling, but a clinging little sort of thing who needs perpetual kind treatment. She's that awful jealous kind of woman who wants all the men at once. We had a very funny but most uncomfortable evening at the Knoxes', on New Year's Eve. I took Adrian Coates there to dinner, and she tried to make a dead set at him and George at the same time. The sad part was that Adrian didn't care if she were dead or alive as he's head over ears in love with Sibyl, the daughter, and I honestly don't think George Knox would notice if any woman were alive or dead, so long as he had an audience. But that's just the danger. He might quite easily marry her without noticing he was doing it. Then I should lose George and gain nothing, and it would be most uncomfortable for the Risings, where she is universally loathed. It's a dismal look out.'

'But won't Mr Knox see what a tartar she is and send her away – make an excuse that his book is finished or something?'

'She is so cleverly dug in, Amy. To begin with, she has no relations to go to – one of these young women alone against the world – which of course rouses George's chivalry. It's rubbish, of course, because he could give her long notice, say two months, and she'd find another job, but George doesn't see that. And as for the book being finished, that's all right, and as a rule he goes off on the Continent with Sibyl when he has finished a book, and thinks about the next one. But she has managed to push him into beginning another already, and he is going to feel that he can't get on without her. It is a mess, Amy. Anne Todd seemed to think you might have some helpful ideas.'

'Why should I have ideas? But I should like to see your incubus. She sounds more interesting than assistant-masters' wives.'

'Of course you shall. I'll ring up the Knoxes now.'

Accordingly she went into the hall and rang up the Knoxes.

'Mr Knox's secretary speaking,' said Miss Grey's voice.

'Oh, I am Mrs Morland. Is Mr Knox there?'

'Could I take a message for you?'

Damn your impudence is the answer I'd like to give, thought Laura, but aloud she said, 'Shall I find you all in tomorrow if I come over to tea?'

'Mr Knox is working terribly hard over his last chapter just now,' said Miss Grey, in an expressionless voice.

'Yes, I know,' said Laura, keeping her temper with difficulty, 'but he always comes down to tea. Tell him I'll look in tomorrow with a friend.'

'I am afraid he is busy just now, Mrs Morland, but I will tell him later and ring you up.'

Laura rang off. 'I'm not a proud woman,' said she to Amy, sitting down by the fire again, 'but I can't stand that woman's impertinence. I've known George Knox for twenty-five years, and here is an Incubus telling me he is too busy for me to come to tea, and she will give him the message and ring me up later. I could burst with rage.'

Just then Tony came violently in.

'Oh, Mother, here is Sibyl, and Sylvia is so pleased to see the dogs. They are all making great friends.'

'Sibyl, dear, how nice,' said Laura, kissing her. 'This is my old friend Mrs Birkett, Tony's headmistress. Sibyl, I am demented with rage – yes, Tony, you can take some cake and go to the dogs – I have just rung up your house, and the Incubus answered – yes, take some sugar for the dogs, too, and go away – and said your father was so busy he couldn't have me to tea tomorrow, and couldn't come to the telephone. I nearly burst.'

'Oh, Mrs Morland! how *too* bad. Daddy is never too busy to see you, and of course you must come tomorrow and bring Mrs Birkett. And Daddy can't have been too busy to come to the telephone because he wasn't there at all. He was over at Castle Rising this afternoon, looking up something in Lord Stoke's library.'

'Then she said he was too busy just out of innate viciousness, I suppose,' said Laura. 'It is really too hard on your father if he isn't to be allowed to see old friends. Then I may bring Mrs Birkett tomorrow?'

'Yes, of course, and Tony, and that lovely cocker spaniel. What a darling she is, Mrs Birkett. Did you breed her?'

The conversation then became highly technical and quite unintelligible to Laura, who only gathered that all judges were notoriously ignorant and prejudiced, if not actually venal, and that a cocker called Marston Hero, who was the best prize-winner of the year, was in every way inferior to Sylvia.

'I do like that girl,' said Amy when Sibyl and the dogs had gone. 'She will be splendid for Mr Coates. He needs something that isn't too complex.'

'Yes, I'll be glad to see him married,' said Laura, smiling at her own thoughts.

On the following day Laura, Amy, Tony and Sylvia walked over to Low Rising. Sylvia had, entirely against orders, spent the night on Tony's bed and had later, for a great treat, been allowed to watch the newly acquired Princess Elizabeth doing her trial trip on the railway. It was difficult to find the right audience for one's train, in Tony's experience. Grown-ups would look on for five minutes, and then say, 'It's lovely, darling,' and go away without having taken the least pains to understand. Other boys showed more proper interest, but they were too apt to want to run the railway themselves; an intolerable situation. Sylvia was perfect. Lying comfortably in front of the play-room fire, she followed the engine with her amber eyes, and listened with a deep appreciation, and without a single interruption, to a monologue on the subject of the relative merits of the Cornish Riviera Express and the Cheltenham Flier, for seventy-five minutes. As a reward Tony had run a branch line up to where she lay, and sent the tank-engine, the Adrian Coates, with a truck full of biscuits, right under her nose. Sylvia was too well bred to snap at the biscuits, but when Tony explained to her that the truck-load was a little middle-of-the-morning snack for her, she yelped with delight, plunged her nose into the truck, and upset the Adrian Coates, which lay on its side with its wheels revolving wildly.

'Look, Mrs Birkett,' cried Tony as Amy came in, 'Sylvia has made a marvellous accident. Oh, Mrs Birkett, I wish you had seen the truck of biscuits running up to Cocker Station – I called it Cocker Station because of Sylvia – Cocker, you see, and Sylvia was so pleased. It was marvellous to see the truck coming right up to her. Oh, my darling Sylvia!'

Sylvia had then got up and stretched herself, causing the Totley Tunnel, the longest in England, consisting of piled volumes of George Eliot covered with green crepe paper, to collapse, and had then sat down amiably upon St Pancras Station which, being built mostly of coloured stone bricks from a box called Ankerbaukasten, relic of the late Mr Morland's childhood, was not calculated to stand the strain. But dear Sylvia could do no wrong, and she kindly watched Tony clear up the debris, while he told her about the dazzling future possibilities of an electric system, to be run off the lights, with a transformer.

When the party got to Low Rising, they found George Knox at work in the garden. George, whose dramatic sense was not one of the least factors in the success of his biographies, liked to dress his part, and at the moment was actively featuring Popular Writer Enjoys Hard Work in Garden of his Sixteenth-Century Manor House. He had perhaps a little overdone the idea, being dressed in bright brown plus-fours, a gigantic pair of what looked like decayed football boots, a very dirty and worn high-necked sweater, and a tweed shooting coat with its buttons and pockets flapping. Large as George Knox was at any time, this wilful collection of odd clothes made him loom incredibly. From his seven-league boots the eye travelled upwards to the vast width of his plus-fours, to the huge girth of thick jacket over thick sweater, only to find, with a start of surprise, that his large face, with its knobbly forehead and domed and rather bald scalp, completely dwarfed the rest of him. He had decided to devote that afternoon to heavy digging, and was excavating, unscientifically and laboriously, a piece of the kitchen garden. The sky was coldly pink in the west where the winter sun was setting behind mists, George Knox's bare-branched trees made a delicate pattern against the sunset flush, George Knox's smoke from the chimneys of his Lovely Sixteenth-Century Manor House was going straight up into the air, a light or two shone golden in George Knox's windows, his feet were clogged with damp earth, his hands were very dirty, and a robin was watching him dig.

'It couldn't have been better arranged, George,' said Laura as she approached. 'Perfect setting for author, down to the robin. I shall have to write a book about the lovely *vendeuse* who marries the strong, noble son of the soil, and use you as a model.'

On hearing this, the robin flew away.

George Knox stuck his spade into the earth, straightened up painfully, in the manner of one who has been devoted to life-long toil in the agricultural line, and mopped his brow with a large red handkerchief with white spots.

'That's the worst of the country,' he remarked. 'Lady

authors coming round unasked, frightening away one's little feathered friends. Who frightened Cock Robin? I, said the Laura, with my feminine aura. Laura, dear, I cannot offer you my hand as it is all earth, but you are as welcome as ever.'

'This is Mr Knox, Amy,' said Laura, exhibiting George to her friend with some pride. 'And this, George, if you will stop rubbing mould into your eyes with that preposterous handkerchief, is Mrs Birkett, whose husband keeps Dotheboys Hall and breaks Tony's spirit.'

'If I am to take your statement as one and indivisible, Laura, it is a lie, because no power on earth, nor indeed any demons under the sea, could ever dissever Tony from his profound self-satisfaction. But if I may separate your sentence into its component parts, I am more than willing to believe that this is Mrs Birkett, whose acquaintance I am honoured and delighted to make, and who, or whom, I look forward to shaking hands with when I have cleaned up a bit.'

'I'm so glad you get mixed about that "who", George. It is the death of me. That, and commas, are the bane of my life. The only way one can really express what one wants to say is by underlining every other word four times, like Queen Victoria, and that appears to be bad taste now. What are you digging, George?'

'Earth?'

'Yes, but I mean what? Potatoes, or bulbs, or asparagus beds?' asked Laura, who cared little about gardening and knew less.

George Knox looked guiltily round.

'The gardener has gone over to Stoke Dry to fetch a parcel from the station, so I thought I would dig for exercise while his back was turned. He doesn't like me in his garden when he is here. I dug up a lot of things that smelled like onions. Come into the house and we'll find Sibyl.'

'Probably it was onions,' said Laura, as they went into the sitting-room, 'or else leeks. You can send me some on St David's Day, and I'll wear them in my bonnet.'

'Are you Welsh, then?' asked Amy Birkett.

'Oh, no, but it's nice to wear things on the right day. Only the right day – yes, Tony, take Sylvia and go and find Sibyl, only keep Sylvia on the lead in case Sibyl's dogs jump at her.'

'Oh, Mother, Sibyl's dogs wouldn't jump at Sylvia. Dogs always know a friendly dog, Mother. They are marvellous. It's a kind of instinct. Mrs Birkett, did you know about instinct? Mr Ferris told us about it in maths, one day.'

'But why in maths, Tony? Is instinct a kind of algebra?'

'No, no, but Mr Ferris is very sensible and tells us all sorts of things in the maths period. His father used to be a doctor in the country, and when the sheep were all buried in snow in the winter, the dogs had an instinct to find them and they leaped on their backs and licked the snow off them.'

'But where does Mr Ferris's father come in?' asked George Knox, slightly bewildered.

'*He* doesn't come in, sir, it was the dogs,' said Tony pityingly. 'They have a marvellous instinct—'

His mother gently pushed him and Sylvia out of the room, and returned to her seat, remarking placidly:

'As I was saying, and I am going to say it, because it is too interesting to lose, the right day and the right flower never seem to come together. One can't possibly expect roses to be out on St George's Day, at least not if St George's Day comes on the twenty-third of April. Unless, of course, in Shakespeare's time April was much later on account of Old Style, or people had hothouses, which we never hear of.'

'Where does Shakespeare come in?' asked Amy, as bewildered by the introduction of the bard as George had previously been by Mr Ferris's father.

'Well, Shakespeare's birthday was St George's Day, so it all somehow goes together. And as for St Patrick's Day, shamrock may be in season then, I don't know, not in Ulster, I suppose, but anyway in the Irish Free State, but one can't tell, because what they sell in the streets looks like compressed mustard and cress. Luckily one doesn't have to wear thistles for St Andrew, and as for St David—'

But here George Knox, who had been simmering with a desire to talk for some time past, took the floor, drowning Laura's gentle voice entirely.

'St David, dear Mrs Birkett,' he began, 'had no nonsense about him, and knew that a leek was about all his countrymen were fit for. I do not offend you, I trust, in saying this. I would quarrel with no one for being Welsh, as I, thank God, am French and Irish by descent, and am far removed from petty racial feelings, but for a nation who are, or who is – damn those pronouns, Laura – time-serving, sycophantic, art nouveau, horticultural and despicable enough to try to change the leek to a daffodil, words fail me to express my contempt. You were alluding just now to Shakespeare's birthday, my dear Laura. What would Shakespeare have thought if Burbage had proposed to substitute a daffodil for a leek in *Henry the Fifth*? Where, Mrs Birkett, would be Fluellen and Pistol? The whole point of that scene would be lost – lost, I say,' he repeated, glaring affectionately at Sibyl who came in with Tony. 'As well might you have substituted the leek for the daffodil in the *Winter's Tale*. Imagine Shakespeare writing that leeks come before the swallow comes – except, of course, when you are eating them – or take the winds of March; for though doubtless they may by the calendar, though on that point I profess no special knowledge, poetically it is impossible. No, dear ladies, the Welsh are utterly and eternally damned for this denial, worse than whoever's it was in Dante, of their national emblem.'

Sibyl, seeing her father in full flood of eloquence, was pouring out tea and feeding the guests. Tony took a large cup to George Knox.

'Thank you, Tony, thank you, my boy,' said George. 'Tea is most welcome.' While he buried his face in the cup, Amy took occasion to put in a good word for the unhappy Welsh nation, on account of its musical proclivities.

'Music!' shouted George Knox, emerging from his tea-cup, which was a special cup of Gargantuan size with FATHER in Gothic lettering on it, one of those presents given by his loving child before her taste was formed, and which had outlived all more valuable crockery.

'Music, did you say? Dear lady, allow me. You are utterly deluded by that most preposterous of principalities. I have heard them singing, and though my pity for those unfor- tunates who walk the streets of London, blackmailing the kind English public into giving them pennies, which however never have the desired effect of making them cease their cacophonous hootings – deep as is my pity for these unfortunates, I say,' George repeated, fixing Tony with his effulgent eye and frightening him considerably, 'it is not music.'

'What is it, then?' asked Amy courageously.

'What is it?' repeated George, to give himself time to think what it was. 'It is this. They all sing in parts, and not one of them sings a tune. The words are gibberish, yes, gibberish, Laura, and in no country but this blessed England would such an offence to taste, such a holding up of the traffic for these ear-splitting impostors be tolerated.'

To emphasise this point he clashed his cup upon his saucer, so that Sibyl came and took it away from him.

'Where is the lady secretary?' asked Laura, quickly changing the subject.

'She was very sorry to miss seeing you,' said Sibyl. 'She meant to be here, and I told her Mrs Birkett was coming over, but then she found she had to go to town to look something up at the museum for Daddy, and she won't be back till late.'

Laura longed to ask if there had been a scene when Miss Grey discovered that she was coming to tea at Sibyl's invitation, but with George Knox there it was too difficult. Sibyl and Tony went off to the stables again to inspect puppies, and the three elders were left alone. George, having worked off some of his fireworks, became less behaviourist, and did his best to entertain his guests. As he and Laura gradually stopped talking nonsense, Amy was surprised and interested by the intimate quality of their talk. George obviously appreciated in Laura a fineness of mind which was untouched by her incursions into second-rate literature. Of the second-rateness of these incursions there appeared to be no doubt in the mind of either. Laura accepted them as a bread-winning necessity, and without being at all ashamed of her peculiar talent, frankly admitted that she envied people who were so placed that they did not need to exploit that side of themselves. Everyone has a second-rate streak somewhere, but there are many lucky ones to whom circumstances have been so kind that nothing has evoked it. If George Knox had been forced to exploit the second-rate in him, it would have overflowed and swamped him, but writing being, from a material point of view, luxury, as his merchant father had left him very well off, he kept his standard where it suited him and, largely through Laura's constant encouragement, kept it high. Laura humbly admired the artist in George, whom she could never hope to emulate, and her open humility sat very becomingly upon her, though she was at all times ready to crush George in all his other aspects. Where she respected the artist, she took no nonsense from the man. George respected the hard worker that she was, and thought very affectionately of the woman; so that his feelings for her were altogether more strong than hers for him. Laura's kindness to Sybil since his wife's death had touched him more than anyone, except perhaps Anne Todd and Dr Ford, could understand. Always ready to take people at their face value, he had luckily found in Laura a friend who was worth quite as much as he imagined her to be, and might very likely prove to be worth more.

Ever since Miss Grey had come to him as secretary he had been vaguely conscious of something missing, in spite of the zeal and efficiency with which she surrounded him. The something was of course the delightful companionship of a woman nearer his own age, discouraged in devious ways by a jealous girl. How little Miss Grey would have had to fear from Laura, she did not realise. Laura, the most generous and unpossessive of creatures, would have felt real pleasure at seeing George Knox happily remarried, and hadn't the slightest intention of appearing as that bane of second wives, the bosom friend of the first. Indeed she had never known intimately that pale and shadowy lady, who enjoyed ill-health till she went too far and let herself die. But Miss Grey, quick and violent in affection, was also quick to jealousy, and had determined that Laura would be an enemy before they ever met. 'That Mrs Morland,' was her inner name for Laura, and the sinister implications of that otherwise harmless demonstrative pronoun are only fully understood by the female mind. If Miss Grey could have hovered unseen over the sitting-room at Low Rising, her spirit would have been incredulously mortified by the fact that no one was thinking about her at all. George Knox wasn't missing her; Laura had forgotten her; and Amy Birkett certainly gave no thought at all to her that afternoon, though Anne Todd was possibly quite right in her idea that Mrs Birkett might help.

When Laura and Amy sat peacefully together after dinner that night, Tony in bed with Neddy and Foxy, and Stoker away at the Women's Institute, which she occasionally attended in a lofty and disparaging way, their talk, not unnaturally, fell upon George Knox.

'He really is very lucky in some ways,' said Laura. 'He manages to work off all the froth of his character, as you might say, in his foaming manner of speech. Do you know any of his books?'

'Yes, I read his *Life of Charles the Fifth*.'

'Well, was he like that book?'

'Not a bit. I expected a kind of ascetic scholar, a kind of Vernon Whitford, only of course not so dull. It was a great surprise to find something like a French editor of a second-class English Sunday paper.'

'How true,' said Laura, disarranging her hair. 'You give all the bluster and cock-sureness and speechifying in one breath. But that is only one George. The other is much more what you thought. He will kill his secretaries over a book, but he doesn't spare himself. He was laughing at the New Year about his difficulty in finishing his book about Edward the Sixth, but that book will have been written with his life-blood, like the quotation from that horrible Milton that people have on book-markers. As if anyone ever used book-markers either – they only tear the pages. But I wish Edward the Sixth were written with that Incubus's life-blood. I haven't seen George look so happy or comfortable all these holidays as he did tonight.'

'I wouldn't worry about that Incubus, as you call her, too much, my dear.'

'Oh, but you would if you lived so near and had her snubbing you all the time. I must get Anne Todd over to see you. She saw the danger at once.'

'What danger exactly does Anne Todd, for whose judgment I have great respect, see? That the Incubus should try to marry Mr Knox, or that Mr Knox should try to marry her?'

Laura considered. 'What Anne said was, "She'll get him if she can." That's enough, isn't it?'

'Not at all. This unknown Incubus isn't going to get Mr Knox unless she kidnaps him. She may make life very difficult for him, and bring an action for breach of promise for all I know, but she can't make him care for her. He is too well protected.'

'Sibyl, do you mean? Oh, but she will marry Adrian, I hope, sooner or later, and then what about poor, deserted George?'

'That's exactly what he will ask you, Laura.'

Laura sat up wildly, raining hairpins on the carpet.

'Don't be a fool, Amy,' she said, quite angrily for her. 'How can I help?'

'Either by accepting him, or turning him down – probably the latter.'

'Amy – I'm ashamed of you, and mortified. It's bad enough to have one man— Well, anyway, it's bad enough to have Miss Grey vamping George without you thinking the man wants to marry me – at my age, too.'

Whether Amy noticed the Incubus's real name, there is not time at present to inquire. 'I'm sorry, Laura, if I've mortified you,' said she. 'For a very intelligent woman you have lapses of sense which are quite remarkable. Mr Knox is extremely fond of you. Even an idiot could see that. And I, who have seen assistant-masters getting engaged for the last twenty years, am no idiot. My darling Laura, don't you ever realise that you are very attractive?'

Laura began to laugh. 'I ought to,' she said, with such a schoolgirl's giggle that Amy had to beg her to explain, but with astounding loyalty to Adrian, or perhaps rather to Sibyl, who must never know of Adrian's punch-inspired lapse, she shook her head.

'Never mind,' she said weakly. 'Anyway, you are quite wrong about George, and it would be a very silly thing.'

Amy might have liked to pursue this fascinating subject further, but was interrupted by Stoker, bearing a tray with cups of cocoa.

'I was making cocoa for myself,' she announced, 'so I thought you might both as well have some too.'

'Thanks, Stoker. What did you do at the Institute tonight?'

Stoker uttered a groan and threw her eyes up to heaven in a manner which compelled the fascinated Amy to ask what had happened.

'Folk dancing,' said Stoker, with a sniff.

'Was it good?'

'Good?' queried Stoker, with ominous implications. 'Depends on what you call good, Mrs Bucket. I've known some that would call an egg or a bit of fish good, when the intentions were in every way contrary, and smell it a mile off. I've nothing to say against a proper dance while you're young. There wasn't many could dance me down when I was a girl and a bit slimmer than I am in my present condition, though I keep wonderfully healthy and have no cause for complaint if it wasn't for my nerves. Listen, Mrs Bucket, I don't hold with that Institute. We're all better in the home than out of it, but young Flo she wanted to go along, and I said I'd go along with her and perhaps give a song if they needed cheering up, poor things, all sitting there at the lecture, or what not, all evening. And when I got there, the vicar's wife said, "Pleased to see you, Miss Stoker. We are just about to commence a dance and hope you'll oblige."'

'Did she really say that, Stoker?' asked Laura, with interest.

'Words to that effect,' replied Stoker, with lofty condescension. 'So I said Miss was for them the cap fitted, meaning, of course, those two vicarage girls, Mrs Bucket, and Mrs I had been ever since I got my ring,' she added, with a comedian's wink, 'and not wishing to encourage her, I said I'd have a look first and see if it was all right for young Flo. Well, by that time young Flo had gone right off somewhere with Sid Brown from the railway, so I sat down in my coat and hat to have a look. But when I seen what they were doing, my nerves gave way, just like I told you at Christmas,' she said, turning to Laura.

'Stoker's back was opening and shutting all the way down at Christmas,' Laura explained gravely, 'because of the way Flo did the work.'

'How awful,' said the enthralled Amy. 'And what happened next?'

'Two rows they stood in, like the photos in a paper after a wedding, and believe me or not, Mrs Bucket, they had bells, same as like a cat's bell on its collar, you know, tied round their legs with ribbands. And there they were, jumping and kicking and carrying on, and Mrs Mallow that's old enough to know better and had buried a husband too, which is more than those two vicarage girls will ever be able to say,' added Stoker venomously. 'So when Miss Todd stopped playing the piano, I got up and shook myself' – here Stoker gave a pantomimic representation of the shaking which would have brought down the house at any music hall, and was nearly too much for her present audience – 'and I said, "Well, I mayn't have bells on my toes, but I have a ring on my finger, and this is no place for decent women." So Miss Todd started in to play again, so I said I'd join in a bit to oblige, and keep an eye on young Flo.'

'That was very good of you, Stoker.'

'That's right. So then Sid Brown he said he'd see young Flo home, so I dare say she'll be no better off with him than she was at those folk dances,' said Stoker, whose chaperonage appeared to be of a sketchy description. 'And then I came home to get myself a good cup of cocoa, and as I was saying, I didn't see why you two shouldn't have some, as I was.'

'Thank you very much, Stoker,' said Laura. 'Goodnight. We're going to bed now.'

'Night,' said Stoker collectively and withdrew, and the ladies went to bed. But in spite of the lure of a very good book called *The Hulk of the Hidden Blood*, Laura was unable to get her mind off what Amy had said about George Knox. When she had told Anne Todd that she sometimes had hankerings for a Platonic arm round her waist, was she, she wondered, thinking at all of George? On careful consideration she decided that she wasn't. An arm was desirable, but what one really wanted was something to lean on, and that George was not. She wished Amy hadn't mentioned her suspicion of George's attachment, as it might diminish the harmony of their present relations, but if George did find her attractive, it would certainly be a good counterblast to the Incubus. Bother the Incubus. If it weren't for her, life would be far simpler.

Amy Birkett, trying to finish a newspaper crossword in bed, also gave a few moments' thought to the Incubus. Like Anne Todd, she had an idea that she might be able to help, but the idea was only in the back of her mind, and required time to germinate. In any case she only stayed with Laura two days longer, and they didn't see the Knoxes again, so the subject of the Incubus was not raised.

Then Tony went back to school, and Laura and Stoker shut up the house and went up to the flat for the winter months.

8

Lunch and the Gentlest Art

For nearly three months, that is to say for most of the winter term, Laura was working hard in London. Adrian she saw once or twice, and gathered that he heard from Sibyl occasionally. He had hoped that she might be in town, but she said nothing about coming and ignored what he hoped were his delicate hints about running down to Low Rising for a day.

'I can't go on much longer like this,' he said to Laura one day, over lunch. 'Letters aren't enough. Sibyl writes darling letters, but they are so short, and don't tell me anything. I do so want to see what she is writing, too. I'm sure it's delicious, and I'd love to publish it, and then perhaps she would be grateful.'

'Gratitude isn't what you need, my good man,' said Laura. 'What you need is the love of a pure girl.'

'But wouldn't gratitude be a step on the way?'

'Man, man, it would be no step at all. And anyway why

should she be grateful? Love or no love, you're not going to publish her book unless you see money in it. You are a Jew and a shark, you know,' said Laura dispassionately, 'who battens on widows. Though I must say I never think of myself as a widow. I'm just myself. Have you noticed how real widows go all crumpled up after their husbands die? They seem to shrink and cave in. But I don't crumple a bit. I suppose I haven't the real widow spirit. Besides, it is so comfortable to live alone – except just now and then, when one feels a superfluous woman and would like to have someone to go to parties with. But you are too young to understand all that, Adrian, and anyway it's Sibyl you want to talk about, not me.'

'Darling, you are a heavenly fool, as I once had occasion to tell Knox.'

'You told George Knox that? Oh, well, I dare say you're right. Only you don't mean I'm like Parsifal, with a nightgown on over my armour, and walking two steps forward and one step back while the scenery moves along, do you?'

Adrian reassured her.

'Also,' he said, 'it would be one in the eye for Johns and Fairfield if I got hold of Sibyl's work. I wonder if they know she is writing.'

'If they don't know, it won't be for the want of telling, while her father is alive. You ought to get something in writing from her to say you are to have first claim, or something.'

'Well, I have got a kind of promise, Laura. I'll show you her letter if you like.'

'I do love it when you say "her" like that, you amorous

136

fool,' said Laura politely. Adrian's dark skin flushed, but he made no reply, and, taking out his pocket-book, he handed a letter to Laura.

'Am I the confidante in this piece?' she asked.

'You are.'

The letter said: *Dear Mr Coates,*

'Good heavens, haven't you got any further than Mr and Miss?' asked Laura.

'I think it is so delicious of her not to plunge into Christian names at once,' said Adrian fatuously.

'Oh, do you, Mr Coates? Well, I suppose it's a change. I imagine that with most of your friends you would be hard put to it to know what their surnames are. But to continue.'

Dear Mr Coates, she read:

> *Thank you so much for your letter. Yes, the dogs are very well. Sheila had puppies last week. I'm going to sell the dogs, and keep the other one for breeding.*

'I like the delicacy of that "other one",' said Laura.

> *I suppose you wouldn't care for a puppy? They are perfect darlings, and of course I don't mean I'd sell it to you. I'd give it you for a present.*

'What are you going to do about the puppy, Adrian?'

'I don't quite know. I must say yes, because it is so adorable of her, but it will be an infernal nuisance in my flat.'

'Why don't you ask her to keep it for you? That would make an excuse for your going down to see it.'

*Daddy is very well and going to start a book about
Queen Elizabeth. Perhaps we'll go to town to stay with
Grannie later, but I don't like to leave the dogs. Thank
you so much for the book you sent me, it is lovely, but
I've hardly had time to read it yet, because Jane had
distemper, poor darling. It was very nice of you to want
to see my story, but I don't think it's good enough, but I'd
rather show it to you than to anyone.*

Yours very sincerely,

SIBYL KNOX

Laura handed the letter to Adrian, who put it reverently back in his pocket-book, and asked what she thought of it.

'I suppose you realise that you'll have to live in the country when you're married, on account of those dogs? As for the book, it seems clear enough that Johns and Fairfield aren't in it at all. Let me see it, Adrian, when she sends it.'

'All right. You shall be my reader and give me your impressions.'

Laura was by now entirely absorbed, as usual, in the subject in hand, and entirely oblivious of her own appearance, sitting with her elbows on the table, and a foot curled round each front leg of her chair. 'I'll tell you what I'll do, Adrian,' she said. 'I'll ask you down in the Easter holidays. Anne Todd and I will keep the Incubus off, and you shall go on primrose paths with Sibyl, and hear the cuckoo, and pluck a cowslip and a violet, and smell the warm earth, and gaze on lakes of bluebells, and be in love in spring.'

Here Laura, to her own great surprise, brimmed over with tears.

'Laura, darling,' said Adrian, much concerned. 'Don't cry. I know spring is very upsetting, but don't take it to heart.'

'Spring and young love are terribly upsetting,' said Laura, all untidy, with a pink, shining nose and suffused eyes. 'It's always like Heine every spring, and I love you to have it, but it makes me feel a bit old. Oh, well, I expect the Incubus will remove all vernal sentiment. Now I must go. Oh, but first I must show you a letter from Tony. I wouldn't have bored you, only you showed me Sibyl's, so it's only fair. It was a Valentine,' said she proudly, 'and it came yesterday, a fortnight late.'

'I have had a professional eye on Tony, ever since that poem about the moorhen,' said Adrian. 'Let me see it.'

The letter was written with much care and a shocking calligraphy in red and blue ink, and copiously decorated with hearts, pierced by arrows, dripping blood. It said:

Dear Mother,
I humbly apologise for this being late, but you cannot find anything out at this ancient mouldy place. So

Valentine will you be Mine
In the Moon-Shine
Near the Foamy Brine
Where your hairs Entwine

Like unto a Vine
As the great Einstein
Once upon a Time
Remarked unto a Shrine
But still that's out of Rhyme
So once again O Valentine
WILL YOU BE MINE.
   Your loving son,
   TONY
   P.S. This is completly original.
   P.S. No. 2. We have our boxing match on March
23rd. I hope you are coming. Centurio dixit me
meliorem esse quam ultimus terminus. γοοδβίέ.

'It's a lovely Valentine,' said Adrian, while Laura's eyes shone with pride. 'But the classics never were my strong point. Can you expound?'

'Well, thank God I'm uneducated, but I think *centurio* must mean the school sergeant, who takes the boxing.'

'But why should the sergeant say Tony is better than last term? It doesn't seem a reasonable comparison. Oh, I see, he means Tony is better than last term.'

'Yes, better than last term,' said Laura, wondering why men were so dense. 'And I could do the last bit,' she added, with modest pride, 'because he has written it before. I once thought I'd learn some Greek to help the boys with their homework, but not being able to master the alphabet, I gave it up, and it was just as well, because whatever I helped the boys with, we always lost our tempers. Well, goodbye, Adrian, and thank you for lunch. Before I began being a female author, I always thought one's publisher gave one a lot of free meals, but lunch twice a year is about the most I get out of you, and then I have to ask for it. Oh, Adrian, what was that book you gave Sibyl that she didn't read?'

'The Testament of Beauty.'

'You poor fish,' said Laura, compassionately. 'And a special binding, I'll be bound. Well, well, I hope that your love she will refuse, till the conversion of the Jews, if that's your idea of courting. When I was young it was the Sonnets from the Portuguese, but those were dashing days ...'

A few days later, Anne Todd sent up a parcel of typescript for Laura, with a letter enclosed.

Dear Mrs Morland,
I am sending you pp. 120–157. I think you will find them correct. I would have sent them sooner, but Mother was pretty ill last week. Dr Ford was here every day and was angelic to Mother. I don't know whether to want her to live or die. She does love being alive, but those heart attacks are no joke, and she is much weaker. When she is dead I shall have no real reason for being alive myself, except your work, but I dare say I'll go on running the Institute. I suppose Stoker told you about her triumph at the Folk Dance evening. She came to curse and remained to dance for a solid hour, but in her coat and hat, to show she wasn't really taking part. She brought the house down, and I shouldn't be surprised if Brown at the garage asked her to walk out with him.

I haven't seen much of the Knoxes. Sibyl looks very fresh and appealing – results of the tender passion, I suppose. Tell Mr Coates he needn't worry about rivals. The Incubus appears to be making a deader set than ever at Mr Knox, but at the same time she doesn't lose sight of Sibyl, and keeps her at home when she can. Whether as chaperon, or to prevent Sibyl attaching any other likely young man, I don't know. Mr Knox seems a bit restless. He has come in here several times lately, and is a great success with Mother, who perks up like anything and flirts violently with him. He wants me to help him over his Queen Elizabeth, but I think I'd better keep out of it, or the Incubus might murder me. Mr Knox has a touching belief that anyone who knows about modern clothes must know about ancient clothes, but I'm afraid I can't help him with ruffs and farthingales. But I should like to have seen Queen Elizabeth's wardrobe all the same. Dr Ford doesn't quite approve of Mr Knox coming so often, but I don't see how it matters. It is much better for Mother to enjoy herself than to be shut up with me always.

I shall be sending the next instalment early next week. How are American sales?

Yours,
ANNE

Laura was glad that George Knox should cheer up old Mrs Todd, and quite agreed with Anne that it was better for the old lady to be amused. Rather interfering of Dr Ford, she thought, but quickly forgot about it in her preparations for attending Tony's boxing match, for which she was to drive down to lunch with the Birketts.

Lunch at the headmaster's house was a flurried affair, as Bill Birkett was to be referee, and Edward was in and out of the room with messages from the sergeant all the time. Also, Wesendonck had chosen that morning to climb on to the back wall of the fives court, which was strictly forbidden, and there dance a war-dance to a crowd of admiring friends, till he fell off and had a sprained ankle and various bruises; while young Johnson, the owner of the hair fixative, had gone down with influenza, so that all the rounds had to be rearranged.

After lunch Amy took Laura over to the school hall. A few front benches were reserved for masters and favoured guests. The rest of the hall was packed with parents, boys stood up on the back benches, and the gallery was so full that Laura expected to see bodies being squeezed out between the bars, like toothpaste. Behind the ring was a huddled mass of little boys in white vests and shorts, their blazers or jerseys slung about their shoulders in a devil-may-care way.

'We've had an awful time,' said Amy, 'getting them clean. Matron, like a fool, made them wash their knees before lunch, so of course after sitting still for half an hour they were filthy again. You know how boys are.'

'I believe,' said Laura, 'that every human boy is born with a bag of dirt inside him, and until it has all exuded, they can never be clean. There's no other way of accounting for it, because you can wash them all over and shut them up in an empty room, or even put them to bed, and ten minutes afterwards they'll be black. Some have a bigger bag than others, and my family seems to be peculiarly favoured.'

'Oh, I don't know. John was always fairly clean; Gerald was filthy, though. Is he still exploring?'

'How clever of you to get it right this time, Amy. Yes, he is still in Mexico, and his Americans want him to go back to New York with them and help to write a book. I might get over and see him in the autumn if American sales do well. Oh, hush; Bill is going to roar.'

The headmaster now uttered his famous bark, and the whole gathering calmed down into whispering silence, while two shrimplike figures entered the ring. A master, Mr Ferris as a matter of fact, then dived under the ropes that marked off a square in the middle of the hall, and began to speak, but the high excited voices of little boys drowned his speaking with shrieking and squeaking. The headmaster half-rose to his feet and gave one horrible look round. The twitterings subsided, and Mr Ferris concluded, '... on my right is Swift-Hetherington, J. W., on my left Fairweather, A. L.' He then made a courteous gesture to each side, repeating, 'Right, Swift-Hetherington, left, Fairweather,' and ducked out under the ropes. Another master hit the boarding-house gong, saying 'Seconds out of the ring', and there advanced to the centre of the open space Swift-Hetherington and Fairweather.

Swift-Hetherington wore a red sash, Fairweather a blue sash. They were in the class under four stone, and Swift-Hetherington may have turned the scales at three stone twelve as against Fairweather's three stone eleven, and possibly their united ages may have reached fifteen years. Their white socks were neatly rolled down over their gym shoes, and their boxing gloves were ridiculously large at the end of their little arms, which looked about as strong as boiled macaroni. There is something very touching to the sentimental mind about the weak and strong points of little boys. So many of them have sturdy footballing legs and manly chests, but when you come to their arms and necks, they are still in the nursery. The size of a little boy's collar, viewed dispassionately with a tape-measure, is heartbreakingly and unbelievably small.

After a manly handshake the combatants set to in earnest, dabbing at each other's pink face with flapping arms, and dancing about on tiptoe in the best tradition of the fancy. In the excitement of being in the ring, all the sergeant's teaching gradually went for nothing, and Swift-Hetherington adopted a flail-like swing which rarely landed anywhere, while Fairweather, in his frenzy, used a downward clawing motion which occasionally brushed Swift-Hetherington's chest. Both were breathing heavily, and looked deeply relieved when the gong sounded. They fled back to their corners, where they tasted real glory, lolling majestically, arms outspread on the ropes and feet dangling well off the ground, while their seconds, elderly gentlemen of twelve and thirteen, flicked them sympathetically with towels, and sponged their faces and tongues.

'The sponging part used to worry me,' said Amy to Laura, 'but now I rather approve of it, because when you have seen the same pail of water being used for thirty different tongues in one afternoon, you realise that it is quite unnecessary ever to take precautions against infectious diseases again. What is the use of disinfectant gargles against influenza when this sort of thing goes on?'

'One couldn't put disinfectant in the pail, I suppose?' asked Laura.

'No, love, you couldn't. First, sergeant wouldn't allow it; secondly, it would be against all our school traditions. Anyway, no one has ever been the worse, and if the water gets too full of blood, Edward sometimes brings a fresh pail.'

While Laura was pondering this, the second round began. The backers began to cheer, waving their arms and legs frantically through the bars of the gallery, and were barked into silence. Swift-Hetherington was doing his best, but his lower lip was trembling ominously, his eyes beginning to fill, and his flapping arms becoming wilder and wilder. Laura clutched Amy, remembering the many boxing matches at which she had been obliged to see one or other of her boys in similar plight. But just as it was becoming unbearable the headmaster jumped up, saying, 'That's enough,' and gave the victory to Fairweather. Swift-Hetherington had spirit enough to shake hands, and then fairly broke down with mortification. The admirable Edward took charge of the tearful warrior, kneeling beside him in a corner, mopping his tears and cheering him up.

'Thank heaven for Edward,' said Laura. 'And thank heaven for Bill stopping the boxing.'

'I don't know if real referees are like that,' said Amy. 'Probably not. But Bill won't let them go on if they get tearful. He says it only spoils their nerve for next time. It certainly worked with your Dick. The poor child used to break my heart with his miserable face when he began, and then he turned into one of our best boxers.'

'Yes, it used to be pretty awful watching him box. I don't know how one can bear to do it. But he was always terribly keen, even if he did cry, and when boys haven't got a father, you feel you ought perhaps to let them do bloodthirsty things to make up for it.'

'Dear idiot,' said Amy affectionately. 'But you were very brave. Poor Mrs Watson, one of our house-masters' wives, simply can't bear it, though Watson is a terribly good fighter, and she always leaves the hall when his round comes on, and hides in a classroom with her face to the wall till it is over. You'll see her presently.'

Gradually the weights rose from four to six stone, and the macaroni arms became stronger, and the blows harder, and one young gentleman actually bled. To Laura's secret relief both Tony and his opponent got through without blood or tears, and though Tony was defeated, it was an honourable defeat. When once this sickening moment was over, Laura was able to give her attention to the scene more peacefully. Tony being safely disposed of, the real interest of the afternoon to her lay in the three sergeants who were present. Two of them had come over from the upper school to judge. The first was the present instructor, a broad-shouldered, light-treading, handsome man, who reminded Laura of Trooper George in *Bleak House*. He sat like a rock all the afternoon, his legs a little apart, a hand on each knee, only moving his eyes from fighter to fighter. Opposite him was the ex-instructor of the upper school, once a great army boxer, lovingly known to masters and boys as Benny. His sight was no longer good, and he peered through thick glasses at the shrimplike figures on the floor, occasionally turning round to explain a point to some of the little boys near him, which made them go pink with pride and pleasure.

As for Mason, the lower school sergeant, he was rapt away into another world. His eyes were glued to every movement of his pupils, his loosely clenched fists followed every movement of their gloves, while his lips moved silently with the instructions and warnings he was panting to give.

'I really believe,' said Amy to Laura, 'that if Mason's house were burned down, and firecrackers fastened to his jersey, he wouldn't notice it in the least, so long as the boxing was going on. Once, when your Dick and a boy called Jones were in the finals—'

But what happened to Dick and Jones remains unsung, for Laura's attention was distracted by a slight scuffle in the audience, just behind her. Amy turned round.

'Oh, that's Mrs Watson,' said she, rather proud of her exhibit. 'She has shut herself up in Mr Ferris's form-room and she won't come out till Watson's fight is over. Edward always goes to tell her. And now, look! Mr Watson is leaving the judges' table, though I don't think it is so much a fear of seeing his infant gored, as his delicate feelings, which make him morbid about giving a decision for or against his own offspring. When you see young Watson you'll realise how funny it is, because he adores boxing, and is never –happier than with the gloves on. How two such rabbit-hearted parents produced a child who is a glutton for fighting, I can't imagine.'

Indeed, young Watson, who stepped modestly but assuredly into the ring at this moment, was the last person about whom even a parent could ever, one would think, be anxious. He danced at his opponent with the joy of battle in his eye, drove him round the ring, placed scientific blows in the right place, and appeared positively to enjoy the trickle of blood which was running down his own face. Mason wore a transfigured expression which may possibly have been approached by St John on Patmos, and almost embraced Watson as he left the field of victory. Edward was seen worming his way through the crowd to Mr Ferris's classroom. Mrs Watson emerged, pale but happy. Mr Watson resumed his seat at the judges' table, and the entertainment proceeded.

Laura only had time for a few words with Tony, as she had to get back to town. He received her congratulations with marked want of interest, and was obviously bursting with something he wanted to say.

'Oh, Mother, do you think I could possibly have old Donkey down in the holidays?'

'Wesendonck?'

'Yes. Oh, could I, Mother? He has lots of lines and a methylated spirit engine, and we could have a huge railway in the garden. Oh, Mother, could he come? He's quite a decent chap, and he knows a chap who has a fifteen-inch-gauge railway with trucks that you can sit in. Oh, Mother, can he?'

'I should think he might, Tony. Do I write to Mrs Wesendonck?'

'Yes, please. Oh, Mother, wouldn't it be lovely if we could have a ten-inch-gauge railway in the garden, and I could take all Sibyl's dogs for rides, Mother.'

Kissing her monomaniac son, Laura hurried away to say goodbye to Amy.

'Come again in the holidays, Amy,' she said, 'and bring Bill if he'll come. I wish I could manage the girls too, but there it is.'

Amy promised for herself, and more vaguely for Bill.

'How is the Incubus?' she asked, as Laura got into her car.

'Going strong.'

'What did you say her name was?' called Amy, as Laura started the car.

'Miss Grey,' shouted Laura.

Amy went back into the school, and talked to hundreds of dull parents who all looked exactly alike, and congratulated Mason on his pupils' prowess, and soothed matron who was agitated beyond measure by the number of white shorts and singlets which were covered with dirt and gore, and visited Wesendonck's ankle, and inquired after young Johnson's influenza, and thanked Edward for helping, and told the maids how nicely everything had gone, and cheered Bill through the cold supper which was the inevitable aftermath of a school festivity, and wrote to Rose and Geraldine who were abroad somewhere living with a family to learn the language, and did a few other odd jobs which are part of the unpaid work of a headmaster's wife. But all the time she was thinking a thought at the back of her head, and wondering if she should tell Laura about it. It might only worry Laura even more, and besides there was just the chance that she was wrong in her thought, though putting two and two together it seemed impossible that she should be. Anyway, it was usually better to let things simmer down: difficulties often solved themselves if you let them alone. But the thought was there, and might be left to itself till the Easter holidays. Then if Laura, or that nice Knox girl, needed help, why there it would be.

9

Embarrassing Afternoon

A few days later Laura was walking in the Park, looking at
the riders in the Row. A large party came trotting up from
the Kensington Gardens end, obviously from a riding
school. Laura was fascinated by the riding-master, one of
the gigolos of the *haute école* so to speak, darkly handsome,
with a touch of the sombrero in his hat and a suggestion of
the plains of the Argentine about his slim, supple figure.
Rather D. H. Lawrence-ish, thought Laura vaguely. The
sort of person that would turn into a half-caste Indian, full
of black, primal, secret something-or-other, and subjugate
his mate. But it seemed improbable that he would be able
to exercise his powers in Rotten Row, and his voice, raised
as he threw a criticism back to a pupil, was so healthily
Cockney that the lure of the he-man vanished. So Laura
turned away, and as she did so bumped into something
which said:

'Why, Mrs Morland!'

Laura, summoning her wandering wits, saw Miss Grey before her.

'Oh, how do you do?' she said, pulling her mind back from pueblos, or haciendas, or whatever they were, where strong, slightly half-witted, primitive men were darkly breathing in the tidal earth-force, and seemed from their description to be all loins and hair, and only had to raise a finger to have women all over the place in swarms, panting for the deep, secret affinity of their pulsating, animal – in the higher and more refined sense of the word – bodies.

'I didn't know you were in town,' said Laura.

'I am looking up some things for Mr Knox at the British Museum. You know we are getting well into Queen Elizabeth.'

'What fun,' said Laura stupidly.

'I am staying with old Mrs Knox in Rutland Gate,' continued Miss Grey. 'Won't you come in and have some tea? I know she'd love to see you.'

As usual the gentle Laura was so flabbergasted by the Incubus's aplomb that she said yes, without effort or resistance. It was surprising enough that old Mrs Knox, who was famous for ill-nature and senile crabbedness, should have her son's secretary to stay with her at all, but that Miss Grey should be on terms which enabled her to ask anyone in to tea was incredible. In all the years that Laura had known Mrs Knox she had never felt really at ease with her, and here was the Incubus calmly assuming the airs of a daughter of the house. Wishing that Anne Todd were with her, Laura walked with Miss Grey across Knightsbridge and down Rutland Gate, doing her best to respond civilly to

Miss Grey's far too competent inquiries after the boys. But the day's surprises were by no means over. As they went up the front-door steps, Miss Grey opened her bag and took out a latchkey. This was indeed daughter of the house with a vengeance. Laura felt herself deprived of all power of speech. It was quite obvious to her that Miss Grey was making the best use of an opportunity to show Mrs Morland how very much at home she was in Mrs Knox's house. Laura had rather forgotten about the Incubus trouble, and was always inclined to take life as placidly as possible, but now the whole uncomfortable situation was to be forced upon her attention. She wildly thought of saying she felt sick, or faint, or had forgotten an engagement, but her invention was paralysed, and she followed Miss Grey upstairs, hearing, as in a dream, George Knox's secretary encouraging George Knox's old friend to come up to the drawing-room, as if she were a shy little girl at her first party.

Mrs Knox's drawing-room was a splendid relic of the last century. When old Mr Knox committed the one unusual act of his extremely conventional career in marrying a Frenchwoman, he brought his bride home to the house where his father and mother had spent all their married life. Mrs Knox, who had a sublime disregard for exteriors, accepted the heavy Victorian furniture, the pier glasses, the dark curtains, the gas chandeliers, with complete equanimity, putting all her personality into her clothes and jewels. As years went on a few changes were introduced, but always ten years later than anywhere else. Electric light had finally replaced gas, a telephone was installed just before the War, but servants were still summoned by a cross-country system of wiring which ended in a row of bells hanging in the kitchen passage, heavy trays were still carried up and down the kitchen stairs, meals were still cooked on a great coal-burning range which also supplied intermittent hot water, and scuttles of coal were carried up to the drawing-room and bedrooms all through the winter. It was in the nature of a miracle that Mrs Knox was able to get or keep servants, but she always did.

Laura had been to many a frozen dinner party in old days, when her husband and George Knox's wife were still alive. George had married, as far as any of his friends knew, entirely to escape from his mother; willingly giving up the hideous house to her in exchange for his freedom. His wife had never made the faintest impression on her redoubtable mother-in-law except by dying, upon which occasion old Mrs Knox went into such deep mourning, and had such deep edges to her notepaper, that George took Sibyl abroad for six months. He was on good terms with his mother, and paid her an occasional duty visit. Sibyl, sweet-natured, and not clever enough to see how terrifying her grandmother was, was the only person who got on with her really well. She was apparently quite happy to spend a fortnight – provided none of the dogs were having distemper or expecting puppies – with old Mrs Knox, playing cards, going for little walks in the park, and talking French, which she and her father both spoke by nature.

When they came into the drawing-room old Mrs Knox was seated on a hideous sofa near the fire. Velvet curtains, lace curtains, half-drawn blinds darkened the room. Velvet

155

curtains were draped over the tall mirrors opposite the fire, and over the arch between the front and back drawing-rooms. The familiar smell of stuffy, dusty materials greeted Laura, making her think for a moment of her unlamented husband with whom she had so often entered that depressing room. But thoughts which contain little affection or regret are only passing affairs.

Miss Grey approached Mrs Knox and said in the charming voice which it would have been so agreeable to hear more often, 'I have brought a very old friend to see you, Mrs Knox.'

Laura felt that the very old was perhaps unnecessary, but with as good a grace as possible she shook hands with the old lady and sat down beside her.

'Enchanted that my little friend has brought you here,' said Mrs Knox. 'Where did you find her, dear?'

Laura was not sure to which of them the dear was directed, but before she could answer, Miss Grey had taken it to herself.

'In the park, Mrs Knox, looking at horses.'

'Aha,' remarked Mrs Knox, who had a disconcerting way of using this interjection, leaving the hearer in complete doubt as to whether approval, interest, or condemnation were intended.

'It was quite a surprise to see Miss Grey,' said Laura, still feeling at a loss. 'I didn't know she was in town.'

'She is staying with me and makes me laugh,' said Mrs Knox. 'You don't make me laugh, Laura. Why not?'

'I suppose I'm not funny,' said the candid Laura. At this remark Mrs Knox burst into wild cackling, and Miss Grey shot a quick, angry look in Laura's direction. Mrs Knox put out a wrinkled, bejewelled hand from the sofa and pulled the painted china bell-handle to the right of the fire, waking reverberations all over the house. While they waited for tea, Miss Grey entertained her hostess and Laura with an account of her day's work at the Reading Room, using that faintly exaggerated brogue which is so attractive to an English ear when politics are not involved, and a very amusing story she made of it. If Laura had not suspected that the charm was being deliberately exercised, she would have fallen under it completely, but the remembrance of New Year's Eve and the thought of the various indignities which Miss Grey had unwisely inflicted on her made her immune to the spell. It was very clever of Miss Grey, she thought, to make herself so delightful to old Mrs Knox, who might be a valuable ally. Mrs Knox had often openly deplored the fact that George showed no wish to marry again. She was probably too fond of Sibyl to want to give the child a step-mother so near her own age, but if Sibyl married Adrian, and George were alone, she might feel inclined to push him into Miss Grey's arms. If she did, it might not make any particular difference to George, who was the kind of man who would hardly notice if he were married or not, but to George's friends it would make a great deal of difference.

Tea was brought up by a butler and footman, with a staggering apparatus of heavy silver teapot and muffineer on a gigantic silver tray. Mrs Knox told Miss Grey to make the tea. Laura, sitting on the low sofa beside her hostess, had a feeling that Miss Grey, facing her across the tea-table, competently pouring out tea and handing cakes with maddening graciousness, looked much more like the mistress of the house than a paid secretary.

'Tell me,' said Mrs Knox, 'all about your boys, Laura.'

Laura gave her, as succinctly as possible, biographies of the four boys since she had last seen Mrs Knox. In spite of Adrian's remark about praising famous children, she really hated to talk about her sons except to a few friends, and was apt by her apologetic manner to make people feel that she was being rather dull.

'You hadn't so many children when I first knew you,' said Mrs Knox. 'Only two small sons when you and your husband used to dine with us here. You were much too good to that man, Laura. He was just *nul*, nothing at all. How you lived with him is quite beyond me. A good-looking worthnothing, nearly as stupid as poor George's wife. It was a pity those two didn't marry each other, only then they would certainly have suckled fools, whereas you have clever, intelligent children. As for George's Sibyl, she inherits partly from her mother. She is not an intellect, but she is a good child. She will have all my jewels when I am dead. Why didn't you marry George, Laura? Then I would give you some of the jewels. You could wear pearls very well. Diamonds, no. Sibyl should have the diamonds. Why not think of it? You and George would get on nicely.'

'Well, he never asked me,' said Laura, in her deep abstracted voice.

'Bah!' said old Mrs Knox, with great contempt. 'Ask, indeed! You, Miss Grey,' continued the old lady, turning with what Laura thought a shade of malicious pleasure to her other guest, 'what do you think? Would not my dear Mrs Morland make a charming wife for my poor George?'

Miss Grey obviously found it very difficult to make any answer, which encouraged Mrs Knox to add, 'Wouldn't it be a charming *ménage, hein*? They would work together and make double fortune. Don't you agree?'

Miss Grey was heard to mumble something unintelligible about its being very nice. Laura, distressed by her embarrassment, plunged into the breach.

'You can't marry people off like that, Mrs Knox,' said she. 'At least in France I believe marriages are arranged, but not here, whatever it may say in *The Times*. George would drive me mad in a month. We have both got other things to think about.'

'Any fool could marry George,' said the fond mother. 'And some fool will, before long.'

'Then it won't be me,' said Laura, conforming to English usage. 'I have other fish to fry.'

'What fish, my dear? The little publisher?'

Laura couldn't help laughing.

'No, not that kind of fish at all. Books, Mrs Knox. I've got to keep up my contracts if Tony is to stay at school. Let's leave George alone now.'

'Frankly, my dear, you disappoint me. I had quite a hope that you and George would marry. But I don't blame you. He is a great unintelligent lump, isn't he?'

Miss Grey at last found her tongue.

'Oh, Mrs Knox, how can you say such things about Mr Knox? All those books he has written. You can't write books without intelligence, can you, Mrs Morland?'

'Well, I can,' said Laura, 'but then I'm just a good hack.'

'But Mr Knox's books are splendid. Sure, you were just joking, Mrs Knox.'

'George can make books,' conceded his mother, 'but he has no genius. Laura has. But neither of their books will live. Laura at least spins her books out of her own entrails,' said old Mrs Knox, glancing at Miss Grey to see if she was shocked, and finding considerable pleasure in the fact that she evidently was, 'but George needs someone else's entrails to help him. He has never written a book without a secretary.'

'That's quite true,' said Laura, considering the statement impartially.

'Oh, Mrs Knox, secretaries are nothing. I only look up things for him and make notes, but he dictates it all, and works frightfully hard,' said Miss Grey indignantly.

'Well, child, if you didn't look them up, someone else would, and if nobody did, George wouldn't take the trouble to write the book, that's all. He'd better marry you and save the expense,' said old Mrs Knox with the impertinence of the aged.

Much as Laura disliked Miss Grey, she could not bear this badgering. She got up and shook herself tidy.

'Goodbye, Mrs Knox,' she said in rather a loud voice, because old Mrs Knox hated to be thought deaf, and Laura felt she needed punishing. 'I must go home now. I've got a lot of work to do.'

Mrs Knox put out a hand ungraciously and said goodbye. Laura went downstairs, accompanied by Miss Grey. At the bottom of the stairs she stopped and said very kindly, 'Don't take any notice of Mrs Knox. She is always like that, and loves making people uncomfortable. Don't let her tease you.'

Miss Grey's face softened for a moment, as if she were considering being grateful for Laura's sympathy, but it quickly hardened again as she answered, 'Thank you so much, Mrs Morland, but I know Mrs Knox so well that I quite understand her ways. And I can quite well take care of myself – against anyone,' she added, with such meaning, such an undercurrent of venom, that Laura wished she hadn't spoken.

'Oh, well, it doesn't matter,' she said vaguely, and drifted out of the house. But as she walked home, she considered the situation again, and didn't like it. Miss Grey dug in so firmly at Rutland Gate, boasting of her intimacy with old Mrs Knox, an intimacy which Laura had never achieved during many years' acquaintance. If Mrs Knox did really get it into her head that George ought to marry Miss Grey, she was quite capable of arranging it all and marrying them out of hand. If Miss Grey really cared for George Knox, it was something to have his mother on her side, even if it was very uncomfortable. What was the most sinister part of all was Miss Grey's too evident dislike of herself, a dislike which would not be lessened by Mrs Knox's calculated remarks about George marrying her. The unconcealed hatred in Miss Grey's face as they parted had been rather alarming. Laura wished she knew what George felt, but as he very rarely knew that himself, there didn't seem to be much chance of finding out, and one couldn't ask point blank. If only people would ever think about anything but being in love, it would be so much simpler, was Laura's thought.

However, it was no good worrying, so she went back to the flat and had a bath and a small but excellent supper, and a gossip with Stoker. Then she devoted the evening to literary composition, forgetting all about George and his troubles.

10

Modern Love

Term came to an end all too soon, and Laura, with Stoker and Tony, went down to High Rising. A few days later Master Wesendonck arrived with a small suitcase of clothes and a large suitcase of railway lines and rolling-stock. It was a late Easter, the weather was fine, and Laura told the little boys that they might make the railway in the garden, which occupied them from morning to night. Laura wished that Tony were less overbearing, or Wesendonck more self-assertive, but as they didn't quarrel she had no complaints to make.

Meanwhile at Low Rising all had been tumult and affright, because George Knox had had influenza. Like most healthy men he thought that any illness was death. For two days he had talked of nothing but his own symptoms. The family thermometer had refused to be shaken down, though Sibyl and Miss Grey had nearly dislocated their wrists over it, so Sibyl telephoned for Dr Ford, who sent George off to bed, saying that if he got any worse they must have a nurse. Against this Miss Grey and Sibyl had protested, so Dr Ford gave in for the time being.

'That Incubus,' said he to Anne Todd, whose mother he was visiting unprofessionally a day or two later, 'is the most curious mixture I've ever seen. She is as jealous and neurotic as they make them, but she is a wonderful nurse. In fact, professional honour makes me admit that she is as good as you are. She is tidy and punctual, and she understands that when I say a measured table-spoonful every three hours, I don't mean the patient is to have what she thinks is a table-spoonful whenever it occurs to her. Poor Sibyl is very little use except to read aloud, and I don't see why the woman should be shut up with an infectious patient. They'll all get it, and then they'll have to have a nurse, so they might as well have one to start with.'

'It will strengthen the Incubus's position a good deal if she nurses Mr Knox through this,' said Anne Todd.

'I should think it would. With Knox's sense of the dramatic, I wouldn't put it past him to have a deathbed marriage.' After a slight pause, he continued abruptly, 'I'm not very pleased with your mother, Miss Todd. She isn't responding to the warmer weather as I hoped she would. I knew you'd rather I told you.'

'Can I do anything?' asked Anne Todd.

'I'm afraid not. It's only a question of conserving her strength, and you do all that can be done in that direction. You poor child,' said Dr Ford, and he held Anne's hand.

'Thank you,' said Anne, not withdrawing it. 'If it weren't

for you, and for Mr Knox coming in, and looking forward to Mrs Morland, it would be too lonely to bear. But I'm all right really.'

'I'm glad Knox has been visiting you. You need more change.'

'I have enjoyed his visits very much,' said Anne, quietly resuming possession of her hand. 'Anyone so self-centred as Mr Knox is very bracing. He makes me feel how extremely unimportant my own troubles are. And I'm very fond of Sibyl.'

'I've often wondered why Knox didn't ask Mrs Morland to marry him,' said Dr Ford, who liked nothing better than gossip. 'Does she ever talk about him?'

'Oh, yes, but not in that way. I can't think of any couple more unsuited. Mrs Morland is as kind and gentle as can be, but she has made a life of her own, and I don't think she would like at all to change it, or get on with anyone with such a boisterous personality as Mr Knox. And I don't think he wants to marry. He would as soon think of marrying me as Mrs Morland.'

'Perhaps he does think of marrying you. There could be stranger thoughts.'

Anne Todd laughed. 'On the strength of a few calls lately, Dr Ford? Oh, no. Besides, I'm not that sort.'

'Which sort?'

'The sort people marry.'

'Oh,' said Dr Ford.

There was a silence. Then he got up, and gently kicking Mrs Todd's revolting little dog away from its place on the hearthrug, he stood up with his back to the fire.

'Anne Todd,' he said, 'I didn't mean to say this just yet, but frankly this conversation has alarmed me. If Knox, with his delightful, overpowering personality, gets you into his clutches, it will be goodbye to all my chances.'

Anne Todd was looking at him, but said nothing.

'I suppose,' he went on, 'you haven't thought much about me, except as the middle-aged G.P., but I've thought a good deal about you. I've seen you with that exasperating old lady, your mother, being kind and firm and considerate, putting yourself aside in every way. I know what perpetual attention to a rather peculiar old lady means. I've admired you more than I can say. I've thought of your future. How much money will you have, Anne Todd, when your mother dies?'

Anne Todd, in no way disturbed by this abrupt question, said, 'Father's pension goes when she dies. I shall have about two pounds a week.'

'And what will you do on that?' he asked, crossly.

'The best I can. I am pretty sure of work for Mrs Morland as long as she goes on writing, and I shall get more work. Lord Stoke would be quite glad to have me look after the library at Castle Rising as a part-time job, and I can always write fashion articles in my spare time.'

'You aren't big enough to be so plucky,' said Dr Ford angrily. 'And what kind of hand-to-mouth life is that going to be? A job here and a job there till you are ten years older and the younger women crowd you out. That's not good enough.'

'One has to make things do. And I'm pretty tough.'

'Yes, so long as you have your mother. You'll keep up till

you're ninety if she goes on living. I know your type, Anne. All wire and whipcord while they have someone to sacrifice themselves to, and then a breakdown, and then trying to start again level with women of twenty-five, whose health and nerves have never been tried.'

'Well, I can't help it,' said Anne calmly. 'One just has to do one's best.'

'What about marriage?'

'I've told you once that I'm not the sort that gets married. It doesn't worry me.'

'But you are the sort if you wouldn't be such a blithering fool,' said Dr Ford, so furiously that Anne looked up in astonishment. 'Haven't you noticed that I've been admiring and caring for you more and more, the more I've seen of you? Hasn't it ever occurred to you that a middle-aged G.P. has human feelings, that he can't watch a dear creature giving up her life and youth and not want to help? Have I got to tell you, Anne, that I love you?'

'Yes, I think you have,' said Anne. 'This is so sudden.'

'Don't laugh at me, fiend in human shape,' said Dr Ford, more furiously than before. 'It isn't sudden at all, or if it is, it's only because you are so silly. I know I'm not much, but I might be worse. You could go on helping Mrs Morland if you wanted to. Mrs Mallow would like to have someone to spoil. We could be very happy, Anne. Is it worth considering?'

Anne looked at him with brimming eyes.

'Oh, well worth, well worth; but not for me.'

'Is it your mother? You can bring her to my house and nurse her there.'

'No, it's not Mother,' said Anne, swallowing her tears. 'And anyway it wouldn't be fair to bring her to your house. She is very trying, poor darling, and I'm better alone with her.'

'Your mother can't live for ever, Anne. I will wait till you are alone if you like, and never say a word to trouble you again until that day. Will that do?'

'No, no. Don't wait for me. It would be no good.'

'Listen, Anne,' said Dr Ford, sitting down on a chair in which the revolting little dog was lying. The dog shrieked. 'Oh, damn that dog,' said Dr Ford, and picking it up by the scruff of its neck he dropped it unsympathetically into its basket, and sat down again. 'Listen, Anne, and look at me. It has taken me about four years to say this, and I may never have the courage to say it again. Will you marry me? If you say yes, I'll wait till Domesday.'

'I'm very, very sorry, but I can't.'

'Is that final?' asked Dr Todd, getting up again.

'Quite, quite final,' said Anne Todd, also getting up.

'Was I right about Knox, then? I know it's impertinent to ask, but I'll have to know some day.'

'Mr Knox wouldn't notice me,' said Anne. 'He wouldn't notice anyone.'

'I see. Well, Anne Todd, that's all. I shan't trouble you again. I care for you a good deal too much. When I next come to see your mother, it will be as a G.P. And if you ever need me, just mention it. It couldn't be too soon, or too late. God bless you.'

So he took Anne Todd in his arms, pressed her rather suffocatingly against his old tweed jacket and went away. Miss

Todd tidied her hair and went upstairs to her mother, to whom she read aloud till supper. After supper she played cribbage with the old lady till her early bedtime, and then she did some typing for Laura. About half-past eleven she went up to bed. As she sat before her glass, she looked into it, to see what Anne Todd looked like, who had refused a lover. Anne Todd looked much the same except that her eyes were misty, and her face blurred. Tears poured down her face. 'Not because of loving him,' said Miss Todd aloud to herself, 'because I don't, I don't. Only because of being sorry for him and grateful for his kindness. As for what he said about Mr Knox, that is rubbish. Mr Knox wouldn't notice if I were dead or alive.'

And Miss Todd, who had just refused a lover whom she didn't love, crept into bed and cried herself to sleep.

Dr Ford spent the evening playing bridge at the Vicarage, and came home about midnight, to find sandwiches and hot coffee left for him in the consulting-room by Mrs Mallow. If life was occasionally lonely for him, with Mrs Mallow to soothe and cheer, it must be damnably lonely, he thought, for a woman who bore the burden of an ageing, childish mother, and had a penniless future before her. A woman as fine and courageous as Anne Todd deserved a better fate, but if he couldn't please her, there was no more to be said, and good luck to any decent fellow who could. Dr Ford's face looked worn in the unshaded light of his consulting-room, and Mrs Mallow complained next day to Stoker, whom she met at the butcher's, that the doctor was walking up and down like a grampus for hours and hours after he come in, upon which Stoker suggested indigestion, which caused a slight coolness, till Stoker had the tact to say that it was probably the Vicarage cooking done it, and all unpleasantness was forgotten in hearty combined condemnation of the Vicarage cook.

An Author in the Sick-room

For a few days after her arrival Laura saw nothing of the Knoxes, as she didn't want to risk influenza with Tony and Master Wesendonck about, but she had news of them from Anne Todd, as well as a telephone message from Sibyl. Anne had been over to inquire and seen Sibyl alone. Her description of the household was distressing. Miss Grey had taken over the sick room and practically barred the door to Sibyl. George had written little daily notes to Sibyl, sending her loving messages, and telling her not to visit him till he was better. Sibyl begged to be allowed in, but Miss Grey had been so cold and forbidding that she hardly liked to ask again. The servants were furious and resented Miss Grey's orders, but were too loyal to Sibyl to show their real feelings.

'But I got in,' said Anne placidly.

'You would,' said her admiring employer. 'How?'

'By intrigue,' said Miss Todd. 'I asked Dr Ford to run me

over, and I stayed in the car. Then while Dr Ford, by arrangement, told the Incubus he wanted to see her in the drawing-room, I slipped out and went up to Mr Knox's room. He was as pleased as Punch to see me. He is really all right now, but very weak and limp. He awfully wants you to go and see him, Mrs Morland, and I think it would do him a lot of good.'

'But I can't. The Incubus would be there with a Flaming Sword.'

'Oh, yes, you can. I made Dr Ford frighten the Incubus and tell her that she must get some fresh air, or she would be ill, and then he'd send a nurse. So when I got home, I rang her up and said would she come for a walk with me tomorrow, and she said yes.'

'What luck, Anne.'

'Well, I did also mention that you would be away all day, so I suppose she felt it would be safe. And it's quite true that you are going to lunch at the Castle, but that is no reason why you shouldn't come on to Low Rising at three o'clock and stay till four, or half-past, is it? I shall keep the Incubus to tea with me, and that will give Sibyl a good chance to talk to you, too.'

'Oh, Anne,' said Laura admiringly.

'I always told you I was a bit of a sleuth,' said Miss Todd.

When Laura arrived at Low Rising the following day, with rather a beating heart, she was greeted by Sibyl, who rushed into her arms.

'Oh, dear Mrs Morland, this is too lovely. I was beginning to think we'd never have you here again. Miss Grey has been a wonderful nurse for Daddy, but she keeps him shut up as if he had distemper, and I know he's been longing to see you. You are to go up to him now, and I'll bring up tea about four o'clock and we'll have a lovely time.'

'Did Miss Todd fetch Miss Grey?'

'Oh, yes, and there was nearly a scene, because Miss Grey suddenly said she couldn't go, she must stay with Daddy. I think she suspected something. But Miss Todd was marvellous. She actually said, "Don't be a fool, my good woman,"' said Sibyl, her eyes shining with awe and admiration, 'and she flattered Miss Grey so awfully about how useful she was, and how Dr Ford said she must take care of her valuable self, that she went off like a lamb. And I happen to know, Mrs Morland, that Miss Todd is taking her round by Stoke Dry and giving her tea at her own house, and she can't possibly get back before five. Hurrah, hurrah!'

'Well, I'll go up to George,' said Laura, taking off her coat. 'And what about you, Sibyl? Have you sent your manuscript to Adrian yet?'

Sibyl became pink. 'Yes, I sent it last week,' she said. 'I'm afraid it's rotten, but I didn't like to say so when he was so kind.'

Laura noted with approval the way her voice lingered on the word 'he'.

'Have you heard anything about it yet?' she asked.

'No. He wrote to say he had got it, and he would read it himself and tell me when he came down to you. When is he coming?'

'The week after next. Is that too far off?' said Laura laughing, and went upstairs to George Knox's room. George was sitting in a chair before the fire, looking all the worse for his bout of influenza.

'Well, George, you do look a misery. Don't get up,' said Laura, settling herself opposite him. 'How are you now?'

'The better for seeing you, my dear. This has indeed been a purgatory, an inferno, where my body and brain have been consuming deliriously for days and nights; how long I do not know; I have lost all count of time.'

'Well, today is the eighth, if it really interests you.'

'The eighth. Blessed eighth, Laura, that brings you. I have been longing for you as pants the hart, but I have been helpless, a swaddled babe in the hands of women.'

'You seem to have been very nicely looked after,' said Laura handsomely.

'The iron has entered into my soul,' announced George Knox impressively. 'Let me tell you, my dear Laura, that when I lay here weak and ill, unable to raise a hand in my own defence, I begged for a nurse, a hireling who would do her day-labour as a machine, and not worry a sick, ageing man. But even this was denied. Miss Grey, all kindness and sympathy and, I must say, Laura, an infernal bore, insisted on nursing me herself. Degrading enough in any case, but the worst you have not heard. Could I ask my secretary to shave me? No. As a matter of fact, I did, but she wouldn't, or couldn't. Imagine me, Laura, becoming more like a pard day by day, prickly and revolting to myself, mortified beyond words to be seen in this condition, but helpless.'

'Why didn't you get the gardener to do it? Or use a safety razor?'

'My dear Laura,' said George Knox in a hurt voice, 'you do not seem to realise how weak I was, how very weak. For two days my temperature had been over a hundred, and when the fever had left me I lay powerless, as a new-born babe, and the woman triumphed over me. She would not let me shave, she fed me on slops, she would not even give me clean pyjamas till the third day.'

'Don't cry, George,' said Laura bracingly. 'It was a bit awkward for Miss Grey. She couldn't very well put you into clean pyjamas, could she, if you were as ill as that? And anyway three days isn't so very awful. And you are nicely shaved now. Count your blessings.'

'I count you as one, dear Laura. But about the shaving. I rebelled at last, Laura; I revolted. Yesterday and today I staggered to the bathroom and shaved myself. Tomorrow I shall come downstairs and assert myself.'

'I'm sorry for anyone who has to nurse you,' said Laura candidly. 'I wouldn't. But why do you let Miss Grey bully you? She is only by the month, isn't she?'

'Nominally, yes; really, no. The month, Laura, is but a fiction, a John Roe, or do I mean Richard Doe? Willingly, after the mortification I have suffered at her hands, would I let her go, but what can I do? A friendless girl. I had found an excellent post for her with my dear old friend Miss Hocking, who requires a secretary to help her in the work of entertaining overseas students, but I have not dared to mention it to her. The bare suggestion of leaving Low Rising is so upsetting to Miss Grey, and she is so much attached to Sibyl. What can I do, a helpless pawn in the hands of fate?'

'Helpless idiot,' said Laura. 'Send Miss Grey to see Miss

Hocking next time she goes to town for you, and if Miss Hocking likes her, settle the affair at once. There's nothing criminal in changing your secretary, and she'll be able to vamp the overseas students and have a splendid time.'

'I will, I will,' said George Knox ecstatically. 'Laura, you are always my saviour. I think of you as a beacon light shining calmly upon troubled waters. Your courage, your wit, your defiant best-sellers, your beauty, I adore them all. Weak, helpless invalid as I am,' said George, getting up and walking vigorously about the room, 'I still have the strength to worship you, as Petrarch worshipped another Laura.'

'Well, that's all very nice of you, George. But I will bet you anything you won't get Miss Grey off to Miss Hocking. She will marry you if you aren't careful,' said Laura, taking the bull by the horns.

George Knox stopped short and looked at Laura, panic-stricken.

'By God, Laura, you are right, as you always are. Fool that I am, it never occurred to me before. Authors always marry their secretaries. Am I compromised already by her sick-room attendance? Good God, good God!'

'Sit down, George. You aren't compromised at all and, as usual, you can't take a joke. No one can marry you unless you ask them to. Women don't really run at a man and force him into marriage, except in novels like mine. They wait till they are asked, though they may help things on a bit.'

George Knox subsided into his chair again, and mopped his forehead. 'I am weaker than I thought,' he said, with great feebleness.

'Don't try to impress me, George.'

'I can't. I know I can't. You always keep me straight, Laura; you support and strengthen me. Laura, there is so much to say, but I can't begin to say it in this lazar-house, this plague-infected abode, with Sibyl liable to come in with tea at any moment and Miss Grey coming back soon. Laura, are you to be in town next week?'

'Probably,' said Laura, a little surprised. 'I have to go up on Thursday for some business, and shall stay the night.'

'Then if I go up on Thursday, will you go to a play with me?'

'I'd love to. Are you going to Rutland Gate?'

'No. I shall go to my club. Mamma will be away then, and the house, I understand, will be all dust-sheeted – only inhabited by the kitchen-maid, a repugnant woman who cannot cook.'

'Your mother seems to like Miss Grey, George.'

'No one knows, dear Laura, what Mamma does or doesn't like. If she likes anything, it is being extremely interfering and making other people uncomfortable.'

George spoke so warmly that Laura wondered if old Mrs Knox had been offering Miss Grey to him as a possible bride.

'Thursday night, then, Laura. You will dine with me and we will go to a theatre. What shall it be?'

'I suppose one ought to go to the repertory performance of *King Lear*,' said Laura tepidly.

'Anywhere you like, my dear Laura. *King Lear* it shall be, though the play is in itself inherently improbable and in parts excessively coarse and painful. But they may do it in modern clothes, or in the dark, or all standing on step-ladders. You never know. *King Lear* it shall be. Dear Laura, it pours fresh life into my veins, ichor, elixir, to think of an evening with you, away from this house of disease and corruption. My mind is a foul and stagnant fen. Even Wordsworth was more interesting than I am at this moment. I should be working on Queen Elizabeth, but I cannot think, I cannot concentrate. It is all gone, gone, gone. I am finished,' said George, groaning and clasping his massive head in both hands.

'Not a bit, George. Only post-flu depression. Take Sibyl abroad. You could give Miss Grey a month's notice and lots of extra wages and go whenever you liked.'

'I could, Laura, I could. But not until we have had our evening together. To that, Laura, I look forward infinitely. With that as goal, I shall struggle towards health, making daily a little progress, sitting in the sun, if there is any, walking daily in the garden, if it doesn't rain, fitting myself for this crown of my convalescence. And here is Sibyl, dear child, so tactlessly coming in with tea, just as I had so much, so much to say to you.'

And in came Sibyl, followed by Annie with a tray. George Knox showed, for an invalid author, a remarkably good appetite, and enjoyed himself hugely, talking, eating large mouthfuls of teacake, and swilling great gulps of tea all at once.

'There's nothing wrong with your father, Sibyl,' said Laura, 'except that he enjoys being sorry for himself. I've told him to push Miss Grey off to Miss Hocking on board wages, and take you abroad.'

178

'But not before I've seen Mr Coates,' said Sibyl anxiously.

'Why Coates?' asked George Knox, in a very mouthful kind of way.

'Oh, Daddy, you know he wanted to see what I was writing, and you were so keen for me to try, so I must wait and hear what he says.'

'Ah, yes, I remember. Laura, this child of mine will never let me see a word that she writes. But I know she has it in her. She is not my child for nothing.'

'Really, George,' said Laura indignantly, 'you are too conceited. Probably people will soon talk about you as the father of Miss Knox.'

'Will they, Laura?' asked George, rather depressed. 'Shall I indeed go down to posterity on the hem of her robe?'

'Oh, no, Daddy,' cried Sibyl, indignant at this cheapening of her father. 'Mrs Morland doesn't mean it. You are a million times better than ever I could be, isn't he, Mrs Morland?'

'I can't tell, Sibyl, till I've seen your book. I expect you'll both do each other credit, and I am as anxious to know what Adrian thinks as you are.'

'After all,' said George, cheering up, 'it is only in the course of Nature. Each year fresh flowers grow from the rotting remains of last year's blossoms, the years renew themselves, Zeus dethrones Cronos and is in his turn dethroned, Ragnarok swallows up the Gods, the world's great golden age returns, seven cities have been built where once Troy Town stood.'

'Oh, do stop talking like an encyclopaedia, George,' said Laura, in her deepest voice. 'You might as well say that spiders eat their husbands, and mice devour their young. I must go now, before Florence Nightingale comes back and finds me here.'

'I hardly grasp your allusion, Laura, to the Lady of the Lamp.'

'For heaven's sake don't talk in clichés, George. I mean your kind nurse, your secretary, your Miss Grey.'

Laura got up, stared at herself in the mirror over the mantelpiece, pushed a few wisps of hair under her hat, and said goodbye.

'Come over to lunch today fortnight and spend the afternoon,' was her farewell to Sybil. 'Adrian will be here. But we'll meet before then.'

In self-defence Laura had arranged for Messrs Morland Jr and Wesendonck to have a high tea at half-past six, so that they could more fully discuss the work upon which they had been occupied all day. She herself usually had a meal on a tray in the drawing-room, while they were indulging in their interminable and ineffectual ablutions. Next evening Stoker brought her supper in and put it beside her in silence. Stoker's silences were always so audible, and so fraught with meaning, that Laura waited to see what was coming.

'I've brought you in the Burgundy,' said Stoker gloomily. 'It wants finishing, and I dare say you'll need it when you've heard.'

'Heard what?'

'That's what I said to Mr Knox's Annie.'

'Well, what had Annie to say? Something about Flo, or the Institute, I suppose.'

'I shouldn't concern myself about the Institute, being as I'm on the committee,' said Stoker haughtily.

'Well, I don't follow your argument, Stoker, but what was it all about?'

Stoker leaned herself against the writing-table and prepared to hold forth.

'Mr Knox's Annie come over on her bike,' she began, 'and had tea with me. And you'd hardly credit what she heard.'

'Well, I can't credit anything if you don't tell me, Stoker,' said Laura, seeing that Stoker was determined to be encouraged.

'Well, it's like this. Annie was very upset about Mr Knox having the flu, and the way madam was in and out of his room all day. Barely decent.'

'Someone had to nurse him, Stoker. Don't be absurd.'

'I dare say. But there was Miss Knox not allowed in, and madam whisking about, morning, noon and night, and giving orders to cook, who knows what a gentleman requires when he's an invalid as well as anyone. So one night madam was having her bath and Annie happened to be passing Mr Knox's door and heard him call out, so she looked in to see if the poor gentleman wanted anything, and what do you think he was doing? Calling your name, mum,' said Stoker, forgetting in her excitement to withhold Laura's title. '"Laura, Laura," he said, so plain that Annie said it fair give her the creeps.'

'I expect he was dreaming, Stoker, or a bit delirious with a temperature.'

'Some dreams go by contraries, others don't,' said Stoker

darkly. 'My aunt used to talk in her sleep, and one night she was calling "Henry, Henry", and next day her Uncle Alf died. Shows you, doesn't it?'

'I can't exactly say that it does, Stoker, but I'm sorry Mr Knox had bad dreams.'

'That's not all. When madam come back yesterday afternoon from having tea with Miss Todd, she saw three cups going downstairs.'

Stoker paused to let this sink in. Laura wondered if Miss Grey had been drunk or seen visions and dreamed dreams, but realising that this was only Stoker's way of saying that Annie had been carrying the tea-things down to the kitchen, she waited with interest for the sequel.

'And she said to Annie, "Who's been having tea here?" And that Annie was fool enough to tell her, and Annie says madam let loose it was a treat to hear. And Miss Knox she run away into her room, and Mr Knox he poked his head over the banisters to ask if the house was afire, and madam she run up to her room and slammed the door.'

Laura's face of horror was ample reward for Stoker.

'So then Annie picked the pieces up.'

'What pieces?'

'The tea-cups. When madam pushed the tray, the cups and saucers fell off. And Annie and cook are going to give notice. Annie told her mother, and she said high time, too, with such goings on.'

'Oh, Stoker, how awful. But do tell Annie to wait a bit. Miss Grey might be going soon. Only don't say it came from me. Tell her and cook to wait till after the Easter holidays, anyway. And don't talk more than you can help yourself,

Stoker, and stop Annie talking if you can. It will be so horrid for Miss Knox.'

'Silent as the grave,' said Stoker, which Laura could not for a moment believe. 'And did you wish the young gentlemen to use the old dog-kennel for their railway, because I found them with it, and Master Tony says he is going to knock the back out so the trains can go right through.'

'No, I did not, Stoker. At least not to knock the back out. I'll tell Tony tomorrow. And don't let them have anything out of the kitchen without my leave. You remember how Tony took all our salt last year to make a snowdrift for his train.'

Stoker sang a few unrestrained notes and went back to her kitchen.

After this Laura and Anne Todd began to feel that they were involved in a heavy, endless nightmare, in which Miss Grey met them malignantly at every turn. While they were working on Monday morning, Sibyl came in, tearful and indignant. It appeared that Stoker's account of the scene at Low Rising was hardly exaggerated at all.

'She hit the tray Annie was carrying so hard that the cups fell off and were broken, Mrs Morland, and she slammed into her room and wouldn't come out for the rest of the evening. Daddy heard the noise and he was furious, and said she must go tomorrow, but of course when tomorrow came he weakened, as he always does, and Miss Grey cried a lot and said she was all alone in the world, so Daddy said he would see about it. And then, Mrs Morland, an awful thing happened.'

Sibyl paused so long, with large tear-stained eyes gazing

piteously at them, that both the elder ladies said, 'What?' simultaneously.

'It came out that you were going to a play with Daddy next week, and she said she'd never seen it, and never could afford to go to plays, and—'

'So your father asked her to come, too, I suppose,' said Laura.

Sibyl nodded hopelessly.

'Well, I'm not surprised. Your father, Sibyl dear, is perhaps one of the world's most mentally deficient men. That is that. And I've a good mind not to go myself.'

'Oh, but Mrs Morland, you must. You can't let her go to a play with him alone.'

'Don't be silly, Sibyl. She can't kidnap him, and it might make him even more sick of her than he is. Today is Monday. Of course with luck she might get influenza before Thursday.'

'I'm sure she won't,' said Sibyl. 'And she'll never leave us. If only she weren't so nice when she isn't being nasty.'

'I know,' said Laura sympathetically. 'When she is nice it is all I can do to remember how nasty she is. But stick to it, Sibyl. By the way, Anne, you must have come in for some of the wrath.'

'No, I didn't,' said Anne Todd. 'I took care not to. I knew you were lunching at Stoke Castle, and it wasn't my fault if you nipped away and rushed off to see Mr Knox on the sly. The Incubus and I had a lot of talk about how hard it is to be alone, and I'm afraid I told her a good deal about Mrs Hocking, and how she has her house always full of young men from the colonies, and the Incubus listened attentively. One good shove from this end and we might get rid of her.'

'But who is to give the shove?' asked Laura.

'Time, possibly. Mrs Morland, is Mrs Birkett coming down these holidays?'

'Yes, the last week, after Adrian goes.'

'Well, I shan't lose hope till then. I have an idea she may be a kind of mascot.'

'I must go home now,' said Sibyl. 'I feel so tired and shivery ever since that dreadful Saturday evening.'

'Don't you go and get influenza too,' said Laura anxiously.

'It might be the best thing she could do,' said Anne Todd.

Sure enough Sibyl did go down with influenza, that evening. Dr Ford was sent for on Tuesday, and said it was only a mild attack, but she must stay in bed for a few days. Being that rare and desirable kind of man who can take a refusal in the spirit in which it is meant, he had not interrupted his friendly visits to old Mrs Todd and her daughter, and this evening he told them about Sibyl.

'That Incubus is nursing her like an angel,' said Dr Ford. 'She appears to want to go to town for a night on Thursday, Anne, but Sibyl will be quite all right with Annie. She isn't a serious case, only we might as well be careful. I'll tell the Incubus tomorrow that she can go with a clear conscience.'

'I think the Incubus had much better nurse Sibyl,' said Anne deliberately. 'Don't ask me why, Dr Ford, but take my word for it. Will you tell her that only her nursing will pull Sibyl through, or words to that effect?'

'Words to any effect you like, Anne, but they won't have any effect on her.'

'They might. And will you tell her that I send my love –
my dear love you might say – and I am coming to see her
tomorrow. And if I can't fill her up with the notion that she
is doing a beautiful and chivalrous deed, which will impress
Mr Knox, in giving up her own pleasure and staying with
Sibyl, I'm a Jew,' said Anne.

So Dr Ford promised. And on Thursday morning Anne
was able to give Laura the welcome information that the
Incubus was behaving like a lamb with a swelled head, and
going to stay and nurse Sibyl and show devotion. It was a
pity, she added, that Mr Knox was so obviously impressed by
the devotion, but that couldn't be helped.

'You are a marvel, Anne,' said Laura.

'I do my best. But I shan't feel safe till tonight has come
and gone. I feel she may still have an outburst – ride
through the air on a broomstick perhaps, and cast spells on
you.'

186

1 2

The Shakespeare Tradition

Laura didn't very often get a treat. Her London life was one of hard work, and she was often too tired to want to go out at night. Unless one goes about a good deal, one doesn't make fresh friends. Also, a woman who can't bring a man with her is apt to be, if not unwelcome, at least the sort of person who doesn't head one's list of guests. Laura faced this fact quite placidly. She had had plenty of going about while her unlamented husband was alive, and was content to slip back into spending her evenings in slippered ease, or go to the nearest cinema. She was still young enough to have attracted men if she had cared to take the trouble, but that she most emphatically didn't. One man had been enough trouble to last her for a lifetime. So she led a very peaceful existence, only broken by festivities when one or other of her sons came home. Then she tried to dress well, had her hair waved, evoked old friends, made advances to new ones, went to plays, had people to dinner, and kept late nights.

Then when Gerald, or John, or Dick had gone off, she would shed a tear, breathe a sigh of relief, and have her meals on a tray again.

So it was a distinct treat to dine with George Knox and go to a play, even if only Shakespeare. Laura dressed almost in a flurry, while Stoker, whom she had brought up for the night, leaving Annie's mother in charge of the boys, attended on her toilette, and gave her unvalued criticism. It was one of Stoker's grievances against her mistress that Laura would not have a permanent wave in her long, heavy hair.

'You wouldn't look not half so old with a perm,' said the faithful handmaiden.

'I dare say not, Stoker, but I know only too well what I would look like. You can have a perm, if you like.'

'Dare say I shall, one of these days,' said Stoker, eyeing herself complacently over Laura's shoulder as she sat in front of her glass. 'Might suit my style. But you did ought to have a Marcel wave for the theatre tonight.'

'Well, I hadn't time, Stoker, so that's that. And I've got the key, so if you want to go to a cinema, you needn't hurry back. Leave out something for me in case I'm hungry, and I might bring Mr Knox back for a drink.'

Laura emptied the contents of one bag into another, clutched her fur coat round her, and went off to meet George Knox. George was waiting for her, and had secured a table and ordered dinner.

'I'm so glad you have arranged what we are to eat,' said Laura. 'It makes it a much better treat not to know what I'm going to have.'

'I may not be a popular author, Laura, but I can at least claim a little knowledge of food. My mother has transmitted the gift to me with her French blood, I suppose. Sibyl, too, understands the pleasures of the table. She is an admirable housekeeper. What shall we drink, my dear Laura? Something to celebrate my recovery, to celebrate this delightful occasion. Champagne, I think, is indicated.'

'Not for me, George. Champagne makes me feel misunderstood at once. Also it makes my knees bend the wrong way. Water, please.'

'But, Laura, I entreat. May I not pledge you? And to see your knees bend the wrong way would be excessively interesting. Let me be indulged for once.'

'You can pledge me as much as you like, George, but I'm not going to pledge you. I don't mind having a terribly expensive liqueur afterwards, with the coffee. You go ahead and drink what you like.'

George turned to the wine waiter and ordered champagne. Just as the man was going away to get it, Laura called to him to stop.

'Just listen a moment, George,' she said in a deep, clear voice which filled the small restaurant. '*Not* champagne for you. You will be weak in the head after that influenza and I'm not going to run any risks with you. A bottle, a *small* bottle, of red wine will be very nice for you, or, if you like, a whisky and soda; but that's all.'

'But, Laura, I am no drunkard, no tippler, no alehouse debauchee,' protested George, in a voice as clear as Laura's and far more powerful. 'Do I downwards fall into a grovelling swine? No. Waiter, bring the champagne.'

'One moment,' said Laura to the waiter, petrifying him with her Mrs Crummles air. 'This is my treat, George, not yours. *Not* champagne.'

George looked annoyed for a moment, but, recovering himself, said, 'You are right, Laura, perfectly right as usual. Waiter, bring me half a bottle of No. 43. Laura, I am grateful to you. I live a lonely life. I become rustic, earthy, gross, unfit to associate with such women as you. I need your calm good sense, your admirable candour. Without it I am as naught.'

'That's all right,' said Laura. 'I do like caviar, George. Not so much because it is nice, as because I feel it ought to be. I shall have some caviar in my new book. Do you think we shall enjoy *King Lear*?'

'Frankly — if frankness is what you require, my dear Laura — no.'

'Oh, George.'

'Well, you know what it will be. It is astounding, Laura, how loudly Shakespearian actors can talk, and yet be perfectly unintelligible.'

'I suppose it's part of the Shakespeare tradition.'

'Tradition! A loud booming noise that no one can make head or tail of. An elocution competition between bitterns. Why can't they talk English?'

'Do you think, George, that Elizabethan actors talked more distinctly than ours do?'

'My dear Laura, there is no doubt about it. Absolutely none. If they didn't, no one would ever have known what Shakespeare plays were about till the Quartos began to appear. And even then their extraordinary spelling and repellent appearance must have put people off. They were not, emphatically not, Laura, the kind of book to slip into your pocket and read, while you waited for the Globe early door. No, we may take it that the stage under Elizabeth, or perhaps more accurately under James the First, for, as you know, Shakespeare's plays were not printed during the reign of Elizabeth, was remarkable for its clarity of speech. This I intend to enlarge upon in my new book.'

'Well, don't pretend it's your idea, George. I suggested it. Oh, George, I do like quails. You are a splendid host.'

'Never had host such a guest,' answered George Knox, after the manner of Sir Richard Whittington. 'My dear Laura, how you outshine those poorer beauties of the night whom I see around us. It is one of the few excellent features of this deplorable phase of civilisation through which we are now passing, if civilisation it may be called, when it is indeed rather a return, a *dégringolade*, to the Dark Ages, that the appreciation of mature beauty is more developed than at any other point in history.'

'I suppose what you mean,' said Laura, who was getting the best out of her quail by finishing the legs in her fingers, 'is that there are heaps of novels with middle-aged women for heroines. Disgusting I call it. They have rejuvenating operations and lovers and what not. All most unsuitable. If you think I'm looking nice tonight, that's very nice of you, and I'm much obliged, but don't make such phrases about it. Stoker says I ought to have a permanent wave.'

'Never,' said George Knox, hitting the table with his fist. 'Could I see you oiled and curled like an Assyrian bull?'

'No, you couldn't. Not that I'd look like a bull in any

case, and I have no intention of following Stoker's advice. I never do. But she likes giving it.'

Conversation then, in a not unusual way, took its course towards George Knox's new book, and Laura was able to enjoy her very expensive liqueur in peace, while George's booming periods rolled over her head. That they attracted the attention of most of the diners did not at all upset Laura, who was used to the publicity which George's presence conferred upon his guests, and she let him roll on till it was time to go to the theatre, when she remarked, 'Time, George,' and beckoned the waiter.

George stopped abruptly and paid the bill.

'What I do like about going out for a treat,' said Laura, 'is that someone else does the tipping. I shall never stop being frightened of tipping. When I have made a fortune I shall over-tip everybody, just to show off, and to obtain servility from them.'

'There should be no difficulty,' said George, struggling into his overcoat. 'Ten per cent, on the bill, and more if you feel generous. Get me a taxi.'

'But I can't do ten per cent,' said Laura piteously. 'If I had a pencil I could, but otherwise it is too hard, and they see my lips moving while I calculate, and despise me. I do hate being despised.'

'You couldn't be despised, Laura,' said George, pushing her into the taxi.

'Oh, couldn't I? And talking of tips, what did you give the commissionaire?"

'A shilling, of course.'

'Don't say "of course" at me like that. What is a shilling

ten per cent of? Ten shillings. Why are the commissionaire's services worth a capital sum of ten shillings?' said Laura, with an extremely business-like manner.

'My dear Laura, I am tempted to apply to you an expression which Coates once used of you, but that it would hardly become me, as your host.'

'Heavenly fool, do you mean?' asked Laura, much interested. 'You needn't look sheepish, George. Adrian told me himself. I rather like it.'

George Knox kissed her hand with as much gallant courtesy as can be shown in a rather jolting taxi. 'Thus,' said he, 'I express my devotion to the heavenly fool.'

'Thank you very much,' said Laura, as the taxi drew up at the theatre. 'And what is ten per cent on one and three-pence?'

'It will be ninepence when I have a lady with me.'

'Oh, gosh,' said Laura as they reached the entrance to the stalls. 'It's begun. We shall disturb everyone, and be hated.'

'Not if I know Shakespeare,' said George sardonically.

He was perfectly right. If all the trumpets had sounded for Laura and George as they walked down the aisle, their entrance would have passed entirely unnoticed in the blasting, ear-splitting noise that was coming from the stage. As George had said, not a single word was distinguishable, though the actors were taking infinite pains to give the impression of saying something. As they sat down Laura whispered to George, 'Shakespeare tradition.' George rather liked to have her hair so close to his ear, and nodded his head violently in approval. After some ten minutes their ears began to be accustomed to the peculiarities of

Shakespeare, and they could enjoy the play, so far as *King Lear* can be said to be a play that one enjoys. Laura, who rarely went to a theatre, became entirely absorbed in the scene, sitting bolt upright on the edge of her seat, her eyes glued to the stage, feeling herself each character in turn. Unobserved, her gloves and bag slid to the ground. George, who never felt stage illusion very strongly, divided his attention between the actors and Laura's profile, young in the subdued light that came from the stage, eager and intent. When the first act came to an end, Laura's tension relaxed. She sat back, and for the first time noticed the loss of her gloves and bag.

'Oh, my goodness, I've dropped everything,' said she wildly, and began rummaging on the floor.

'What is it, Laura? Let me get it,' said George Knox, also stooping down, but Laura had already retrieved her property and arisen from the depths, considerably dishevelled.

'It's all right, George. I've got them, but if you see any hairpins, I'll be glad. They all fell out when I was under the seat.'

George Knox dived again, and emerged with several large tortoiseshell pins, which Laura twisted into her hair, appearing to be quite satisfied with the result, though George was a little disturbed.

'It will all be down again in a moment, Laura,' said he, anxiously. 'And there's a large piece sticking straight out behind. Could you do anything about it?'

'You haven't got a spare hairpin on you, have you?' said Laura hopefully.

'My dear Laura, do I carry hairpins?'

'Yes, sometimes, to clean your pipe with. I've bought penny packets for you at Woolworth's before now. But never mind, I'll manage.'

With considerable exertion she retrieved her back hair and skewered it down triumphantly, before the lights went out. As the play passed from gloom to gloom, Laura sat like a carved figure, till the moment arrived when Gloucester's eye is to be put out, when she startled George and her neighbours by saying urgently, 'Tell me when it's over,' and putting her hands over her ears, while she shut her eyes tightly. So firmly was she entrenched in her determination neither to see nor hear that George had to shake her arm violently to recall her to the world. In the interval she apologised.

'I'd rather forgotten the eyes part,' she said earnestly. 'Is there much more, George?'

'Aren't you enjoying it, then?'

Laura struggled with politeness. 'It's a wonderful play, George, but it takes a lot out of one, don't you think?'

'Would you like to go?'

'Oh, George, could we really?'

With alacrity she bundled herself into her coat, seized her loose property and forced her way out through the stalls, followed by her host. They left the theatre and picked up a taxi.

'You'll come back and have a drink, George, won't you?' said Laura. 'Tell the taxi to go to my flat. George, I'm terribly sorry to be such an unworthy guest. I did mean to enjoy it, but what with the noise at first-hand then that awful eye scene, I really couldn't. Do you mind?'

'No, I don't,' said George Knox in his loudest voice. 'If there is one pleasure on earth which surpasses all others, it is leaving a play before the end. I might perhaps except the joy of taking tickets for a play, dining well, sitting on after dinner, and finally not going at all. That, of course, is very heaven.'

The taxi drew up at the block of flats where Laura lived. George Knox over-tipped the driver to that extent that the grateful creature detained him, to give him a sure thing for the two-thirty next day. When he rejoined Laura in the hall, he found her majestically annoyed.

'I do wish, George, you would remember that I am a defenceless widow,' she said plaintively. 'There you were, consorting with greasy mechanics, leaving me to be murdered.'

'Were you murdered?' asked George Knox anxiously.

'No, but I might have been. I was waiting patiently for you while you were showing off to the taxi-driver, and someone came hurtling downstairs and nearly knocked me down, and I've dropped my bag again and my gloves.'

'Who was it?'

'I didn't notice. Just someone scurrying downstairs in a frightful hurry, and the hall is rather dark. I'll turn the light on, and you can find my bag and things for me. If you hadn't preferred the society of a taxi-man to that of a cultured woman of uncertain age, this wouldn't have happened.'

George Knox penitently collected Laura's scattered property and they went up to her flat, where the good Stoker had left out food according to directions, and banked up the fire.

'Give it a poke, George,' said Laura, dropping her coat on

to a chair and sitting down. 'You've known me for more than seven years, so it's all right.'

'To one it is ten years of years,' said George gallantly, hitting the fire violently with the poker as he spoke. The mass of coal collapsed and settled down into a clear blaze.

'What do you mean?' asked Laura. 'I suppose it's a compliment, but it might have been better put. Give me some coffee, George, and you can have a whisky and soda.'

They ate and drank in comfortable silence for a few minutes, by the glowing fire.

'Golly, what a play,' said Laura suddenly, alluding to the masterpiece of the Bard from which they had just fled, 'but very unfair to daughters. I never had one, but I am sure they are very nice, really. Darling Sibyl is sometimes nearly as silly as Cordelia, but one can't imagine her behaving like Regan, whatever the provocation.'

As she said the words, it flashed across her mind that Miss Grey might be capable of very Reganish behaviour. Whether the same idea occurred to George she could not guess, but in any case neither of them made any allusion to it.

'Sibyl is as loving as Cordelia,' said George Knox with dignity, 'but no one could be such a fool.'

'Of course they couldn't, George. I only meant she was a darling, clinging creature without many brains. The Cordelias always have to have someone to cling to. If it isn't their father, it is France. Not, of course, that you would turn Sibyl out of doors. But France might be there all the same.'

'France?' said George, still rather dignified. 'France who? Or perhaps I should say Who France?'

'Nobody France, George. But there always might be Somebody France.'

'Dear Laura, my mind is still enfeebled by the grave indisposition which I have not yet fully shaken off. Somebody France? Could you, in pity to an ageing man whose intellect is clouded by disease, make yourself a little clearer?'

'Well,' said Laura patiently, 'Cordelia married France, didn't she? The King of France, you know, but Shakespeare calls him France, to save time, or because it is what one calls kings, like Cleopatra being Egypt.'

George Knox looked, if possible, more confused than before.

'So,' continued Laura, ignoring his studied air of bewilderment, 'if Cordelia, who adored her father, married a king because she was turned out of doors, Sibyl might marry too, mightn't she? Not a king, of course, because you have to be turned out of doors to do that, but some nice commoner.'

'Laura,' exclaimed George Knox, theatrically, 'what are you saying?'

'You heard perfectly well. I said Sibyl will probably get married before long. She is very attractive and if she is rather silly, that is no bar to matrimony. You needn't look offended.'

'But the child is yet in her teens.'

'No, she isn't. She's twenty. Of course, if you like to say twenteen you can, but no one will understand you. Do you ever think that she is grown-up, George?'

George Knox stared at her, poured himself out another drink, stared again, and exploded.

'But you are right, Laura. So right. I had never thought of my child as grown-up. Child, friend, companion, yes: grown-up, no. And it needs a stranger – no, Laura, forgive me, no stranger, for have our paths not lain side by side ever since your very uninteresting husband first brought you as a bride to Rutland Gate and Mamma was so rude to him? – let us say a dear friend, though we are not bound by ties of blood, to point out to me that my own child is grown-up. Why have I never seen it?'

'Well, you could have any day, if you had looked, George, but you are so dense.'

'Why,' repeated George Knox, ignoring this interruption, 'have I never seen it? What kind of father am I? I go on my own way, selfish, unheeding, while this exquisite bud comes to blossom in a single night. The child is marriageable, nubile—'

'That's enough, George,' said Laura firmly. 'A little more and you'll be Shakespearian, or even Biblical, which is worse. I merely wished to point out to you that Sibyl can't be expected to stay at home all her life, so you might as well get used to the idea.'

George Knox rearranged himself as the pathetic, ageing greybeard, alone by a desolate hearth. Already, Laura could see, he had a vision of himself, living only for the rare visits of his married daughter and the patter of childish feet. Fresh young voices brought life into the old home, and in their joyous youth he renewed his own, till they faded away, those Dream Children, and left him solitary as before. But no, not altogether solitary, for who was the gracious figure who advanced towards him from the house, as he stood straining his eyes after the departing dear ones? A noble, matronly figure, in heavy draperies, her still abundant hair sprinkled with silver. 'George,' she cried, in the low but resonant tones he loved so well, 'come in. The night dew falls fast and the air grows chill.' He turned, and accompanied her to the house.

'Laura,' said George, with a jolt, 'does dew fall? I thought it came up from the ground.'

'How should I know? You are as bad as Tony with your questions. It falls in poetry, but I have never felt it falling myself. One would be apt to mistake it for rain. Perhaps one has often been in a dewfall and only thought it was a shower. Why?'

'Just a thought I had,' said George Knox absently. 'Laura, when Sibyl is married, I shall be very much alone.'

'You'll have to get used to that. And even when Sibyl does marry, it won't mean that the Black Death has come to Low Rising. There is the vicar, and Dr Ford, and Anne Todd, and me if you come to that, and Lord Stoke not so far off, and—'

'Yes, Laura, my friends will still be there, and you not least among them. You won't desert me, will you?'

'I think *King Lear* has gone to your head,' said Laura, eyeing him suspiciously, as she stuck a few hairpins further in. 'Why should anyone desert you? I'm not an unhatched, new-fledged – at least I mean a new-hatched, unfledged – comrade, beware. I've known you for about a quarter of a century, and I've no intention of dropping you because Sibyl, who isn't even engaged yet, may get married. Don't be so silly, George.'

'When I think what old friends we are,' said George Knox, 'and how you were the one bright spot of light in Mamma's appalling dinner parties, and how gay and alive you always were, in spite of your suet pudding of a husband, and how gracious to my poor colourless wife, I feel that your continued friendship is all I have to live for.'

He drained his glass moodily and gazed at the fire.

Laura stood up in some dudgeon.

'George Knox,' she said, 'poor Rhoda was certainly colourless, and you have a perfect right to say it, but in calling poor Henry a suet pudding, you go too far. I can only excuse you by reminding myself that people frequently go mad after influenza. Now you have made my hair come down and I shall have to go and do it up properly. When I come back you will apologise, and then,' she added, melting at the sight of George's miserable face, 'we will go on as before.'

Leaving George Knox sunk in gloom, Laura went out of the room. As she passed through the little hall, she looked automatically at the letter-box which hung on the front door, and saw something in it. Stoker had evidently gone out before the last post came, otherwise any letters would have been put on the hall table. She fetched the letter, which was apparently some bill or circular with a typewritten address and no stamp, and took it with her into her room, where she sat down before the dressing-table and began to do her hair again. When she had finished she picked up the envelope and opened it. Typewritten on a sheet of ordinary typewriting paper were the words:

Mrs Morland,

'The man you are thinking of marrying is no good at all.
He would make love to anyone. Think of your family
and have nothing to do with him.

A FRIEND

Underneath it the date, THURS., AP. 13TH, had been stamped with a rubber stamp.

Laura sat aghast, going hot and cold. Her first feeling was fury against the anonymous writer. 'But, you fool, I'm not thinking of marrying *anybody*,' she said aloud in an indignant voice to her own reflection. She was utterly at a loss. Could some person who was fond of Adrian have heard of his abortive proposal and written this note in a fit of jealousy? It seemed impossible. She had told no one but Anne Todd, and on Anne's proved fidelity she would stake her soul. Adrian certainly would not go about telling the world what a fool he had made of himself, and in any case he thought of nothing but Sibyl now. For a moment her thoughts flew to that source of all troubles, the Incubus, but the Incubus knew nothing of it, and couldn't be traipsing about London, putting anonymous communications into people's letter-boxes while she was nursing Sibyl in the country. It was all most puzzling and uncomfortable, and Laura wished Anne Todd or Amy Birkett were at hand to consult. George would only fly into a verbose rage and probably tell everyone about it in his indignation. Poor Laura, hot, ashamed, angry, miserable, took up the letter furiously, crumpled it, and threw it into the waste-paper basket. Then she gave herself a shake and returned to the drawing-room, her cheeks flushed, and her eyes sparkling with impotent rage.

'George,' she said. 'I'm very sorry, but I am going to turn you out. I have a fiendish headache, in fact I shouldn't wonder if I were going to have influenza, and I must have a lot of aspirin and go to bed.'

George Knox's face showed genuine concern. 'I don't like to leave you all alone, Laura, if you are feeling unwell,' he said. 'Wouldn't you like me to stay here till Stoker comes in? I wouldn't disturb you.'

'It's sweet of you, George dear, but I don't need anyone. It has been a lovely evening and I enjoyed it frightfully and thanks ever so much, but I shall go mad if you don't go.'

George Knox, roused for once from his usual self-absorption, was seriously concerned by her feverish appearance.

'Very well, Laura,' he said, getting up obediently. 'I can't tell you how sorry I am that our evening has ended so badly. And I had so much to say to you – things that it is difficult to say unless we are alone. When shall I see you again?'

'Oh, soon, any time. I am going back to High Rising tomorrow if I am well enough, and I'll be there till Tony goes back to school. Goodnight, George.'

'I find I shall have to stay in town for some time, unfortunately,' said George Knox, 'but I'll ring you up.'

'Yes, do, at any time, only for goodness' sake go away now.' And Laura shoved him into his coat, shook hands warmly, and pushed him out of the flat. George, to his eternal honour, went downstairs and sat for three quarters of an hour on a hard, narrow, backless bench in the hall, to await

Stoker's return. He was so used to depending on Laura that the sight of her ill and upset had upset him too, considerably. He had had some idea, not very well formulated, of feeling his way towards a suggestion that Low Rising would be less lonely after Sibyl's theoretical marriage if Laura cared to share it with him, but the idea was as yet extremely nebulous. As he sat, stiff and not over-warm, in the little hall, reflection cooled his blood. Much as he loved and admired Laura, he was slightly in awe of her, which is not a good basis for matrimony, from the man's point of view, at any rate. Then he began to reflect on her large family. The noble figure calling him to come in out of the dew was all very well, but flanked by four large step-sons it lost some of its attractiveness. And it was even possible that if Laura accepted him she might want him to give Low Rising to Sibyl and her imaginary husband, and come and live at High Rising, which would never do. He must have peace to work in. Sibyl's dogs were bad enough occasionally, but Tony's conversation and his railways, not to speak of Gerald and John and Dick coming home perpetually on leave, would make concentration impossible. If Laura, dearest and best of women, had no children and a good knowledge of shorthand, she would be the perfect wife. More like Miss Todd. It was almost unfair that Laura should have so excellent a secretary as Miss Todd as her private property. By marrying Laura he might get Miss Todd thrown in as a kind of marriage settlement. He had admired Miss Todd's efficient handling of her mother immensely. Obviously she would be Useful – and charming – in so many ways, if only one could get hold of her. It might be worth offering her the cottage again, if and when her mother died. It then struck Mr Knox for the first time that Dr Ford was nearly always at the Todds' house when he called, and would be a suitable match for Miss Todd; so suitable that it was probably already an arranged thing, only waiting for old Mrs Todd to die. With these and other profitless musings, not uncoupled with anxiety about Laura, he whiled away the time till half-past eleven, at which hour Stoker's ample form came billowing up the steps.

'Don't be frightened, Stoker,' said he rising. 'Mrs Morland didn't feel very well, so I have been sitting in the hall.'

'Lot of good that will do,' said Stoker, with genial contempt. 'What's wrong with her?'

'She said she had a headache and might be getting influenza.'

'Well, you'd better go home,' said the devoted handmaid. 'You can't do no good setting here. *She*'ll be all right in the morning.'

With which bracing words Stoker shut herself into the lift and soared upwards in majesty, while George Knox went back to his club.

Laura had gone straight to bed. She knew she couldn't sleep, but bed was a refuge from circling harms. A very good book called The Bucket of Blood, or The Butcher's Revenge, was helping her to try to forget her troubles, when Stoker hit the door and walked in.

'Headache?' said Stoker.

'Rather,' said Laura. 'I'll be all right tomorrow, but I knew it would get worse if Mr Knox went on talking, so I went to bed.'

Stoker left the room without a word, and presently returned with a large cup of tea.

'Oh, thank you, Stoker, you are an angel really.'

'How long had Mr Knox been setting in the hall?' asked Stoker.

'In the hall? But he went nearly an hour ago.'

'Hall downstairs,' said Stoker briefly. 'I told him he hadn't no call to worry about you, so off he went.'

Laura considered this mark of devotion silently. It was really dear of George, if rather silly, to sit in the hall because her head ached.

'Well, well,' said she for all comment. 'Oh, Stoker, give me a crumpled-up letter out of the waste-paper basket before you go.'

Stoker produced the letter and handed it to her mistress, adding, 'Marleen was lovely.'

Taking this, correctly as it appeared, to be a tribute to the physical and moral charms of Fraülein Dietrich, Laura expressed her gratification that Stoker had had a pleasant evening and said goodnight. Before trying to go to sleep, she considered again the anonymous document. It was not her first experience of anonymous letters, vicariously at any rate, for Madame Koska hardly counted any week well spent unless at least one of these missives reached her, but it had never happened to Laura herself, and she didn't like it at all. She tried to think what Madame Koska would have done. Sometimes she would tear the letter contemptuously across and throw it into the fire; sometimes, on the other hand, she would put it away in her private safe with a slow, enigmatic smile, until such time as she could

206

produce it for the confounding of her business adversaries. Not having a fire in her room, Laura decided on the slow enigmatic smile, and, folding the letter up, replaced it neatly in its envelope. Slumber, as she had feared, shunned her couch, and it was two in the morning before she went to sleep over the last chapter of *The Bucket of Blood,* with the light still on. She woke cross and tired and was glad to get down to High Rising again, with the horrid document, which she locked up in a drawer, determined to show it to Anne Todd at the earliest opportunity.

13

Spring Interlude

On the Friday morning of the following week Laura received a parcel and a letter from Adrian. The parcel she immediately identified as manuscript, or rather typescript. Adrian was apt to send her novels for her shrewd if unorthodox comments, and this was probably one of them. And so indeed in a way it was, but not in the way she had expected. Adrian's letter said:

Dear Laura,
You promised you would read Sibyl's manuscript and give me an opinion. Here it is, and I am quite in despair. When you have read it, you will see what I mean. What can I say or do? It is the most appalling predicament a man could be in, and I adore her with all my heart, and nothing can change that, but I am now in terror that she will never speak to me again. From a business point of view publication would, of course, be impossible, but

what can I say as a friend? If you can make any
suggestions I shall be more than grateful. I have showed
it to no one else – one couldn't. Don't write, as I shall be
with you on Saturday for lunch, but if you can help me,
for God's sake, do. I've been worrying for days over this
thing, and I can't even write to Sibyl.

Ever yours,
ADRIAN

Filled with forebodings Laura contemplated the parcel.
Had Sibyl the peculiar talent of the young for producing
obscene literature? Or had she caricatured all her friends so
maliciously that libel actions would flow like water? Or was
it so exquisite, so slight, so precious, that it could never
have any market at all? The only, and obvious way to find
out, was to read it, so seeing that Tony and Master
Wesendonck were safely employed in making railway
embankments with sand, borrowed from Mrs Mallow's
cousin the builder, and hurrying through her morning talk
with Stoker, she took the parcel upstairs to her room and
settled down to read it.

Anyone who knew Laura well could have gathered from
the state of her hair that she was sorely perplexed and tried.
What with running pencils through it, and pushing it off
her forehead, and absently sticking in pins which emotion
had caused to fall, she looked, by the time she had finished
Sibyl's story, like Medusa on a heavy washing-day.

'Oh, my God,' said Laura, who rarely used strong language, aloud to herself and the shade of Adrian. 'My God,
my God, what are we to do? Why did Adrian have to be

such a half-wit? Why couldn't he leave the girl alone? Oh, damn, oh, damn. We shall never get over it, and I did think everything was going so well.'

And now everything was going so badly. Anne Todd hadn't been able to come up since Laura's return, because old Mrs Todd had been weaker and more trying than usual, and the typewriting was all in arrears. George was still in town. Sibyl was getting over her influenza, but Laura didn't care to go over and find the Incubus acting hostess. And now Sibyl's manuscript, and Adrian coming tomorrow. There was nothing for it but to call on her creator again, which she did with some vehemence, but no result. Then she went and put a call through to Adrian.

'Adrian,' she said, as soon as they were connected, 'I can't talk on the telephone, but listen. You must cut your work and be down here by half-past twelve tomorrow. Sibyl is coming to lunch, and I must see you first, it's absolutely essential.'

Adrian's voice sounded pale and shaken over the wires, as he briefly assured her that he would be with her faithfully by twelve-thirty. She then rang up Dr Ford, who by great good luck happened to be in.

'Dr Ford, can you angelically do something for me? Could you possibly bring Sibyl over to lunch tomorrow – drive her over yourself, I mean? And come to lunch too, of course. I have got Adrian down specially for Sibyl, and I don't want any interference from the Incubus.'

'You aren't the first on the job,' said Dr Ford, chuckling.

'How do you mean?'

'Anne Todd has got the Incubus coming to lunch with

her tomorrow, and I have orders to fetch her, so that she shan't escape. I'll fetch them both and bring Sibyl on to you. I'm sorry I can't stop to lunch, but I've got to be over the other side of Stoke Dry by two o'clock, so I'll go home for a meal.'

'Thank you very much. How's Mrs Todd?'

'I don't like it at all,' was all Dr Ford would say.

In vain did Laura try to compose herself for the morrow's ordeal. The childish prattle of Tony and Master Wesendonck drove her nearly insane. Work was impossible, food a mockery. A brand-new library book called *The Windingsheet of Blood* had no charms, and she found it impossible to care whether the person who had cut off the gentleman's face with a razor and burned most of him beyond recognition in the old brick kiln was the blonde typist, or Ti Lung the Parrot-faced Ape. Finally she took the little boys to a cinema at Stoke Dry and, merely to pass the time away, sat with them through two and a half hours of slapstick and horrors which they rapturously enjoyed.

Saturday morning dawned fair and bright. The sun shone, the cuckoo bellowed from a copse hard by, other birds less easy to recognise made suitable bird noises. In the little wood primroses grew in vulgar profusion, a drift of blue mist showed that bluebells were on the way, glades were still white with wind-flowers. All the trees that come out early were brilliant green, while those that come out later were, not unnaturally, still brown, thus forming an agreeable contrast. A stream bordered with kingcups made a gentle bubbling noise like sausages in a frying-pan. Nature, in fact, was at it; and when she chooses, Nature can do it.

But what avails the sceptred race, or indeed anything else, when the heart of man is oppressed by care? If icy winds had blown from dark storm clouds, if thunder had crashed, if sleet had stripped the fruit trees of their blossom and broken the fritillaries in the meadow, Laura could not have felt more depressed. Tony, attempting to read her a detective story of one page which he had recently composed, was savagely snubbed and accused of base plagiarism and a commonplace mind. Stoker was told to be quiet and give them what she liked for lunch. Even Master Wesendonck, who had only brought, with considerable personal exertion, a bucketful of coal to put in the goods yard to make it look more real, was harshly told to pick it all up off the grass and put it back where it came from.

As the hour of half-past twelve approached, Laura was prowling up and down the drawing-room like a mad panther. Luckily for her sanity, Adrian drove up to the gate with perfect punctuality, jumped out of his car, slamming the door, shouted an injunction to the little boys to leave it alone, and rushed into the house. In spite of a toilette to which he had evidently devoted considerable attention, he looked worn, haggard and sleepless.

'Laura!' he cried.

'Adrian!' shrieked Laura with equal fervour. 'My dear, I'm so thankful. Nothing so awful has ever happened to me in all my life. Here it is, and I don't know what we can do about it.' She pointed to Sibyl's typescript upon a table, but Adrian made no movement towards it, gazing at it as if it were a snake which had hypnotised him.

'Isn't it ghastly?' he managed to get out.

'Too ghastly for words. Sit down. Adrian, when I read it, I couldn't believe my eyes.'

'Nor could I. Laura, it's hell. What can I do?'

'There's only one thing,' said Laura, with immense determination, 'you must tell her the truth.'

'But how can I? How can I? I asked her to send me the thing. I feel responsible.'

'Rubbish. We've hardly any time, Adrian. Listen: as soon as we've finished lunch you must take her into the wood and tell her the whole truth. You'll be quite alone there.'

'Laura, it will be like murder. To tell that darling creature that she hasn't the ghost of an idea of plot, or style, or grammar, or spelling, or anything!'

He wrung his hands in despair.

'You've got to,' said Laura. 'She'll take anything from you, Adrian. When I read it, I thought I'd gone mad. That our Sibyl should be such an incapable, doddering, half-witted, sentimental, sloshy school-girl was too much for me. I read it three times, to try to find something good in it, and not one thing could I find. It might just do for a junior girls' school magazine, but I doubt it. The only kindness you can show is to squash all her hopes at once. If you don't, I'll tell you what will happen: Johns and Fairfield will get it and they'll make a joke of it, and it will have a huge circulation, and people will think Sibyl is being funny, while the poor child is perfectly serious. Her father would see through it at once and go mad. If she had shown him what she was writing, he would have stopped it, but like the great blundering idiot he is, he insisted that she was clever and what not. The only sign of grace I can see in the whole thing is that she has imitated some of my more offensive mannerisms. Adrian, I am devoted to her, and I am devoted to you in a suitable way too, and I tell you quite seriously that this has to be nipped in the bud, now and at once and for ever. She never wanted to show it to you, and you would persecute her, and now you've got it, and you must face the situation. If you don't, I shall tell her how you proposed to me, though I believe,' she added immediately, touched by Adrian's mute misery, 'it wouldn't make any difference. She has never seen you beating starving authors down on royalties, and she believes in you.'

'No,' said Adrian, 'it wouldn't make any difference to her.'

'Though it's hardly for you to say it,' snapped Laura, whose heart and temper had been severely tried.

'I'm sorry, Laura. I didn't mean to sound conceited, I was only judging by my own feelings. Because, though I have gone through hell about this business, it doesn't make the faintest difference to me that Sibyl is a literary nincompoop. In fact, I think I love her all the more for it. It is so adorable of her to be so silly. It is only the hurting her that I can't bear.'

Laura looked at him with a mingling of kindly contempt, affection and envy, thought of saying something, thought better of it, left the room, and returned almost immediately with a glass.

'Brandy,' she said. 'Drink it. I hear Dr Ford's car with Sibyl.'

Adrian raised the glass to her. 'Laura,' he said, drinking, and began to choke.

'Don't do that,' said his exasperated hostess, thumping him on the back. 'No one can love a spluttering idiot.'

By the time Sibyl had come into the room, followed by the boys, Adrian had recovered and, fortified by the brandy, was able to pull himself together. As her lunch party threatened to be embarrassing, Laura allowed Tony to take part in the conversation, which was equivalent to allowing him to monopolise it. The interest of the moment was an exhibition of model railways which was going on, though, alas, in London. Tony and Master Wesendonck read and talked of nothing else, and their highest ambition, in no way encouraged by Laura, was to go up to town for the day and see it. At any other time Tony's detailed account of an electric signalling system on a six-inch model would have driven the grown-ups to frenzy and led to his speedy downfall. Nor were the supporting remarks of Master Wesendonck, who was the electric expert, of any more interest. But all three grown-ups, extremely nervous and ill at ease, were only too grateful for the flow of talk, and rewarded Tony and his friend with a degree of attention to which they were quite unaccustomed.

As soon as they had had coffee, Laura looked wildly round.

'My head is splitting and I hardly slept last night,' said she in a sepulchral voice. 'Sibyl, darling, I must lie down. Will you very sweetly take Adrian down to the copse? The boys have gone to Stoke Dry station for the afternoon, so I can be quite alone and rest. If I hear you talking, I shall go mad.'

Sibyl, looking rather scared, got up at once. Refusing all offers of help, Laura went up to her room and, from behind the curtains, had the pleasure of seeing the young couple go down the garden and through the gate into the wood. With a deep sigh of relief she kicked off her shoes and lay down on her bed. In a few moments *The Windingsheet of Blood* had slipped from her hand, and she was deeply sunk in well-earned repose.

If one wanted a perfect setting in which to offer one's heart to an adored creature, this coppice on this warm April afternoon would have been the place. But to Adrian, as he walked down the narrow path behind Sibyl, the sunshine had no light, the birds were whistling in peculiarly unpleasant derision. 'Juggins,' they said, 'it is all your fault. You might have seen that she was all affection and not much else. What she wants is things to love. Now she has her father and the dogs. If you hadn't been such a fool, she would have had you as well. You have bullied her into showing you her little story. She was cleverer than you are. She knew it was no good, and she was right. Now, what are you going to do about it? Cuckoo, jug-jug, you be a silly fool,' they concluded in rapturous chorus.

'Aren't the birds heavenly?' said Sibyl, stopping.

Adrian, feeling the greatest sympathy for poachers and sportsmen and Italians, and people who snare or cage wild birds, said that they were.

'Let's sit down,' said Sibyl. 'One has to walk in single file here, and it's so silly.'

So they sat down on the roots of a tree. All round them was loveliness. The woodspurge was busy having a cup of three, two of one sort and one of another. Everything else was behaving in the best tradition of English poetry. But it is doubtful whether either of them noticed it. Adrian in particular was feeling quite sick with nervousness, but the plunge had to be taken.

'Sibyl,' he said, and hesitated.

'You called me Sibyl,' murmured the lady faintly.

'You don't mind?'

'I love it. Everyone calls me Sibyl.'

There was a short and embarrassing pause.

'Sibyl,' he began again. 'I let Laura look at your story. You don't mind, do you?'

Sibyl started, and looked at him with large terrified eyes.

'No one else shall see it,' he assured her. 'But I thought I'd like her opinion. She is an awfully good judge and often reads things for me. And she is so fond of you that I thought she'd like it because you wrote it.'

'Was it any good?' asked Sibyl in a low, frightened whisper.

'Well, it's difficult to explain. One can't always judge beginners' work, and I really don't pretend to be a critic,' said Adrian, with a poor attempt at treating the matter light-heartedly. 'I'm only a publisher, a money-making machine. Perhaps Laura could discuss it with you better than I can,' he concluded, in a cowardly way. His voice trailed into silence, as if ashamed to offer such wretched subterfuges. He sat staring at the ground, prodding holes with a twig in the moss upon their seat.

'Mr Coates,' said a very small voice, 'could you please say one thing to me. Is it good or bad?'

Adrian gazed more steadfastly than before at the toes of his shoes.

'Please,' said the small voice again.

Adrian made a desperate effort to overcome the paralysis of throat and jaw which was affecting him, and said in a toneless way, 'Bad. I'd give my soul to tell you a lie, but I can't.'

'Is it really bad?' asked the small voice, now perilously near tears. 'Pretty hopeless, I mean?'

Adrian nodded, dumb with misery.

'Then you think I'd better give up the idea of writing?' continued the small voice, insistently.

Feeling that he was destroying his own happiness for ever, Adrian looked up and said, 'You are the loveliest and dearest thing in the world, Sibyl, and you mustn't ever write anything again. If you will just be alive, that's enough.'

'Oh, thank heaven,' said Sibyl, and burst into loud sobs. Of course, Adrian turned and grabbed her violently into his arms, where she lay crying her heart out all over his exquisite spring suiting and delicately tinted tie, while he rubbed his face against the top of her head and said every foolish and endearing thing he could think of, in a quite incoherent way. 'Now we are engaged,' he said at last, regaining a little sanity.

'Oh Adrian, how lovely,' said Sibyl, making no attempt to sit up again.

'My darling, are you sure you don't mind about that book?'

'Oh Adrian,' said she to the middle button of his waistcoat, 'I have never been so happy in my life. It was all Daddy's fault. He wanted me to be able to write, and I did try, but I couldn't. I knew it was rotten, and you wanted to see it and I did so want to please you, and then I thought you would despise me, and everything was awful.'

'My poor, precious, persecuted angel,' said her besotted admirer. 'You shan't ever write a line again. In fact,' he added loftily, 'I forbid it.'

Sibyl laughed so much that she had to sit up again.

'You won't expect me to be literary?' she asked suspiciously.

'I won't marry you if you are. You shall never do anything you don't like, and we'll live in the country and breed dogs and I'll go up to town every day,' said he, remembering what Laura had told him.

'Not live in London at all?' said Sibyl a little wistfully.

'Would you like to?'

'Oh Adrian, I'd adore it. And go to theatres? And just have about two dogs. I could always sell the puppies.'

So there was nothing for it but another soul-cracking embrace. And it was all just as Laura had said, with spring and birds and flowers, and young love in the middle of it all. All the birds were saying delightful things about how clever and successful Adrian was, and how lovely and adorable Sibyl was, and it might have gone on for ever, except for the call of tea.

'Heavens, it's half-past four, Adrian. I'm so hungry,' said Sibyl.

'Angel, so am I. I couldn't eat much lunch.'

'Oh Adrian, nor could I.'

And at this exquisite coincidence they gazed, enraptured, into each other's eyes.

Going back was not so easy, because of walking with your

arms round each other on a path that is only meant for one, but it was accomplished, with suitable delays, and they arrived at Laura's door. Laura was sitting in the drawing-room with the tea-things when they came in, and one glance at them told her what had happened.

'Oh, I am so glad,' she gasped, gathering them both into her warm embrace, so that all their heads nearly knocked together. 'I can't tell you how glad I am. Bless you, bless you. This is as good a deed as drink. And what about the book?'

'Oh, Mrs Morland,' said Sibyl, 'Adrian says it is *rotten*, and I need never try to write again. Isn't it *lovely*? Oh, Adrian, you are *marvellous*.'

Upon which Laura, who had suffered great trials and anxieties, and was not in the least prepared for Sibyl's attitude, fell away into helpless laughter, while Adrian proudly explained that if there were more women like Sibyl, who knew they couldn't write, the world would be a better place.

After that it appeared to Adrian and Sibyl that they were living in a delightful kaleidoscope. Stoker, coming in to take tea away, was informed by her mistress of the happy news.

'Young blood,' said Stoker. 'Well, it's to be hoped all will go well. I'll come to the wedding, miss. When's it to be?'

'When, Adrian?' asked Sibyl.

'Whenever you like, darling. We must just mention it to your father, that's all.'

Stoker smiled tolerantly on the lovers, picked up the tray, and left the room in a burst of song, identifiable as the once popular melody of 'There Was I, Waiting at the Church'.

Then Dr Ford and Anne Todd came in, and were enchanted by the engagement. Dr Ford electrified them all by remarking that he must claim an old bachelor's privilege and kiss the bride.

'But you've always kissed me, Dr Ford, ever since I was a baby,' said Sibyl.

'Never mind that,' said Dr Ford. 'It's the right thing to say, isn't it, Mrs Morland?'

Laura, as the representative of literature, confirmed his statement.

Then Tony came back from Stoke Dry with Master Wesendonck.

'Tony,' said his mother, 'Mr Coates is going to marry Sibyl. Isn't it lovely?'

'Yes,' said Tony briefly. 'Oh, Mother, could Donkey and I possibly go to London and see the Model Railway Exhibition? Donk has just had a postal order from his uncle, so we could pay for ourselves. Oh, Mother, could we?'

'I'll tell you what, Tony,' said Adrian. 'I'll take you and Mr Donkey to town in my car on Monday morning, and you can spend the day at the show, and I'll put them into the four-fifty to come back,' he added to Laura. 'Will that be all right?'

'Oh, sir,' cried Tony and Master Wesendonck with one voice, both going bright pink, 'thanks most awfully.'

They then scuffled violently together and retired in a medley of arms and legs to the garden, there to admire Adrian's generosity and his extreme wit.

'Well, as we are all mad,' said Laura, 'I suppose they can go, and I shall have a day in bed. I need it. Adrian, suppose you get your car and take Sibyl home. She has had influenza and oughtn't to get tired. And if she asks you to stay to supper, that's all right. And if she asks you to come to break-fast tomorrow and spend the day, don't mind me. Only you must both write to Sibyl's father by the Sunday post.'

'Of course we will,' said Sibyl. 'Had I better tell Miss Grey we are engaged?'

Nobody answered.

'She was awfully kind to me when I was ill,' said the soft-hearted Sibyl. 'She nursed me all the time and was awfully sweet. And she wasn't feeling very well herself either. She had to go to bed all afternoon and evening that day you went to the play with Daddy, but she would get up next day and look after me.'

'What did you call me to George?' said Laura to Adrian. 'I think you can use it for your Sibyl now. She will never be any sillier if she lives to be a hundred.'

Adrian had the grace to look foolish, though without abating any of his pride in his future wife's silliness.

'Yes, tell her,' said Laura. 'If you don't she'll only find out sideways, and that would be worse.'

'She will be very glad,' said Anne Todd suddenly, with authority. 'Take it from one who knows.'

'Then that's all right,' said Laura vaguely. 'Adrian, you can come down here next weekend if you like, if you don't mind using Tony's room, because Amy Birkett will be here. Or if George Knox asks you to Low Rising as an accepted suitor, don't bother about me. Go along now, all of you. I want to talk to Anne.'

When Dr Ford and the lovers had gone, Laura asked Anne to come upstairs, and there showed her the anony-mous letter, with a full account of how it had appeared in her letter-box. Anne was as intrigued and puzzled as Laura could have wished. She also thought of the Incubus at once, but according to Sibyl's statement, the Incubus had a perfect alibi. Also she couldn't know about Adrian.

'But let me have the letter, if you don't mind,' said Anne Todd. 'I'd like to do a little sleuthing on my own. Also I have an idea that we are barking up the wrong tree about Mr Coates. But I must get back to Mother now.'

'I'll run you over. You look tired to death. Tell me, Anne, is your mother much worse?'

Anne nodded with compressed lips. 'I'm sorry about it,' she said, 'because it puts me back with your work. But I'll have the next chapter ready by Monday.'

When Laura returned from driving Anne home, she saw Sibyl's typescript lying on the table. So she rang up Low Rising. Miss Grey answered the telephone, and Laura asked her to tell Sibyl that she had left a parcel behind her. Miss Grey was some time in coming back, and said that she had had to go into the garden to find Sibyl, who asked Mrs Morland to destroy the parcel. 'And isn't it lovely about Sibyl's engagement,' said Miss Grey, with what was apparently genuine pleasure. 'It's a pleasure to see them, the fine couple that they are.'

'Yes, I'm delighted. Thanks so much. Goodbye,' said Laura, who did not quite relish Miss Grey's raptures.

The matter of the little boys' clothes for their Monday expedition then claimed her attention, and by the time she had sorted out two wearable suits with their accessories, and decided how much shopping she would have to do for Tony before next term, it was time for supper. After supper she read Sibyl's story for the last time, and then thrust it into the fire, after which she had leisure to ponder, over a blackening grate, the difficulties, so forcibly described by Mr Max Beerbohm, which must have beset the common hangman when publicly burning a book. About twelve o'clock she was roused by a light tap on her bedroom door, and Adrian's face appeared in the chink.

'I hope I'm not disturbing you, Laura,' said he anxiously, 'but as I'm practically a married man I thought it would be quite respectable for me to tell you that I am back, and that Sibyl is quite divine, and you are an angel.'

'That's all right. Shut the door quietly and go to bed at once.'

And she resumed her reading of the *Omnibus Book of Blood, Torture and Disease* with considerable relish.

14

George Knox Meets his Match

On Monday afternoon Anne Todd walked over to Low Rising. She found Sibyl and Miss Grey in the stables, washing and brushing dogs, so she sat down on the edge of a wheelbarrow and watched them. Miss Grey, always at her nicest with dogs, looked happy and charming, and was bursting with the excitement of Sibyl's engagement.

'Have you got Mr Knox's telegram there, Sibyl?' she asked.

Sibyl rummaged in the pocket of her large apron and produced it.

'Daddy sent a lovely telegram,' she said. 'Read it, Miss Todd.'

Anne Todd unfolded the telegraph form and read:

BLESS YOU DEAREST SIBYL AND BLESS THE HAPPY MAN OF YOUR CHOICE WHO AM I TO SAY YES OR NO BUT IF MY CONSENT IS NEEDED TAKE IT DEAR CHILD WITH ALL

MY HEART PROBABLY COMING DOWN THIS AFTERNOON
AM LUNCHING COATES SHALL ASK HIM WEEKEND
BLESSINGS MY DEAR CHILD YOUR AFFECTIONATE
FATHER GEORGE KNOX.

'I gather,' said Anne Todd, returning the paper to Sibyl, 'that your father approves.'

'You see,' said Sibyl, 'Daddy doesn't mind what he spends on a telegram so long as it's in shillings, but he can't bear odd pence. That's why he put in "your affectionate father George Knox", to make it an equal number. Otherwise he would have said "love Daddy", or something of the sort. Isn't it lovely that he is asking Adrian for the weekend?'

'And how soon are you going to be married?' asked Anne Todd.

'Oh, whenever Adrian likes. I expect Granny will want to interfere about my clothes though.'

'You couldn't have better advice,' put in Miss Grey. 'Mrs Knox is just the person to help. Don't you think, Anne, that Sibyl ought to go up to town and stay with her grandmother while she gets her things?'

'Quite a good plan,' said Anne Todd, rather wondering where this was leading to. 'Then she could see something of Mr Coates, and you and Mr Knox could be getting on with the new book.'

Miss Grey looked gratified.

The conversation then raged round the subject of clothes, on the whole to the benefit of the dogs, whose brushing and combing was less searching than usual, though Miss Grey nearly drowned one of the puppies in her excitement over a daring suggestion of Anne Todd's in the underwear line. Tea was partaken of by all three ladies in a most amicable spirit, and Miss Grey seemed perfectly contented about the whole affair.

'Your father would have been here now if he had come by the three-ten,' said she to Sibyl.

'I expect he's coming by the four-fifty,' said Sibyl, 'because Adrian was going to send Tony and his friend back by it, and probably he told Daddy, so that Daddy could go back with them. He is so kind. Oh, Miss Todd, do you know what Mrs Morland did? She has sent me a wedding present already – at least she says it is only an engagement present, but I count it as my first wedding present. Do come up and see it.'

Anne Todd followed Sibyl upstairs to her room. Laura's present – evidently a reminiscence of her talk with old Mrs Knox – was a pair of old paste ear-rings, with sparkling leaves and flowers.

'Aren't they lovely?' said Sibyl. 'They used to be her grandmother's, and she says they are to be mine because I am like a daughter. Could I wear them, do you think, Miss Todd, or ought I to wait till I am married?'

'If they are an engagement present,' said Miss Todd gravely, 'I should think you could wear them at once. I must get back to Mother now, Sibyl. I am so very glad everything is so happy.'

'It's like heaven. And I know the dogs will get prizes at the show tomorrow, and there's a new nest outside Daddy's window this year. Come and look.'

They went into George Knox's study. Just outside one of the windows there was a nest in the budding wistaria, with a beady-eyed parent sitting on it. While Sibyl enlarged in her sincere but limited vocabulary on the heavenliness of things in general, Anne Todd stood by the writing-table in the window, fidgeting with various objects on it. Presently she picked up a rubber stamp and tried it on the blotting paper. Something seemed to interest her, and she tried it again on a piece of notepaper.

'I didn't know your father used these date stamps,' she said.

'That's Miss Grey's, but she doesn't use it much. It's a bit broken and she said she meant to throw it away. I might get her a new one when I go to town. Perhaps Adrian and I could go shopping.'

While Sibyl shut the window, Anne Todd neatly picked up the date stamp and the piece of paper and put them into her bag, unnoticed. Then she went downstairs, said goodbye to her hostess, and walked home again. Old Mrs Todd was sitting up in bed waiting to be amused, so her daughter helped her to do a crossword puzzle, over which the old lady's wits were not at all wandering. While they were struggling with one of those long words to which every alternate letter gives no clue at all, the front-door bell rang. Presently Louisa came upstairs to announce Mr Knox. Anne told Louisa to stay with her mother while she went downstairs, where she found George Knox in the drawing-room.

'This is very nice,' said Anne Todd, shaking hands. 'Have you had tea?'

'Yes, I had it on the train. Coates, whom it really seems ridiculous to look upon as a son-in-law – imagine me, Miss Todd, as a father-in-law, luckily a shade less ludicrous than a mother-in-law, but not to be considered without some cause for laughter, though why one cannot imagine – Coates, I say, asked me to keep an eye on Laura's boy and his young friend. Never have I heard two boys talk so incessantly. Finally I had to take them to the dining-car and give them tea, to stop their mouths. We arrived here all covered with jam and dirt. I feel an unaccountable shyness in meeting my daughter as an affianced bride – ridiculous again you may say, perhaps – but I feel that a few minutes with you, with your calm sanity, would arm me against the mental perturbation which I so unreasonably feel.'

'I can quite understand your being a little exhausted by Tony and his friend,' said Anne Todd sympathetically, 'but I wouldn't worry about Sibyl. She isn't a bit like an affianced bride – she's just her dear, affectionate, silly self.'

George Knox looked round nervously.

'And how is Miss Grey?' he asked.

'Very well, and in very good spirits. She seems to be as pleased as Punch about the engagement.'

'I wish I knew what to do about her,' said George Knox. 'I would ask Laura, but I should have to face Tony again, and I am not yet strong enough. Never have I met so *acharné* a talker.'

'I expect you are a bit mortified too at having met your match,' said Anne Todd placidly.

George Knox stared at her, and then a great light appeared to burst upon him.

'You are right, Miss Todd, perfectly right. I talk too much. You and Laura are the only people who will ever have the courage, the kindness, to tell me. I have been a bore, a pest, a curse to humanity with my unrestrained loquacity. It is in the blood, you know. We Latins must express ourselves in speech. But in Tony, I must confess, I have met one whom I acknowledge as my master. Never,' said George Knox, becoming quite human at the remembrance, 'have I had such an appalling journey in my life. If it had been a mere question of conversation, of give and take, I could have held my own, with difficulty perhaps, but I could have held it. But I was as a child, a deaf-mute – though unfortunately not deaf – before Tony. What I have not been told about the railway systems of England is not worth the telling. And what made it the more annoying, my dear Miss Todd, was that I strongly suspected a good deal of the information which he lavished upon me to be erroneous, but I had no means of disproving it. And then the effort of listening while the train was in rapid motion. And if ever Tony stopped to take breath, though I must say he appears to be able to speak with equal fluency breathing inwards or out-wards, his infernal friend would begin about electricity. What is electricity to me, Miss Todd? I will not add, or I to electricity? Gratefully do I accept its benefits, though I have not had it put in at Low Rising, nor shall I until enough of us want it to make it worthwhile, because it would mean making it for myself with a machine which I could not work, and which the gardener would infallibly neglect, or ruin through his incompetence, and there we should be, worse off than before; gratefully in the houses of others, in the Underground railway system – ominous phrase which I have already heard too often this afternoon and am as it were condemned to perpetuate in my own speech – in all the thousand uses of daily life, such as vacuum cleaners, and others too numerous to mention, do I accept its benefits, but it is all as a miracle to me. To others, to Mr Ohm, to Mr Volta, to Mr Ampere, for I believe these to have been living persons, though if they were flesh and blood it would probably be more correct to say Herr Ohm, Signor Volta and M. Ampère, to them I leave the task of understanding what it is all about, although, according to what I read in the very unreliable columns of the daily press, no one – *no one*, Miss Todd – yet knows what it is all about, though they can make use of it; all is yet in the empirical stage. I, as a poor man of letters, prefer to admire in ignorance. And then this devilish child,' said George Knox with a sudden revival of fury, 'must needs explain it all to me at the top of his very high, exhausting voice in a rattling train. I give in. 'Tis well an old age is out, and time to begin anew. I am silent before Tony and his friend – silent, subdued.' He sank into a studied apathy.

'You said a mouthful,' observed Miss Todd (who but rarely employed the language of the movies) with some truth.

'I did, I did,' groaned the unlucky George Knox. 'Again you rebuke me, most graciously, but most justly. My fatal gift of speech is the cause of all my woes. I come here weary and jaded to seek the precious gift of repose in your sanity, your cool and balanced mind, and what do I do? I trespass upon your heavenly patience. I exhaust you. I lay all my burdens upon your shoulders. I will be silent from henceforth. When I come to see you, Miss Todd, that is if you ever, after my unwarrantable behaviour, allow me to darken your doors again, I shall attune myself to your atmosphere of peace and serenity. You must teach me to listen. You must force me to listen. It will do me good to forget myself.'

'Not at all,' said Anne Todd.

Encouraged by this non-committal remark, George Knox proceeded to expatiate at great length upon the quality of silence. Anne Todd, not wishing to damp his new-found ardour, sat knitting quietly while his periods boomed above her head. She liked – she very much liked – having him there. There was no particular need to listen to what he said, and she was able to think placidly, under cover of his monologue, how kind and large-hearted he really was, and how easily he could have got out of accompanying two little boys and giving them tea in the dining-car. Although he did talk a lot, he never expected one to attend, never insisted on one's opinion of what he had been saying. And if real kindness were needed, she felt that one could safely go to George Knox. Who but he – except, of course, Laura or Dr Ford – would trouble to visit a dull spinster, for so she called herself, after a tiring railway journey, merely to cheer her up. As for what he had said about coming for rest and peace, that Anne did not believe, though in this she was for once wrong. It was all his own kindness, she felt. And as he was still talking away, and she was thinking of him, with her mind far removed from his presence, who should come in but Dr Ford, explaining that he had rung in vain and had taken the liberty of coming in.

'Well, Knox, this is great news about Sibyl's engagement,' said he.

'It is, it is. Coates is a splendid fellow, and if I am to be left alone, that is but in the course of things.'

Dr Ford, who appeared to be lacking in the finer shades of feeling, ignored this opening for pathos, and inquired cheerfully after Miss Grey.

George Knox looked guilty.

'Well, Ford, you and Miss Todd must know how inconveniently, how awkwardly I am placed. Miss Grey, all zeal and over-devotion, does not, will not take a hint that I should now like to dispense with her kind services. I have descended to the baseness of making certain *démarches* behind her back. I saw my old friend Miss Hocking while in town. She was delighted with what I told her about Miss Grey, and is only too eager to have her. In fact, she would like her to come this day week.'

'Splendid,' said Dr Ford.

'And I suppose you daren't tell her,' said Anne Todd, a little anxiously.

'I daren't, I daren't,' said George Knox, looking far from happy. 'I only have to mention it for her to cry. That weapon of your sex, Miss Todd, disarms me completely. I shall have to steel my heart, but I am extremely nervous of a scene. I had hoped she might have gone to see Miss Hocking when she was in town last week, and settled it all – but no.'

'But she wasn't in town last week,' said Dr Ford. 'She did want to go, but I told her Sibyl really needed her attention.'

He cast a surreptitious look at Anne Todd, who blushed faintly, but held her tongue.

'But she *was* in town,' insisted George Knox. 'I went to Rutland Gate yesterday to collect some letters, and the kitchen-maid – a repugnant piece,' said he with a shudder, 'gave me the latchkey that she had left there on Thursday last week.'

'But that—' began Anne Todd and Dr Ford simultaneously, and as simultaneously checked themselves. Luckily, George Knox, entirely absorbed in his own difficulties, did not notice.

'It was good of her to go up,' said he, 'as I specially wanted some information from the Reading Room, but she shouldn't have left Sibyl against your wishes, Ford. I suppose she thought her duty as a secretary was paramount.'

'What happened to the latchkey?' asked Anne Todd carelessly.

'Oh, I have it. Mamma has decided to stay away till the autumn, so the house will be entirely dismantled. The kitchen-maid, thank God, is leaving to better herself, so she told me, a resolution which it would not be difficult to carry into effect.'

'Then, Sibyl won't be going to stay with her grandmother to get her trousseau?'

'Not unless she goes to Torquay, dear Miss Todd, a most unlikely place for clothes, where Mamma misguidedly prefers to spend the summer months. This wedding is all going to be confusing. For an old *célibataire*, or rather widower, like myself, the preparations for marriage are very terrifying. Frills, tuckers, petticoats, gussets, what do I know? If it were the wardrobe of Queen Elizabeth – with which I propose to make myself familiar as soon as these nuptials are consummated – I might be of assistance, but in this modern world I am helpless, helpless.'

Here George Knox became realistically helpless, in a very alarming way.

'Well, I expect you'll find Mrs Knox will come up to town, even if it's only to an hotel,' said Anne Todd kindly. 'She will want to help Sibyl. And now, Mr Knox, I'm terribly sorry to turn you out, but Dr Ford is waiting to have a look at Mother.'

'Forgive me, forgive me,' cried George Knox, genuinely upset. 'I have never inquired after your mother. Dear Miss Todd, attribute my negligence to the devastating effect of Tony's conversation, rather than to my own want of sympathy. Can you ever pardon me?'

While Dr Ford slipped upstairs to Mrs Todd, Anne took George Knox to the door, George descanting so profusely upon his own shortcomings in courtesy that he never got as far as asking how old Mrs Todd really was. It did occur to Anne Todd, as she stood patiently listening to George Knox winding himself up in a web of verbosity, that he seemed unaccountably nervous, and was talking, not after his usual fashion for the sake of talking, but rather to gain time. When finally she was able to get a word in edgeways, she told him that Dr Ford was not pleased with her mother's condition.

'He says he can't answer for her, Mr Knox. And that's that.'

She found a kind of comfort in the large figure beside her, and in the real concern which showed in George Knox's face.

'Dear Miss Todd,' said he, looking down at her. 'I am sorrier than I can say. If there were anything I could do – if a nurse were needed, and you would allow me the privilege, the very great privilege, of letting that be my care – if there were anything I could do to lighten your burden – if there were a fruit, or a flower, or a jelly – I am vague about the wants of invalids, owing to my unfortunately robust health, but my poor wife, as I remember, did occasionally express a liking for a flower – would you honour me by letting me know?'

Anne Todd, worn by much anxiety and many vigils, always under the shadow of poverty, but not daunted, laid both her hands on his coat-sleeve and looked up.

'Thank you very, very much,' she said. 'I would tell you if there were anything, but there isn't. She is quite happy unless she is in pain, and Dr Ford is kindness itself. Everyone is.'

'Ford is a good fellow,' said George Knox, 'but I don't like him to do everything. I'm a bit selfish about this. Is there nothing?'

Anne Todd shook her head. George Knox felt the weight of her hands on his arm, as if she were mutely seeking support.

'If at any time the cottage would be of any use,' he said diffidently, 'quiet, change of air. And I shall need help with Queen Elizabeth's wardrobe, Anne.'

Did his use of her first name pass unnoticed? Her mouth trembled a little, but she forced it to a smile as she said, 'First get rid of your hare, Mr Knox.'

George Knox went away and Anne Todd went back to the drawing-room, where she was joined by Dr Ford, who had a more reassuring report to give of old Mrs Todd. He sat down to write a prescription and asked Anne what the date was.

'Oh, that reminds me,' cried Anne Todd, opening a drawer and taking out a letter and a rubber stamp. 'Dr Ford, what I am doing is quite dishonourable, but I don't care, and I am going to implicate you.'

'Fire away,' said Dr Ford, quite unmoved.

'Last week, when Mrs Morland was in town, the night Mr Knox took her to a play, she found an anonymous letter when she got back. It upset her frightfully. She thought it was someone warning her off Mr Coates, but I think it was someone warning her off Mr Knox. Look.'

Dr Ford, throwing honour to the winds, read the horrid document.

'A nasty piece of work,' he observed. 'Why should she think Coates was in it?'

'Well, she sees a lot of him in the way of business,' said Anne Todd, not to be disconcerted, 'and she thought some idiot might think it was affection. He's years younger than she is.'

'And why should you think Knox is in it?' asked Dr Ford, dismissing the whole question of Adrian.

For answer Miss Todd took from another drawer an inky pad, pressed the date stamp on it and jabbed it down on a piece of paper. Dr Ford looked on attentively.

'Yes, Madame Poirot,' said he, 'these two dates are undoubtedly from the same stamp, with the same defect in each, but where does that get us?'

'It gets us here, Dr Watson,' said the sleuth. 'This date stamp belongs to the Incubus. I found it at Low Rising. Sibyl told me the Incubus was going to throw it away because it was damaged, and the date is the same as the one on the letter, so it hasn't been used since. Hasn't the Incubus been running after Mr Knox ever since she came here? Isn't Mr Knox a very old friend of Mrs Morland? Wouldn't the Incubus like to make mischief between them?'

'By Jove, Anne, you may be right,' said Dr Ford admiringly. 'But thoroughly unprincipled. Not the kind of woman I could ever ask to marry me.'

Ignoring this insult, Anne Todd continued in a hoarse conspiratorial voice:

'And you heard what Mr Knox said about finding the latchkey at Rutland Gate? Dr Ford, I believe we have found the guilty secret. Sibyl said the Incubus went to bed all the afternoon and evening of that Thursday Mrs Morland and Mr Knox went to town. Well, I think she locked her door and went up to town by the five-thirty with that letter, and let herself into Rutland Gate, where she is known, and stayed there till dark, and then put the letter into Mrs Morland's letter-box and came down here by the late train again. The dogs all know her, they wouldn't bark, and Cook and Annie wouldn't hear if the house was on fire when they are in bed. And there she was next morning, safe and sound. What do you think?'

'Anne, you surprise me.'

'But what do you think?'

'I think it is all probable enough, but not enough to hang her on.'

'No one wants to hang her, James. But one might frighten her.'

'You've never called me James before,' said Dr Ford,

losing all interest in the nefarious conduct of Miss Grey. 'Does that mean that you are relenting?'

'Not a bit. It was only excitement. And after what you said just now about not asking people to marry you, I withdraw it.'

'I hadn't much hope,' said Dr Ford, getting up. 'Well, what do you propose to do about it?'

'Hold it up my sleeve,' said Anne Todd.

Here they were interrupted by Laura, who came in accompanied by Tony and Master Wesendonck, also apologising for having come in without waiting for the door to be answered.

'Oh, Miss Todd, oh, sir,' said Tony, before anyone else could speak. 'What do you think Mr Knox did? He took us first class!'

He paused for this to sink in and to let his audience express suitable astonishment.

'And I and Donk each had a seat to ourselves, and I told Mr Knox a lot of useful things about the railway, and we had tea in the dining-car, and Donk had six cakes and I had five and a whole pot of jam, you know those tiny ones, and Donk had six lumps of sugar in his tea and I had seven, and the waiter poured some of the tea on to the tablecloth because the train joggled so, and some of it went into the sugar basin, so I and Donk ate all the lumps that got wet. Dr Ford, Mr Knox doesn't know what a tank-engine is.'

'Nor do I,' said Dr Ford.

'Oh, sir,' exclaimed the little boys reproachfully.

'Tony,' interrupted Anne Todd, 'Mrs Todd isn't very well, so don't make a noise, but you can each have an apple off the dish in the dining-room and eat it outside.'

'And go home and get ready for supper,' added Laura. 'I won't be long.'

Tony and Master Wesendonck withdrew, their opinion of Dr Ford considerably lessened.

'You looked as if you might have something to tell me,' said Laura, looking from Anne Todd to Dr Ford, 'so I sent the boys off. Anything exciting?'

Anne knew quite well what Laura meant and hoped, but pretended she didn't.

'Very exciting,' she said. 'Look here, Mrs Morland, I've had to take Dr Ford into my confidence – I hope you don't mind.'

In strophe and antistrophe Dr Ford and Anne Todd related the story of Anne's sleuthing, and laid the proofs before her. Poor Laura was so upset and disturbed that Anne almost wished she had let well alone.

'I never thought anyone would be so dreadful,' said Laura piteously, pushing her hair wildly off her fevered brow. 'And fancy her thinking George Knox wanted to marry me, of all people. She must be mad. George mustn't know. He would never get over it. He is very delicate-minded for so large a man. My dears, you must both promise never to tell him. I know I can trust you, Anne. Dr Ford, can I trust you? Oath of Hypocrites, or whatever it is?'

'Every oath of the British Medical Association,' said Dr Ford. 'Seriously, Mrs Morland, I hardly think Anne should have told me, or for that matter have done what she has done, but as she has, it will be a professional secret as long as you wish it.'

'And please destroy the horrible letter and the rubber

thing,' said Laura distractedly. 'I wish I had never let you keep that letter, Anne. Only don't burn the rubber, it smells so frightful. Put it in the dust-bin and let's forget all about it.'

'If you don't mind, I'll keep it till the Incubus really goes,' said Anne Todd firmly.

'Oh, very well. I dare say you know best and you have been very clever, but it is all most uncomfortable and mortifying. Oh, do both come to tea on Saturday. The Knoxes are coming and Adrian will be staying with them.'

'And the Incubus?' asked Anne Todd.

'Oh, yes, I suppose so. It wouldn't be any good not asking her, would it, because she would just come. And Amy Birkett will be here. She is coming on Friday, so it will be a party. Goodbye, goodbye, it's all very upsetting.'

'Ought I to have told her?' asked Anne Todd when Laura had gone.

'I don't know. It doesn't matter much, but I warn you, Anne, you will get yourself into a nasty tangle if you do much more of this amateur detective work. You'll be taking people's fingerprints at tea, next. I won't bail you out when the Incubus brings an action against you for stealing her rubber stamp.'

'I am the Queen Sleuth,' said Anne Todd with conviction. 'I must go to Mother now, or Louisa will give notice. Goodbye, Dr Ford.'

'Not James?'

'No, not James.'

'All right. I'll make up that prescription and send it round to you. Goodnight.'

End of an Incubus

Sibyl's engagement was naturally the absorbing topic of the following days. Under Laura's guidance George Knox put the announcement in *The Times*. Old Mrs Knox wrote from Torquay to say that nothing would induce her to come to the wedding at Low Rising, where there was defective drainage and no electric light, but she sent Sibyl her love and a cheque for five hundred pounds, and told her banker to put all her diamonds at Sibyl's disposal. Laura promised to take Sibyl up to town as soon as Tony was back at school, and help her to buy clothes. George Knox enjoyed himself immensely, helping Sibyl to unpack the wedding presents which began to pour in, and losing the cards which accompanied them, while Miss Grey, radiating good-humour, retrieved the cards and typed out lists of people to be thanked. George also began to plan elaborate additions to Low Rising for the benefit of his grandchildren, all of which Sibyl, who was used to dogs, took very calmly. Adrian and

Sibyl wrote every day and blocked the local line with trunk calls. Johns and Fairfield sent Sibyl an edition of her father's works so gorgeously bound that they shut again like mouse-traps whenever they were opened, and it was impossible to read them unless, following *Caliban's Guide to Letters*, one bent them backwards till they cracked. But this, as Sibyl affectionately said, didn't matter a bit, because she never read darling Daddy's books. George Knox, however, was thrown into a fever of rage because he would never be able to find out whether the binding had come off his royalties. Tony, having seen Master Wesendonck off, shut himself up for two days and produced a wedding address in extremely incorrect Latin, using the Greek alphabet. This he read aloud to Stoker, Mrs Mallow, Mr Brown of the garage, Sid Brown of the railway, Mr Knox's cook, Mr Knox's Annie and Mr Knox's Annie's mother. It was universally agreed by these critics that he was a real little gentleman. Young Flo, who was accidentally included in a reading at which Stoker and Mrs Mallow were present, so far forgot herself as to say he was a brainy kid, but was severely snubbed by her elders.

The wedding was to take place early in June, and Stoker produced a hitherto unknown piece of folklore in the shape of a rhyme running:

Marry in June,
You'll have 'em many and soon.

Lord Stoke, a passionate antiquarian, on hearing from Dr Ford of this interesting find, insisted on coming over to High Rising and having tea in the kitchen with Stoker, in the hopes of recovering the remaining couplets. But Stoker, though entirely at her ease with his lordship, showed considerable diffidence about producing further contributions. Her reluctance may be accounted for by the distinctly primitive nature of the only two lines Lord Stoke could subsequently be induced to repeat:

> Marry in August,
> The first won't be yours, but father it you must.

Lord Stoke then went off at a tangent and tried to find a common origin for himself and Stoker, by whom he was completely enthralled, but as his family had borne the same name and lived at Castle Rising for five hundred years, and Stoker's father, who came from Plaistow, locally pronounced Plaster, was really called MacHenry and had acquired the name Stoker owing to his calling, which was shovelling coke at the gasworks, this research went no further.

But we are going too far.

On Friday Amy Birkett came down, bringing Sylvia with her, much to the joy of Tony, who had sadly missed his audience since Master Wesendonck's departure. After dinner Laura began to unfold to her friend the story of the anonymous letter, but before she was well embarked on it, Anne Todd came in to ask her for a missing sheet of manuscript. It took Laura some time to find, and when she returned to the drawing-room, the two ladies were sitting close together with a conspiratorial air.

'I have been continuing the story of the Incubus,' said Anne Todd with rather a peculiar look.

'What do you think of it, Amy?' asked Laura. 'Here you are, Anne – it had got into *The Noseless Horror* – I must have put it in as a book-marker.'

'I think it is all very remarkable,' said Amy, also with a rather peculiar expression.

'And listen, Anne,' said Laura. 'Leave a gap after page two hundred and three, because I want to put in a bit about smuggling cocaine, only I haven't thought what to smuggle it in.'

'What about rolls of silk?' said Amy. 'Madame Koska – I suppose it's her you're writing about – would probably buy her silk from abroad, and her enemies might get some hollow bits of wood – you know, those things like long rolling-pins that silk is wrapped round – and put cocaine inside them and try to get Madame Koska into trouble.'

'That's an idea,' said Laura. 'Only how would the enemies' agents over here get at the rollers? They'd have to have a spy in the stock-room. You've no idea how difficult it all is,' said Laura, looking really worried.

The discussion on cocaine smuggling lasted, very ignorantly, for some time, without any definite result, till Anne Todd said she must go. Then Laura and Amy talked about the school, and the Incubus was forgotten. Not till Laura was in bed, and a page turned down in *The Noseless Horror* reminded her of the evening's talk, did the peculiar attitude of Anne Todd and Amy Birkett occur to her again. They looked as if they had a guilty secret. But this was so obviously unlikely that Laura dismissed it from her mind, and went on with the chapter in which the Horror appears, disguised with a false nose, in the hero's garage.

Laura's tea party were all punctual next day. Amy was still in her room writing letters when the party from Low Rising arrived. Adrian drove Sibyl over, picking up Anne Todd on the way. This would not have been his own choice, but when kind Sibyl suggested it, he was so overcome by the beauty of her nature that he willingly consented. Dr Ford came in next, followed shortly by George Knox and Miss Grey, who had walked over together. Everything was joy and rapture. Laura embraced most of her guests in a combination of absent-mindedness and congratulation, but they all knew their Laura, and were not in the least surprised.

'And why should we not kiss?' asked George Knox, and did not wait for answer. 'Kissing has in many ages been a recognised form of salute. Savages, it is true, rub their noses together, a repellent action, but then savages are repellent, grossly so, and the less we hear of their customs the better. If savages, who after all have been just as long on the earth as we have, have got no further than knocking their front teeth out, and in general leading a life of dirt, ignorance, and an abject fear of all natural phenomena, they should have made better use of their time. The marriage customs, my dear Laura, of the Arunta tribe, a revolting set of Australian aboriginals, are alone enough to justify their extirpation by rum, missionaries, or any other destroying element. When I tell you—'

But the whole company decided unanimously that George Knox should not tell them whatever it was; and rightly, too. Dr Ford and Miss Todd began to talk about the dog show, Adrian studied his own name on the back of a row of Laura's books, while Laura and Miss Grey discussed Sibyl's wedding presents.

'Lord Stoke sent the loveliest present this morning,' said Miss Grey, as the conversation became general again. Everyone turned to listen.

'What was it?' asked Laura.

'Such a lovely piece of old silver, a kind of dish, all carved, wrapped up in a piece of old lace, real Mechlin, just as if the lace were a piece of paper.'

'I shall wear the lace with my wedding dress,' said Sibyl, 'and Adrian and I shall have fruit on the silver dish, shan't we, darling?'

'Of course we shall, darling,' said Adrian. 'It will be delicious to see you taking a peach from it.'

'But, Adrian darling, I don't really like peaches.'

'Then anything you like, darling,' said the lover.

'"Nothing, darling, only darling, darling,"' remarked Laura, in a quotation.

By this time George Knox had been in the background quite long enough.

'Wine from gold, fruit from silver,' he remarked sententiously. 'How fitting for youth and love. To think that in six weeks or so I shall be alone. But I shall occupy myself,' he said courageously. 'Books, work, the daily round, an occasional guest, these will fill my empty days.'

'I suppose I shan't be able to stay long with Mr Knox, now,' said Miss Grey.

Everyone's ears pricked.

'Are you leaving us, then?' asked Dr Ford with interest.

Miss Grey almost simpered, 'Well,' she said to Dr Ford,

confidentially, but with appalling distinctness, 'when Sibyl is married, my position will be a little difficult, won't it?'

'Why?' asked Dr Ford stupidly.

This was just the opening Miss Grey wanted.

'Well,' she continued, lowering her voice, but still holding her audience spellbound, 'it will be a little awkward for me to be alone with Mr Knox. Not that I would mind, but you know how people talk, and I am so friendless.'

Blank silence fell upon the room. Poor George Knox went quite purple with embarrassment. Adrian and Sibyl, most chicken-heartedly, had oozed out by the French window into the sunny garden. Before anyone could collect him or herself sufficiently to speak, the door opened and Amy Birkett, followed by Tony, came in. Looking round the room, her eye lighted upon Miss Grey.

'Well, Una,' said she, advancing with hand outstretched, 'it is a surprise to see you here.'

'I didn't know you knew Miss Grey,' said Laura.

'Of course I do. And so does Tony.'

'Of course Tony does,' said Laura, deeply perplexed. 'He has known her ever since Christmas. You know the others, don't you?' she added, turning. But Dr Ford and George Knox had also melted away through the window.

Miss Grey, all her assurance gone, was staring white-faced at Amy Birkett.

'What on earth is the matter?' asked Laura. 'Miss Grey, aren't you well?'

But Miss Grey, with an almost animal sound of rage, rushed through the window and down the drive, out of sight.

'We always said her brain was wonky,' remarked Tony, with the air of one who observes the peculiarities of grown-ups dispassionately, from a higher sphere.

'What are you all talking about?' asked Laura.

'Only about Una Grey,' said Amy Birkett. 'Bill's old secretary.'

'Do you mean she was the one you told me about before Christmas? The one that went mad and you had to send her away?'

'That's the one,' said Amy cheerfully. 'Not really mad, but very neurotic.'

'Why didn't you tell me, Amy? Tony, why didn't you tell me you knew Miss Grey?'

'But I did, Mother. I told you we said her brain was wonky.'

'But I thought you meant you and Stoker.'

'Oh, old Stokes thinks she is wonky all right, but all the boys said so, too. You should have seen her go off pop when she was in a temper.'

'Well, I suppose I'm mad,' said Laura. 'Go to Stoker, Tony, and tell her we'll have tea as soon as it's ready. Heaven knows we need it. It's four o'clock, anyway.'

Tony went off to give Stoker the message and help her, and himself, with the cake. For a few moments he was pen-etrated by that ever-recurring sense of the unreasonableness of grown-ups. Of course he knew Miss Grey, though she had never known him among so many little boys. One was never surprised at anything grown-ups did. Miss Grey had been at school, being old Birky's secretary: well and good. Then Miss Grey was at Low Rising, being Mr Knox's secretary. Also well and good. One was much the same as the other. Grown-ups must live somewhere. Whether they lived at school, or at Low Rising was all one to Tony. The main fact was that she was wonky in the brain. But she liked dogs; that was in her favour. So he dismissed her from his mind, where indeed she had never held any very prominent place, and favoured Stoker with a repetition of his Latin address to Sibyl.

Meanwhile, Laura was divided between anxiety for Miss Grey and a desire to have an explanation from Amy.

'Where do you think she has gone?' she asked. 'Oughtn't we to go and find her? She might drown herself, or get under a train.'

'Not she,' said Amy with decision. 'You are too soft-hearted, Laura.'

'But why didn't you tell me you knew her, Amy?'

'I didn't know myself that I knew her till yesterday. You told me that your friend, Mr Knox, had a troublesome secretary, but there are plenty of those. If you remember, she went to London when I was here before, so we never met.'

'But, Amy, 'said Laura, turning reproachful eyes on her friend, 'I told you her name was Grey. You asked me yourself what it was, after the boxing finals.'

'Yes, my dear, but Grey is not an uncommon name, and I didn't want to worry you unnecessarily. It wasn't till yesterday evening when Miss Todd told me about the letter that I could put two and two together properly. We had no end of trouble with her at school. She got it into her head that she adored Bill. She said she worshipped the very ground he trod on, and it was very trying. Then she took to writing anonymous letters to me, to tell me I was neglecting and ill-treating poor Bill, but she wasn't good at it, and I knew at once who it was. So there was nothing for it but to send her back to her mother. She came to us with good references, so I suppose she used those for Mr Knox.'

'But, Amy, she hasn't got a mother. That is one of George's difficulties. If he sends her away, she has nowhere to go.'

'Rubbish, my dear. She has a mother in County Cork who is quite alive and very glad to have her to stay, but the poor girl prefers to go about falling in love with her employers.'

The appearance of Stoker with tea put a temporary end to these disturbing revelations. Adrian and Sibyl, looking very silly and blissful, then rejoined them, with George Knox, and they were presently followed by Dr Ford, who took Anne aside and told her something.

'Did you go into the wood, Adrian?' asked Laura, trying to make conversation with an abstracted mind.

Adrian stared blankly at her, smiled charmingly, and said yes, he thought they did.

'No, darling, it was along the field-path,' said Sibyl.

'So it was, darling.'

'Adrian Coates,' said Laura, so sharply that her publisher almost leaped from his seat, 'if you don't stop looking like a mooncalf and pay a little attention to your most important author, I shall break my contract on the ground of lunacy, and go to Johns and Fairfield.'

'He can't help it, Mrs Morland,' said Sibyl. 'He's terribly in love; aren't you, Adrian? It just makes him rather silly.'

'It does have that effect on him,' said Laura, at which double-edged remark, Adrian, remembering New Year's Eve, choked into his tea. Under cover of the disturbance caused by this lapse from good manners, Anne Todd brought her cup to Laura to be refilled and whispered that Dr Ford had driven Miss Grey back to Low Rising at her own request. Laura whispered back that they must go over as soon as they had finished tea, and see if she was all right. A rapid conspiracy took place, with the result that Adrian and Sibyl were dismissed to re-explore the wood, while Dr Ford volunteered to keep George Knox entertained till the ladies came back. Laura, Amy and Anne then set off for Low Rising, Laura only stipulating that Amy should drive, as she felt quite unequal to concentrating. During the short journey she provoked her companions to the point of frenzy by alternately letting her imagination play freely upon what might have happened to Miss Grey, and imploring Amy to turn back and not make things worse than they were. Amy and Anne, who appeared to be united in a single thought, took no notice of her appeals, and in a few minutes they arrived at Low Rising. A rather scared-looking Annie, who opened the door, said in answer to Anne Todd's inquiries that Miss Grey was upstairs in her room, and she thought she was packing, as she had told her to get her big suitcase out of the box-room.

'Perhaps she has cut her throat,' said Laura wildly.

'Don't be an idiot, Laura,' said Amy. 'People don't ask for suitcases to cut their throats into. But we had better go and see, all the same.'

As she spoke, a door was opened upstairs and Miss Grey

came out on to the landing, with evident signs of tears on her face.

'I suppose you've all come to laugh at me,' she said fiercely. 'You can laugh as much as you like. I'm going. You've always hated me, Mrs Morland, and so has Mrs Birkett. After the insult she put upon me I'll not stay here a moment longer. It doesn't need three of you to turn me out. I wouldn't stay here a moment, if you were to beg me on your bended knees.'

'But you mustn't talk like that about hate,' said Laura. 'Please come down and let us explain. Mrs Birkett didn't know you were here, and after all she only said she was surprised to see you, which isn't really an insult, and I dare say she didn't mean it; did you, Amy?'

Amy looked despairingly at Laura. Miss Grey came suspiciously downstairs and passed into the sitting-room, followed by the three visitors. Anne Todd, remarking that Annie was not above listening from the kitchen passage, shut the door.

'Well,' said Miss Grey sullenly. 'What have you got to say? You've nothing against me.'

'Only your letter to Mrs Morland, and the rubber stamp you used for the date,' said Anne Todd. 'I have them both here if you want to see them.'

'I'll not be seeing anything,' said Miss Grey, looking nervously and defiantly from one to the other. 'You can make up all the lies you like.'

'If you don't want to see it, I can show it to Mr Knox,' said Anne Todd. 'You can be there too, if you like, and you can ask Mr Knox for the latchkey that you left at Rutland

Gate. The kitchen-maid found it and told him you left it there.'

'Anne, Anne,' begged Laura, 'don't be so cruel. Miss Grey didn't mean anything I expect – the letter was all a joke.'

'Be quiet, Laura,' said Amy. 'If you interfere once more, I shall be very angry. Miss Todd, will you do that telephoning we talked about?'

Anne Todd squeezed Laura's hand and left the room.

'Now,' said Amy, 'let's be sensible, Una. You know quite well what happened at my house last year. It seems that much the same has been going on here. It's no affair of mine what you do in other people's houses, but when it comes to anonymous letters, Mrs Morland must be protected. If you are packing, that is the best thing you can do. Miss Todd is ringing up Miss Hocking to see if she can take you at once. If you go now, Mr Knox needn't be told anything. We will make an excuse.'

Miss Grey's face crumpled and changed. Bursting into tears, she fell on her knees at Laura's feet, much to Laura's embarrassment.

'Mrs Morland,' she cried, 'don't send me away. I must see Mr Knox again. I'd work my fingers to the bone for him. I've borne everything for him. I knew you hated me, and Sibyl hated me, and Dr Ford, too. And you made Mr Coates laugh at me. You could visit Mr Knox when I was away and poison his mind against me, but who nursed him when he was ill? Who helped him with his book? There wasn't one of you was a friend to me. Miss Todd pretended, but she was as black-hearted as the rest of you, lying and leading me on. She'd have been glad enough to get Mr Knox herself. So would you, Mrs Morland, for all your airs, and you a widow. Going to London with him, pretending it was a play you were going to, but it was no play, it was just a trick to get him to your flat at night. I saw the pair of you.'

'It was you that bumped into me in the hall that night, then,' said Laura, drawing back.

'Faith it was, and I wish I could have bumped you off,' said Miss Grey savagely, amid her uncontrolled sobs.

'But, you poor girl,' said Laura, trying to overcome her natural revulsion, and indeed her fear, 'you are mad. Mr Knox has never thought of me in his life. Not in that way. Why, I've known him for nearly thirty years.'

'Mad is it? It's you and your likes that are trying to drive me to the madhouse,' said Miss Grey, twisting her hands together as she still knelt on the floor.

'Amy,' said Laura urgently. 'This is too ghastly. We can't go on with it. Let the poor girl go. She can come and stay with me if she has nowhere to go.'

'Shut up, you idiot,' returned Amy.

'I'd sooner die here, on this floor,' said Miss Grey violently. 'I won't leave this house till I've seen Mr Knox and he has heard how you have treated me. I'm not ashamed of caring for him. I worship the ground he treads on.'

'Well, I hope it is the same ground my husband treads on,' said Amy Birkett coolly. 'That would save you a lot of trouble. Mr Birkett is coming to fetch me tomorrow and Mr Knox can get the truth from him.'

Miss Grey got up, white-faced, shaking and silent.

'Oh, Amy, you couldn't do that,' implored Laura. Anne came back and nodded to Amy.

'I could and would,' said Amy Birkett. 'Una, are you going, or shall we tell Mr Knox everything?'

'I'm going,' said Miss Grey. 'You'll be glad if I starve, you beasts.'

'You won't starve unless you want to,' said Amy. 'Miss Todd has just spoken to Miss Hocking on the telephone. Miss Hocking wanted you to come on Monday, but today will suit her just as well. There is time to get the five-thirty. I will drive you to the station in Mrs Morland's car. We will tell Mr Knox that Miss Hocking wanted you urgently. He shall send your cheque to you at once, and if you are in any need of money till Monday, we will contribute.'

'Oh, do take this, Miss Grey,' said Laura, pressing the contents of her bag upon her. 'It's about two pounds ten, not very much, but just in case you needed it. Please do.'

'I'll starve before I'll take your dirty money,' said Miss Grey contemptuously. 'I've some of my own, thank God.'

'That's enough,' said Amy. 'If you and Miss Todd will get your luggage, I'll start the car. We needn't call Annie in.'

Without a word Miss Grey turned and followed Anne Todd upstairs. They were not long in returning with suit-cases and a typewriter. Anne appeared, in her own peculiar fashion, to be on friendly terms again with Miss Grey, who kissed her tepidly at parting, but ignored Laura's hand.

'You needn't come back for us,' said Anne Todd to Amy. 'We'll walk back. Goodbye, Una.'

Miss Grey made no answer and the car drove off.

'We shall now each have a whisky and soda, if I can find where Mr Knox keeps them,' said Anne Todd. She found everything on the sideboard, poured out two stiff drinks and sat down.

'But, Anne, what have we done?' said Laura, still entirely bewildered. 'She's only a girl, after all, and I dare say she just writes anonymous letters for fun. I don't know why she thinks I hate her. I don't like her at all, and she has made a lot of trouble, but it was awful to see her on the floor crying. It was something we had no business to see.'

'It was something she had no business to do. If Mrs Birkett hadn't been here, she would have got round you again, and you'd probably have asked her to stay with you till Mr Knox married her. You mustn't worry, Mrs Morland. Drink your whisky and you'll feel better. She will be perfectly all right in a few days. She is that unfortunate type who must be in love with someone – any doctor would tell you about them. She will be quite happy with Miss Hocking, and she will do the secretarial work very competently, and see lots of nice young men, and probably marry one of them. If you meet her again in a few months, you'll find her quite friendly again, and quite forgetting all these rampages.'

'But, Anne, I feel like a murderess.'

'You'd have felt more like one if she had stayed any longer. She nearly bluffed Mr Knox into committing himself this afternoon. He was so terrified of being unkind that he might have made her an offer on the spot if Mrs Birkett hadn't come in and recognised her.'

'Did you and Amy arrange that, Anne?'

Anne Todd had the grace to look slightly ashamed.

'We had had a good talk about it the night before, while

you were upstairs,' said Anne Todd, without going into details. 'Come along, we must go back now. I must go to Mother. Why don't you ask the Knoxes to stay to supper? It would take your mind off things. If there's enough to eat, that is.'

'Oh, Stoker can always make enough to eat. Won't you come too, Anne?'

'No, I've neglected Mother too long today already. And Dr Ford is going to look in after dinner to see her.'

By the time they got back to High Rising, Laura had sketched out, for Anne Todd's approval, a scenario for a new novel in which a successful middle-aged dress designer (George Knox) was to fall prey to a vamp (Miss Grey), who by her wiles made him show her all his spring collection in advance, meaning to copy them cheaply and sell them as her own. But she was closely watched by the faithful secretary (Anne Todd), who found that the vamp was also a cocaine fiend, who got her supplies from the Continent in boxes of trimmings with false bottoms, addressed to the dress designer. The discovery of the vamp in the stock-room at midnight, removing the cocaine to her bag, followed by her vain tears and entreaties, was to be the great scene of the book, and the dress designer would marry the secretary. Anne Todd had very little comment to make upon this, and once or twice eyed Laura suspiciously, as if she suspected some hidden meaning, but Laura didn't notice her abstraction, and they parted at Anne's door.

16

The Last Word

When Laura got home, she found Amy in the drawing-room with George Knox.

'I was telling Mr Knox,' said Amy, with the most brazen effrontery, 'how Miss Grey was suddenly sent for, and how lucky it was I could drive her to the station. Miss Hocking had rung her up and begged her to come at once, as she was short-handed.'

'But I thought—' George Knox began.

'So,' interrupted Laura, 'as she had practically promised to go to Miss Hocking on Monday – you told Anne how anxious Miss Hocking was to get her – she thought you would forgive her if she didn't wait to say goodbye. She'll be seeing you again some time, of course.'

'But I don't understand why—'

'And you see, George dear,' continued Laura, 'she would never have left you and Sibyl in the lurch, but she knew Sibyl was coming up to town on Tuesday with me to see about clothes, and she knew you would be too busy to work on the book just at present, so she just went.'

'I am bewildered,' said George Knox, 'but resigned.'

At which both ladies laughed and laughed, he couldn't tell why. So Laura quickly asked him to stay to supper, an invitation which he gratefully accepted. Laura, going to the kitchen to see Stoker about a meal, found Adrian and Sibyl sitting in the dining-room, with their arms round each other's waist.

'It was getting rather cold in the garden, and we didn't like to disturb Daddy and Mrs Birkett in the drawing-room,' said Sibyl, 'so we came in here. Oh, Mrs Morland, we are going to a cinema tonight at Stoke Dry. Won't you come, too?'

'No, thank you, Sibyl. It is very sweet of you both, but I am rather tired. And your father is stopping to supper, so you had better all stay, and we'll have an early meal.'

'What about Miss Grey?'

Laura sat down with a flop. 'Listen, children,' she said impressively, though marring her effect by taking her hat off and running her fingers through her hair till it stuck out in all directions, 'you heard how awful she was being this afternoon, just when you and Adrian slipped out, Sibyl, which was very mean. I don't mind telling you that I thought she was going to force your father to say what his intentions were before the whole lot of us. Well, then, when you had gone, she lost her temper awfully and went back to Low Rising and packed up and went to town, and is gone for good. There's a lot more, but it wouldn't interest you now, you silly young couple, thinking of nothing but each other. And now I must see Stoker.'

She vanished into the kitchen, leaving her hearers vaguely pleased and interested.

To Stoker she merely said that Miss Grey had gone to town and the others were staying on to supper. Stoker, though inwardly consumed with excitement, and determined to see Mr Knox's Annie at the earliest possible moment, affected outwardly the stoicism of an American Indian at the stake, which was very disappointing to Laura. But food was the essential for the moment, so she and Stoker set their minds to the concoction of a high tea which would satisfy everybody. Conversation at table chiefly consisted of interminable arrangements and rearrangements of who was to go in whose car. Finally, it was decided that Adrian should drive Amy, Sibyl and Tony to Stoke Dry, while George Knox should spend the evening quietly with Laura. George said he would prefer to walk home, and would not wait for the return of the cinema party.

Laura and George, both feeling a little elderly, settled down in the drawing-room when the others had gone. There were various matters connected with Sibyl's wedding on which he wanted Laura's advice, his own mother having proved a broken reed.

'Though in a way it is better,' said Laura, 'because your mother would have interfered so awfully, George. And it's a good thing they are to be married soon, because engagements are so upsetting to everyone. And then you'll be able to go on with Queen Elizabeth in peace. I suppose you'll be needing a new secretary later on. Oh, and that reminds me, will you forward letters to Miss Grey, or tell Annie to if it's a bother. She won't have had time to let her people know her new address.'

'I don't suppose there'll be much to forward. She had no friends or relations to speak of.'

'Well, there's her mother.'

'My dear Laura, you mistake strangely. She has no mother.'

'Oh, yes, she has, George, in Ireland.'

George Knox was plunged into such stupefaction that he became temporarily speechless, which gave Laura an opportunity to tell him a little about Amy's previous experience with Miss Grey, without being in any way unkind to that temperamental young woman. But about the anonymous letter she said nothing. That was to be kept in a private compartment with Adrian's proposal and a few other indiscretions of her friends and enemies, which she was too generous to use, even in jest, against them.

'I shall find it very difficult to get back into my stride with Queen Elizabeth,' George Knox complained. 'Miss Grey was an admirable secretary from many points of view, and I shall miss her capable ways, though not her very exhausting personality. I may drop the Queen for the present, Laura. I am thinking of writing a novel.'

'It's the first I've heard of it, George, and the first you've thought of it, I believe. But what fun. What about?'

'The subject, my dear Laura, is quite immaterial.'

'Rubbish, George. You must write about something.'

'I have been giving my mind lately, Laura, to the outstanding successes of modern fiction. They appear to me to be divided into two classes, three, I might say, if we include the thrillers to which you, dearest Laura, are so addicted; but these are apart, *sui generis* I would say if I were sure that the grammar is correct in the case of a plural number. Two classes, then, I repeat. The first, and by far the largest, is frankly, and I hope I shall not offend you by using the word, Laura, but no other expresses my meaning, obscene.'

'That's all right, George. I have used it myself sometimes.'

'Obscene,' continued George Knox, taking no notice of the interruption, 'and that is a thing I cannot be. In private conversation I can be as coarse as anyone if I give my mind to it, but when I write, I find the idea altogether repellent, unlike me. I am therefore cut off from one form of fiction. What remains?'

He paused so long that Laura suggested lazily, 'To write some nice clean fiction like me, George.'

'Ah, Laura, you mock me. Your paths are beyond me. You raise mediocrity to genius. I trust I am not being in any way offensive, but I see at the moment no other way of expressing what I wish to express. You have carved for yourself a niche in the Temple of Fame, Laura, perhaps not more enduring than brass, or bronze would perhaps be more correct, but of pleasing form and honest workmanship. But I will not speak of you. You are very modest about your own work, and I will respect your feelings. Let me rather speak of myself. Where was I? Oh, yes. I have come to the conclusion that there remains one form of very successful novel in which I am eminently qualified to succeed.'

'And what's that, George? Historical novels?'

'You mock me again, Laura. Is not the reproach already levelled at me that my historical biographies are no more

263

than novels in disguise? No, my dear lady, what I mean is: Awfully Dull Novels.'

'Dull novels? But, George, why? Anyone can do that.'

'Laura, they cannot. It needs a power, an absorption, which few possess. If you write enough dull novels, excessively dull ones, Laura, you obtain an immense reputation. I have thought of one. Essentially the plot is, as you may say, nothing, a mere vulgar intrigue between an unhappily married man and a woman of great charm, also unhappily mated. Trite, banal, you will say.'

As Laura did not say it, but sat staring at him, he proceeded.

'But, Laura, and this is where success lies, there will be a strong philosophic vein running through the book. My hero shall be an ardent student of philosophy, a follower of Spinoza, Kant, Plato, a Transcendentalist, a Quietist, what do I know – one can read that up with the greatest of ease thanks to the appalling increase of cheap little books about philosophy edited by men with famous names who do not scruple to pander to this modern craze for education, which is, in sum, only a plan for helping people not to think for themselves. Now, mark me, Laura. What really interests novel readers? Seduction. I scruple to use the word in front of you, but art knows no bounds. Seduction; I say it again. Novel readers by thousands will read my book, each asking her or, in comparatively few cases, him, or his self: Will seduction take place? Well, I may tell you, Laura, that it will. But so philosophically that hundreds and thousands of readers will feel that they are improving their minds by reading philosophy, which is just as harsh and crabbed as the dull fools suppose, until it is made attractive by the lure of sex. Do I make myself clear, Laura?'

'My dear George, what on earth are you talking about?'

George Knox fell into deep despair.

'Perhaps you are right, Laura. Perhaps the idea is far-fetched. *Yet I see a best-seller rising from it.* But Queen Elizabeth, *in* spite of the lures of other and more flowery paths, still tears at my entrails, Laura. I must finish her before I can think of anything else. If only I could induce Miss Todd to work for me. Do you think I could, Laura?'

'I don't know. It's not that I'm at all a dog in the manger about her, but you know how obstinate she is. And really at present she is terribly tied by her mother, and couldn't take on a permanent job. She and I work in a hand to mouth kind of way, but that wouldn't do for you.'

'I shall ask her again, Laura. If the warmer weather suits Mrs Todd, Anne may be more free to get out, and I would like to feel I was helping her as far as money goes. She has a great deal of courage, Laura.'

As he finished speaking, voices were heard in the hall. The door was opened and Stoker announced Miss Todd. Anne, looking very pale and strange, came into the room and began taking off her coat and hat without saying a word. George Knox got up to help her.

'What's happened, Anne?' said Laura, her thoughts immediately turning to Miss Grey.

'I had to come to you,' said Anne, speaking with great difficulty. 'I didn't know Mr Knox was here. Mother's dead.'

'Oh, Anne darling, if I had known I'd have been with you at once. You poor darling. What happened?'

Laura took a step forward, but Anne Todd held her at arms' length.

'Don't touch me,' she said. 'I can't stand sympathy. It was while Dr Ford was with her. I was there, too. It was very quick and horrible and now it's over. Mrs Mallow is there with her. I came to you in the dark, because I couldn't bear it. I ran mostly. I'll go back soon.'

Her white, strained face was so inhuman that Laura, her affection rebuffed, did not know what to do. She looked for help at George Knox, but his eyes were on the rigid figure of Anne Todd.

'Anne,' he said, and opened his arms.

Anne turned, fell against his heart, and delivered herself to such a passion of silent tears as shook her from head to foot.

'We can't have her like this,' said George Knox with authority. 'Laura, tell Stoker to get some tea at once, and if you have any brandy, bring me some.'

Laura raced upstairs, returned with a small travelling flask of brandy which she thrust into George Knox's hand, and ran to the kitchen. In the hall she collided with Dr Ford.

'Is Anne here?' he asked, seizing her arm.

'In the drawing-room with George.'

'Thank God. I didn't know where she was.'

'Come into the dining-room. She's all right for a moment.'

Laura rang the dining-room bell violently. 'Make some tea at once,' she said, as Stoker's face appeared. 'Miss Todd is here and her mother is dead and she is very ill. What happened, Dr Ford? She said you were there.'

'The old lady died quite suddenly, about an hour ago. Anne knew she might go out at any minute. I was there, luckily, and I sent for Mrs Mallow to come and stay the night. Louisa is no use. Anne behaved like a brick. Then I went to talk to Mrs Mallow, and when I came back, she was gone. Louisa said she had seen her go, looking like a ghost. They haven't got a telephone, so I risked her being here and came round. I was honestly afraid of what she might do. She has tremendous self-control and she has been at breaking-point for months. Thank God she is with you. I'd better see her before I go.'

'I'll keep her for the night,' said Laura. 'She can have Tony's room, opening off mine. Oh, thank you, Stoker, I'll take it in. Mrs Mallow is staying at Miss Todd's to look after things, and Miss Todd will spend the night here. Get Tony's room ready for her at once.'

Having thrown this sop to Stoker, whose eye was gleaming at the prospect of an early visit to Mrs Mallow next morning, Laura picked up the tray and carried it across the hall into the drawing-room. Anne was huddled against George Knox on the sofa, crying in long-drawn sobs. The room reeked of brandy.

'Hush,' said George, tightening his hold on Anne. 'I'm glad you've come, Ford. Anne is all in – or all out – words fail me. I have given her all the brandy.'

'The best thing you could do,' said Dr Ford, sitting down beside Anne and taking her limp hand. 'Was that flask full, Mrs Morland?'

'It was. I had just got it filled, because I always take it with me when I drive to London.'

'Well, she is dead drunk by now, I should say, and a good thing, too. If you can get her into bed, Mrs Morland, I'll give her something to keep her doped, and she'll be all right tomorrow, or right enough.'

'Could we get her up between us?' said Laura. 'The bed's all ready.'

George Knox rose from the sofa and picked Anne up quite easily. She laid her face against his comforting shoulder and made no opposition. Stricken with admiration Laura led the way upstairs, Dr Ford bringing up the rear. Stoker had just finished making the bed as they came into the room, and had the exquisite pleasure of seeing a strong man carrying an unconscious heroine just as if she were Marlene. George Knox brushed Anne's wet face with his lips and laid her down in a chair.

'I'll be downstairs if you need me,' he said.

With the help of Stoker, Anne was got into Tony's bed with a hot water bottle. Dr Ford said she would be all right and went downstairs. Stoker was to be left on guard, savouring deeply every rapturous moment of this unlooked-for romance. Laura drew her into the passage.

'Oh, Stoker,' she whispered, 'Miss Grey has gone for good. There was a frightful row. You shall hear all about it.'

Stoker's eloquent face was an impressive tribute to the news, as Laura told in a hurried undertone the outline of the afternoon's catastrophe, so that Stoker might direct village talk in both the Risings into the right channels. She then looked back into the room and saw that Anne was fast asleep.

Meanwhile, Dr Ford and George Knox sat drinking large cups of tea.

'Will Anne be all right?' asked George.

'Perfectly. She is as strong as a horse, but no horse, not even a mule, could stand what she has been through. I admire that woman more than I can say, Knox. I've seen her at all times, always competent, kind; never losing her head, never impatient; without any pleasures, always ready to sacrifice herself to her old Moloch of a mother. It won't hurt Mrs Todd if I say what I feel, and Anne can't hear.'

'What will happen to her now?'

'If she would listen to me, she'd marry me. I've asked her to more than once. I asked again last week, but she won't. You are my rival, Knox, I'm afraid. Good luck to you. If you beat her, I'll put arsenic in your tooth-paste, that's all.'

'What do you mean?' asked George Knox, putting down his cup of tea with a crash.

'What I say. I can't say it again. All this nobility is too much for me. I can be rung up at any time if I'm wanted. Say goodnight to Mrs Morland for me.'

Dr Ford hit George Knox on the shoulder and went out of the room. Almost immediately his clanking two-seater was heard going down the drive, and Laura found George Knox alone.

'My God, what a day,' said Laura, all dishevelled. 'Give me some tea, George. Anne is fast asleep. Where is Dr Ford?'

'He has gone. He left word you were to ring him up if you needed him. I'll do all the business arrangements for Anne, if she'll let me – funeral and so on, I mean.'

'That's very good of you, George. I don't quite know what will happen to the poor child now. She will have about twopence a week. Anyway, when she has got over this she will be able to work for you, too.'

'I don't think I want her to work for me,' said George Knox, assuming an obstinate expression.

'But why not, George? Before all this happened, you said you wanted her.'

'I spoke more truly than I knew, Laura. But she wouldn't be much use as a secretary. Even Miss Grey saw that one can't have an attractive secretary to live with one quite alone.'

'Oh, George, how disappointing. I did so hope you could help. But she could go to you by the day, anyhow.'

'I couldn't bear to have her by the day – nor the month, nor the year.'

'But, George, what is the matter? I thought you liked Anne?'

George Knox gave a tremendous gulp and swallowed all his tea.

'My dear Laura,' he began, 'heavenly fool is an expression which occurs to me very forcefully at this moment. I am, as you know, a man of few words, more apt with the pen than the tongue, no squire of dames, readier to act than to talk, so it is difficult for me to express myself as I should wish, but I must be even more leaden-tongued than I had feared if I have so completely failed to make myself in any way under-standed of you – understood, I mean, and why the dickens I am talking like the Prayer Book I don't know,' said George Knox, in just irritation. 'You, Laura, with your woman's tact, your crystal wit, your quick understanding, would, so I thought, mistakenly it appears, have met me by now on equal terrain, thought leaping to thought, in sympathetic comprehension. That you can have failed me is incredible, so incredible that I am forced to seek the cause, and find it, as usual, in myself. You have had a long and tiring day, you have borne with the difficult ways, the really embarrassing conversation of my late secretary, you have smoothed her departing path, how I do not know and feel it safer not to inquire, you have provided an excellent if light repast at short notice for a company, a great host, of unexpected guests, you have helped an old friend – I allude to myself, my dear Laura – with advice about his daughter's wedding, you have been an angel of comfort and sympathy to our dear Anne in her affliction, and I, brute that I am, wonder that your mind cannot concentrate on my halting conversation. I should rather ought, I mean I ought to, and,' said George Knox reflectively, 'that the excellent and grammatical locutions of did ought and had ought – how like the names of adjacent English villages these sound, Laura, or is it, perhaps, Much Hadham that I am thinking of, are now obsolete, strikes one very forcibly as a sign of the decadence of the language, though to revive them is, alas, impossible, and would merely appear an archaic affectation – I ought rather, I say, to wonder that you have the patience to listen to me at all.'

'I haven't,' said Laura briefly.

'There isn't any of that brandy left, is there?'

'There is not.'

'Your patience,' continued George Knox, waving aside

this interlude, 'could not be surpassed by anyone, even if they were fool enough to sit smiling on a monument, but bear with me, Laura, while I explain what should perhaps have been explained to you before. When I spoke of not desiring Anne as a secretary, I did not, in so saying, deny the possibility of wishing to see her in any other capacity. Rather did I wish to emphasise my wish to see her in another capacity and not as a secretary. Am I clear?'

'If your novel is going to be like that, no one will read it,' said Laura crossly. 'You drive me mad, George. Say what you want to say and have done with it. If you don't want Anne, you needn't have her. I can find lots of work for her. Lord Stoke would only be too glad to have her at Castle Rising for three or four days a week, I know.'

'Damn Lord Stoke,' shouted George Knox. 'Can't you see, Laura, that my whole mind, my conscious being, my volition, is bent upon one thing? And what is that one thing?'

'Don't ask me, George, because I don't know and I don't care. I shall look after Anne.'

'You won't,' thundered George Knox. 'I shall. Now do you understand?'

Laura stared at him, stupefied.

'You mean you will?'

'Yes, I will.'

'Oh, my hat,' said Laura.

She and George looked at each other, George's large face gradually assuming a sheepish expression, tinged with rich, deep pink.

'Well, I'm as glad of this as I ever was of anything,' said Laura, twisting her back hair into an unbecoming knob.

'Bless your heart, George. You weren't such a fool as I thought. Does Anne know?'

'I don't know. No, I don't suppose she does. I shall have to rely, dear Laura, on your womanly tact, your fine sympathy to guide me in this delicate affair. Your hands shall lead me.'

'No, George, they shan't. You can do your own work this time. It isn't as if you hadn't been married before and didn't know how to propose. It would be decent, perhaps, to wait till after the funeral, but after that, don't waste time. Oh, thank goodness, George,' exclaimed Laura, mopping her eyes. 'I do believe you will always be kind to her, and she needs loads and loads of kindness. Bless you, my dear. I shan't say anything about it till you give me leave.'

Just then the sound of the returning revellers was heard. Laura dashed out to the front door, herded them all into the drawing-room, and told them about Mrs Todd's death.

'Oh, Mrs Morland, how awful,' said Sibyl. 'Oh, supposing it had been Adrian. Oh, Adrian, you won't ever die, will you?'

'Never, darling.'

'Will the coffin go in a special saloon?' asked Tony, with sparkling eyes. 'I've never seen a coffin train, Mother. Will Mrs Todd's coffin go in one? Can I see it?'

Amy Birkett took Tony by the hand.

'The best thing I can do for you, Laura, is to take Tony and myself to bed. If I could help I would, but we'll be best out of the way.'

'Thank you, dear,' said Laura, kissing her. 'You've been such a help today. Tony is to sleep on the sofa in my room

273

tonight. You needn't have a bath, Tony, but do wash thoroughly, and don't make a noise, or I'll kill you.'

Mrs Birkett dragged Tony off.

'There is nothing we can do for you, Laura dear, is there?' asked Adrian.

'Only go away, and take your silly bride and your very trying father-in-law with you, Adrian dear. It's been an awful day. I love you all. Go away. We can all ring up tomorrow.'

'Goodnight, Mrs Morland,' said Sibyl. 'Give Miss Todd my love and tell her how terribly sorry I am.'

'Goodnight, dear Laura,' said Adrian. 'We have been very selfish and you have been an angel. Are you still the solitary-hearted?'

'Always.'

'I thought perhaps——'

'Don't think, Adrian. Goodnight. Bless you.'

'Goodnight, Laura dear,' said George Knox. 'Let me know how Anne is. I'll come over tomorrow.'

'For heaven's sake, go away,' said Laura, pushing them all out of the house. There was a shining of headlights, a waving of hands, and she was alone.

'You can go to bed now, Stoker,' said Laura, looking into Anne's room. 'Miss Todd will be all right now, and if she moves I shall hear.'

'I dare say she won't be long for this world neither,' said Stoker, with gloomy relish. 'Those as bears up are often the first to go. Miss Todd won't have no interest like in life, now the poor old lady's dead. Now if only she had a cat, or some of them love-birds——'

Laura said goodnight at Amy's door and went into her own room. Tony, very pink and clean, was lying bright-eyed on the sofa, ready for an agreeable talk.

'Go to sleep at once, Tony, I'm tired,' said his mother, disappearing into the bathroom. As she lay soaking in a hot bath, she reflected with wonder upon the events of the day, and felt very thankful for good friends. Without Amy and Anne the Incubus would never have been routed. Poor Incubus – but one couldn't bother about that now. Without George and Dr Ford she could never have dealt with poor Anne in her misery. Without George there was no future for Anne, and though she knew little of Anne's feelings for George, she felt pretty sure that she would come gladly into harbour after life's buffetings. Kind Amy, who had borne the brunt of the battle with the Incubus, and this evening had so splendidly curbed her own curiosity, to ease Laura's path. She would tell Amy everything, or nearly everything, tomorrow. Dear George, how delightful it would be to see him with Anne at Low Rising, no longer fearing to be alone after Sibyl's marriage. And Adrian and Sibyl, well, they hadn't exactly helped, but they looked so young and happy that it did one good. It then struck her with horror that she might be needing a new secretary herself, but she resolutely put the thought aside, to rejoice in Anne's unknown happiness. Softly she went back to her room, turned on the reading lamp, and composed herself to forget the fatigues of the day in a new book called *Who'll Sew his Shroud?*.

Just as she was sinking into delicious coma, a voice said, 'Mother.'

'Go to sleep.'

'But Mother!'

'Well, what is it?'

'Oh, Mother, you know the Model Railway Exhibition that Mr Coates took me and Donk to? Well, there was a model of the Salisbury curve where the accident happened. Mother, can I make a model of it with sand in the garden before I go back to school? I could have a lovely accident. Mother—'

VIRAGO MODERN CLASSICS

WILD STRAWBERRIES

Angela Thirkell

Pretty, impecunious Mary Preston, newly arrived as a guest
of her Aunt Agnes at the magnificent wooded estate of
Rushwater, falls head over heels for handsome playboy David
Leslie. Meanwhile, Agnes and her mother, the eccentric
matriarch Lady Emily, have hopes of a different, more suitable
match for Mary. At the lavish Rushwater dance party, her
future happiness hangs in the balance . . .

First published in the 1930s, *Wild Strawberries* is a
sparkling romantic comedy from Angela Thirkell's
much-loved classic series.

VIRAGO MODERN CLASSICS

EXCELLENT WOMEN

Barbara Pym

Mildred Lathbury is one of those excellent women who are often taken for granted. She is a godsend, 'capable of dealing with most of the stock situations or even the great moments of life – birth, marriage, death, the successful jumble sale, the garden fete spoiled by bad weather'. Her glamorous new neighbours, the Napiers, seem to be in marital crisis. One cannot take sides in these matters, though it is tricky, especially when Mildred has a soft spot for dashing Rockingham Napier. This is Barbara Pym's world at its funniest and most touching.

'I'd sooner read a new Barbara Pym than a new Jane Austen'
Philip Larkin